A Measure
of Guilt

M K Turner

Edited by Sharon Kelly
Cover design by www.behance.net/lwpmarshala1e9
Photograph: Martyna Bober - Christmas Steps
Font Photography – Katie Harp

ISBN 978-1-9996734-8-2

By M K Turner

Meredith & Hodge Series
The Making of Meredith
Misplaced Loyalty
Ill Conceived
The Wrong Shoes
Tin Soldiers
One Secret Too Many
Mistaken Beliefs
Quite by Chance
Family Matters
Not If You Paid Me
A Measure of Guilt

Bearing Witness Series
Witness for Wendy
An Unexpected Gift
Terms of Affection

The Murder Tour Series
Who Killed Charlie Birch?

Others
The Cuban Conundrum
Murderous Mishaps
The Recruitment of Lucy James

Chapter One

L ife shouldn't be like this. This was punishment for others' shortcomings. Would one of them remember and be decent enough to help? Time was running out, as were the options available. With shaking hands, he crumpled the final demand into a ball and aimed it at the bin, placed to catch the water dripping through the ceiling of the drab studio apartment. Tears of anger appeared as it flew towards the target. When it missed, a roar of frustration joined the sound of rain pounding on the roof above.

There weren't many of them left. One of them must have a shred of decency.

Perhaps fate needed a helping hand.

Again.

He snatched car keys from the hook and yanked a coat from the back of the door before slamming it shut. As he hurried down the three flights of stairs, he struggled into the coat, ignoring the greeting from a neighbour as she rushed into the hall to escape the rain. Puddles had formed in the potholes and he skipped around them as he ran to the car, for once grateful it couldn't be locked. The car was a wreck, held together by rust and goodwill. Even if it passed the next MOT, there was no money for insurance or tax. It was doubtful there was enough to buy fuel.

A fresh wave of anger took hold as the engine spluttered into life.

Two Days Later

Henry Duggan took the two envelopes from the safe and placed them on his desk next to the message pad. The news of Amy Cleaver's death saddened him, she'd been a feisty woman with a sense of humour and a champion of the underdog. Henry always enjoyed his conversations with her, both as a neighbour and a client. It had been a surprise when Amy gave him the envelopes, making it quite clear they were only to be opened upon her death. Only the week before, they had finalised her will, and despite his questions, she wouldn't explain why whatever it was in the envelopes had not been included in her will.

The drafting of the will had not been straightforward, and as Amy insisted that a healthy sum be set aside for Henry himself for services rendered, Tom Blunos a friend from another firm of solicitors had become involved. Duggan had helped Amy in many ways over the years, some of which would have been chargeable if he'd had a mind to do so. He hadn't. Most, he considered to be neighbourly and that he was helping a friend, not working for a client. When Amy refuted his suggestion that the money was quite unnecessary, she'd caused a fair old stink in the office, and refused to leave until they had dealt with the matter. Michelle, his secretary, supplied a constant stream of tea and chitchat for the four hours Amy sat in the small reception area awaiting a satisfactory conclusion. Amy wrote the cheque for Tom Blunos before the ink was dry on her will.

Henry's own bequest aside, the bulk of her estate had been left to four of her favourite charities. The remainder was to be divided between several people she wanted to recognise.

Settled at his desk, Henry picked up one of the envelopes. It was clear it held a small box, and he hoped it was going to be a simple bequest. Amy was evasive when she delivered it, and as she was normally forthright, if not downright blunt, his curiosity wanted something a little more exciting. He smiled as the contents slid onto his desk; it appeared that might be the case.

Henry lifted the small cassette tape and turned it over. Neither the box nor the tape were labelled. Opening the box, he checked there was nothing else inside before unfolding the single sheet of paper in the second envelope.

My Dearest Henry,

If you are reading this, then I am dead. I started writing this several times, to no avail. So, I've decided to speak to you instead. (I can see your eyebrows rising!) Have a listen, I'm confident you'll do what must be done.

Sincere regards,

Amy

PS To reiterate, no slushy nonsense at the funeral, however it is I've met my end.

2

Short and concise, not what one would expect from Amy. Clasping the cassette, he went in search of Michelle. As expected, he found her in the cellar, supervising the boxing of old files. His office space was modest, and storage was running out. Cases over twenty years old were being shipped out to a secure facility. It made him nervous, but he was confident Michelle would know which files were best kept back. Halfway down the stairs, he stopped and called to her.

"Michelle, a moment of your time. Do we still own a handset that will play this?" Presenting the box between his thumb and forefinger, he smiled. "Amy Cleaver has left me a taped message."

"Taped? How intriguing. Why?" Rubbing her hands together to remove some dust, Michelle walked across the cellar.

"I don't know, hence the need for something to play this on."

"Why did she use a dictating machine?"

"Because she was struggling to put her thoughts in writing. Odd but true."

"Yes, she was a little odd. I did like her though, such a shame." Michelle slid a box from the shelf and set it on the floor. "If we've still got one, it will be in here. This is the box where I put the useless stuff that you won't get rid of." Lifting the lid, she peered in. "Yes, thought so. Here's one, next to the petty cash tin with no key, and next to—"

"I knew we'd need it one day. Thank you, Michelle." Duggan smiled and held out his hand. "You see, I'm not always wrong."

"You were. You didn't keep it in case a client left you an outdated tape, you kept it because you didn't think the digital one would work," Grinning at her boss, Michelle handed over the machine. "Batteries in my middle drawer if you need them. Now, if you don't mind, we need to crack on. Dawn has the dentist at twelve, and the man with the van arrives to collect me and the boxes at one. I haven't got time to chat."

"I'll leave you to it. Good work, ladies. Look at those empty shelves."

Back in his office, he fitted the new batteries, inserted the tape, and pushed the play button down.

"Henry,

I'm sorry to lumber you with this. There was little option as will be revealed, and I will try not to ramble, but you know better than most what I'm like. If you are listening to this, I am dead. The question is how? Death comes to us all in the fullness of time, and I don't have that many years left. I'm almost sixty as I speak and have no idea how old I will be when you listen to this. Sorry, back to the point. One would expect me to live at least another twenty years, but even if this is the case, I am asking

3

you to ensure that I did indeed reach that point naturally. I ask this because I believe someone is going to kill me. Ha!

Sounds dramatic, but nonetheless it's true. I almost wish I'd told you in person so I could see your expression, but you might have wheedled a confession out of me. I can't risk that, although, for the life of me, I don't know why. Now I think about it, it strikes me that I could simply tell you now, but I can't bring myself to say the words. Not in full. I'm too ashamed. I should mention that I also feel a measure of guilt. We all do, and in my own way I've paid the price of my actions, or lack of them. The question is, I suppose, was that enough? From my point of view, I feel it might have been, for others, looking at it from another angle, possibly not. No, no, make that probably not. And that being the case, my days might be numbered, that's if we're right of course, and I think we are. You're aware I'm rarely wrong.

Ha! I was wrong back then, we all were. Perhaps that's what gave me clarity of thought, perhaps that's… RAMBLING! Sorry, Henry. I'll get back on course.

You have friends in the legal profession, police officers, solicitors, judges, and I have every confidence that with

them you will bring this matter to a conclusion and see justice done, if there is any to be dished out. But remember, that is only if I didn't die of natural causes.

Or should I get you to do it whatever the circumstances? Hmm.

No, let's stick to the original plan. Do it if they have bumped me off too, don't if it was a heart attack, or the proverbial bus got me."

Shocked, Henry stopped the tape and stared at it for a while. If he drank during the day, he would have had a drink, but it was only half past ten, so he settled for a slurp of tepid water from the glass which had sat on his desk for over an hour. Amy Cleaver had been run over, but not by a bus. The driver hadn't stopped. Had it been deliberate?

Despite the storm that day, Amy had walked to the doctor's surgery. A large van had parked half on and half off the pavement. The thoughtless driver hadn't left enough room for pedestrians to squeeze past the overgrown bushes on the small strip of path still available, particularly with an umbrella, causing Amy to step out into the road to go round it. Unable to see the approaching vehicle, Amy stepped into its path. It didn't stop, or so the police assumed.

There were no witnesses to the event, although a driver who had pulled over to take a call had seen Amy seconds before, struggling with her umbrella as she approached the van. He was concentrating on the latest row with his partner and didn't see the vehicle that hit her. The collision was over in seconds, and Amy was discovered only moments later. No one expressed surprise that Amy had been hit, the rain was torrential, and even if the weather was fine, the van had blocked the view of both the hit-and-run driver and Amy, but all were shocked that the driver hadn't stopped. It was unclear if Amy attempted to look before stepping out, or if she stumbled. It made little difference, as the driver would have had no idea of her presence until it was too late. Despite attempts to resuscitate her, Amy was dead before she reached hospital.

Henry drummed his fingers and wondered whether, given the circumstances, Amy would consider being hit by a car a natural cause. It had only been two days since she died. The death certificate, when he collected it, would show the cause of death to be related to the collision with the car, or perhaps the road. Had the driver stopped, the police would have considered it to be an accident. The young constable who knocked at Henry's door, hoping to find Amy's next of kin, said that the owner of the van would be prosecuted, but not for Amy's death, only some minor motoring offence.

Further consideration was required, and deciding to listen to the rest first, he leaned back in his chair and pushed the play button.

"Is that clear? No. How could it be? You'll need clues... how can I... OK, cards on the table. Listen carefully.

In 1979 someone died. Someone who shouldn't have. It was an awful bloody time. I can't begin to tell you. We considered doing something about it, too late of course, but argued what good would come out of it if we did.

Honesty. Honesty would have, and a slightly clearer conscience. As is often said, honesty is always, always the best policy. Had we been honest right from the start, none of this would be necessary. He would still be alive. Probably anyway, who can say for certain? But so might most of us. But we weren't honest, not even with ourselves. We attended the funeral and wept tears of guilt. Looking back, I have no idea how we had the cheek to go. But at the

time it felt right. We were all there. All with our own measure of guilt.

We all went, a great gang of us, but this is about the four of us. Two of us are already dead, probably murdered, although I can't prove that. By the time I found out it was too long after the event for me to do much about it, and now they, whoever they are, might have got me too. Although you should know if I've been murdered.

Oh, I wish I was there to see your reaction. Has your jaw hit the desk?

I'm not loopy, Henry. If I have been murdered, you must investigate. It's the last one I'm trying to protect. Of all of us, they were least to blame. Innocent of any wrongdoing, but I fear they may be tarred with the same brush and meet a premature end that they certainly don't deserve. I…"

The commentary stopped, and a series of clicking and rustling replaced Amy's voice. Henry tapped the machine in his hand and wondered if the dictating machine Amy was using had developed a fault which she hadn't noticed. Henry tutted and glanced at his notes.

Nineteen seventy-nine - *HE* would be alive - Four of them?

With such scant information, Henry believed even if Amy hadn't been deluded, this tape wouldn't be enough to start an investigation into a murder connected to something which had started forty years ago. In need of caffeine, he got to his feet to go in search of coffee. He'd not reached the door when Amy began speaking again. He hurried back to his desk.

"I've just played that back, it's not much use to you, is it? I've decided to stop beating about the bush, well almost. Check into the death of Jeremy Rossiter. He's the man who

never should have died, although, as we argued at the time, he was a spiteful, arrogant bastard at the best of times, so others might disagree. But did he deserve to die? Did any of them? The answer is no. It must be stopped.

Finally, it's occurred to me that you must be at least five years older than me, and you're threatening to retire at the end of the year, if you're brave enough, of course. That means you too could either be dead, I hope of natural causes, or doolally and dribbling in some care home, singing along to the radio. If this is the case and someone intelligent is listening to this, all of the above stands. Whatever their justification, they must be stopped. I'm sorry I might not get to find out who it was.

That's it, that's all I can say, other than don't think badly of me. We were young, we didn't actually do anything, but I think it was what we didn't do that started this.

If you are listening to this, Henry, thank you for being a good friend. Give my love to Jenny. Oh yes, and good luck."

The recording stopped, and Henry looked at the note underlined on his notepad. At least that was a start, and pulling forward his keyboard, he typed in the name.

Jeremy Rossiter 1979.

Chapter Two

Meredith's phone clattered back onto the bedside cabinet as he slumped back against the pillow and yawned.

"Who was it?" Patsy squinted at the clock as she rolled onto her side. It was almost five thirty.

"Hutchins. A teenager claims to have seen a murder. Rather than disturb anyone, Hutchins went to look with a couple of uniforms, they didn't find a body." Pushing himself into a sitting position, he rubbed his hands over his face. "On that basis, I'm not inclined to rush."

"But … you're going, so you don't think it was just some form of altercation?"

"There was blood. A lot of blood, and no one with major injuries has been admitted to hospital. Sherlock is on his way, and a search team is being assembled." Meredith swung his legs off the bed and stretched his arms above his head. "And I thought I was having a weekend off."

"Frankie? I thought Frankie and Amanda were away this weekend. Have they cancelled it?"

Frankie Callaghan was a senior forensic pathologist, whom Meredith had nicknamed Sherlock many years before when he helped solve a case Meredith was working on. He had recently become romantically involved with Meredith's daughter.

"I have no idea. Apparently, my daughter keeps you better informed of her itinerary than she does me. But Hutchins said he'd spoken to him. If I see him, I'll ask for you. I'm going to jump in the shower. A coffee to go would be nice if you're getting up."

Twenty minutes later, Meredith parked his car in the middle of Lower Park Row, unable to go further due to the police cordon already in place. He left his coffee in the car and lit a cigarette as he walked towards the officer guarding the cordon. The officer recognised him and lifted the tape.

Further down the road, at the top of Christmas Steps, Frankie Callaghan waved a gloved hand. "Wait there, Meredith, there's blood

7

everywhere and I could do without further contamination. I see you didn't kit up."

Meredith held his hands out. "Apologies. No stock on me, send some over." While he waited for Frankie's assistant to provide him with shoe coverings, he squinted at the area where Frankie was working. "That looks like a lot of blood."

"Yep. I doubt whoever it belongs to survived their injuries. Come and look at this and get rid of that cigarette."

Meredith walked forward slowly, dropping his cigarette into the nearest drain as instructed before stepping onto the first tile and making his way towards Frankie. Meredith could make out partial bloody footprints around the larger patch of blood. "This is a bit of a mess, let's hope it doesn't rain."

"Tent approaching from rear." Frankie dropped onto his haunches and pointed at the stone wall which ran the length of the pavement. "Flesh, unless I'm very much mistaken, as is that." His finger swung to an area on Meredith's left. "This was a frenzied attack with a very sharp weapon. I'm guessing it hit an artery. Wherever your victim is, he didn't

get there under his own steam. There are no drag marks, so whoever moved him, carried him."

"A bloke then. That's impressive with only this to go on."

"I'm sure you had the same brief as I did about what the girl said." Frankie looked over his shoulder. "Oh, that sounds promising." Now standing, he turned towards the frantic barking. There were also shouts from the dog's handler.

"I've no idea what they're saying, but do you want to join me?" Turning, Meredith followed the tiles, and once away from the scene walked quickly towards the ruckus.

Halfway down Christmas Steps, the dog handler was kneeling and praising his dog. A few yards ahead, a pair of shoes peeped out from behind the base of an ornate pillar. A little further on, a pile of clothes had been neatly folded. Meredith frowned, wondering what had got the dog so excited.

The dog handler pointed to a row of bins. "In there."

Frankie moved quickly and lifted the lid. "Oh dear. We've found our victim." He turned to Meredith. "I'll get the body to the morgue in the bin. I'm not moving him here. Do you want to look?"

"I doubt it." Despite his words, Meredith stepped forward. "No wonder there was so much blood. Poor sod, he's been butchered."

With a curt nod, Frankie agreed. "Appropriate turn of phrase. Look at the damage to his chest. It's like they've tried to cut him open. After the heart possibly? May even have succeeded, I can't say for certain without moving him." He returned to the pile of clothes and pointed at the blood-soaked shirt. "Stripped after the event, I'm guessing. I need the area that's sealed off, expanded. And no one else should enter this lane, even your officers. There will be traces of blood everywhere. I don't want them disappearing on the soles of feet."

"Done. Let me speak to Hutchins. I'll go back the way I came, and, yes, I'll be careful."

"Thanks, take your lot with you until I give the all clear." Frankie was already dialling out.

~ ~ ~

"I'm going to keep this short because I'm off to see the witness. Her grandmother has confirmed she's awake, and happy to talk. There's not much to share. Hopefully, by the time we get back you will have found out more."

Meredith pinned a single photograph of the body in the bin on the incident board and ran through what they knew.

"At three thirty this morning, Mrs Sarah Sampson called the emergency services. Her granddaughter, nineteen-year-old Jody Sampson, had woken her in quite a state. When she had calmed down, the girl told her she'd seen a murder. Jody ran away from the scene, tried to flag down passing cars who ignored her, and unable to find a taxi she went to her grandmother's house as it was quicker than going home. Before you ask, yes, she had a mobile phone, but it had no battery."

Jo Adler held up a finger. "Where does the grandmother live? How long did it take her to get there?"

"Grandmother lives on Hampton Road, and without speaking to her, the best guess is ten to fifteen minutes. It depends on how long she tried to find someone to help, and what route she took. She was on Colston Street, but at the moment that's all I know. If she went up St Michael's Hill, not long, but as the attack appears to have happened on Colston Street itself, and the body carried down Christmas Steps towards the Centre, she might have doubled back the way she came. Doctor gave her a mild sedative, but she's up and about now."

"Still no ID on the victim, sir?" Trump asked as he placed a coffee in front of Meredith and peered at the photograph taken at the scene. "The murderer must have been strong to lift him in there."

"Nope, not an inkling. We have clothes, mostly expensive. We have shoes, also expensive, and we have his fingerprints, but nothing that tells

9

who he is. Closest Sherlock would guess for age was mid-fifties, hair cut short and almost totally grey, no personal possessions. Although it's doubtful robbery is the motive. This has all the markings of a frenzied personal attack. The removal of the clothes would indicate they wanted our victim to be humiliated, exposed. Not that he'd have known anything about it. Also, the victim has, until very recently, been wearing a wedding band, but Sherlock can't tell how recently. No other jewellery. Height five-ten, slight build, weight around ten and a half stone. Whatever he did to earn a crust didn't involve manual labour, soft, callus-free hands. And that's it. Not much to go on. Adler you can join me, the rest of you get the CCTV from the surrounding area, I want a mile radius minimum. Once you have anything, work your way further out. Trump, get an appeal ready for radio and TV to find out who was in the area, get it out asap. By the way, ask for people who were in the area at the time, but don't think they saw anything to check their dash cams. Better still get them to send copies to us, we might find something. Seaton, circulate the details to all the local stations, find out who, if anyone, has been reported as not coming home last night."

Meredith got to his feet. "And the most important bit: it looks like whoever did this tried to remove the poor sod's heart. He was partially successful." Nodding at the various comments, he added, "So let's search for any other cases where body parts have been taken. Jo, let's move."

~ ~ ~

Jo smiled at Jody Sampson as her grandmother ushered them into the living room. A cup clasped to her chest, Jody nodded acknowledgement.

"Hi, Jody, I'm Jo, and this is DCI Meredith, sorry about the end to your evening, must have been terrifying, if—"

"It was, wasn't it, love? She was in a right state. Never seen her like that before, not even when she was little, doctor gave her something to make her sleep." Taking a seat next to Jody, Sarah Sampson patted her granddaughter's leg. "Not that she should have been out at that time of night, like I told her, that could have been her if she'd been five minutes earlier. I can't bear to think about it."

"I'm not surprised. Can I be a pain, before you get comfortable, is there any chance of a cuppa? We've been on the go since you called this in, not had time to grab anything." Meredith smiled. "Only if it's no trouble."

On her feet before he completed the sentence, Sarah left the room, shaking her head. "I've never had anyone cross that threshold without an offer of hospitality before. That's what this news has done to me. My nerves are shredded. I'll rustle up something for you to nibble on." Her head popped back round the door and she peered at Jody. "Are you alright if I leave you a minute?"

"Yes, of course." Jody forced her smile as her grandmother nodded acceptance. When she'd disappeared, she looked at Jo. "I don't know that much. I wasn't taking any notice. It was only when the man shouted out, I looked up."

"Okay, let's start at how you came to be there, what you heard, and what you saw."

Her eyes on the door, Jody nodded and lowered her voice. "I don't want Nan to hear why I was there. Can I skip that?"

"For now. Might need to know later, but we can always do this somewhere else. How old are you?"

"Eighteen. So, old enough to be where I was, don't worry, it's just you oldies are easily shocked." Jody smirked at Meredith's exaggerated reaction and leaned forward. "No offence."

"Heartbroken, but open-minded. Without the detail of why, tell us how you got to Colston Street and what happened."

Jody settled back into the sofa and drew in a deep breath. Her nose twitched. "Nan's making bacon sandwiches. She never asks if anyone is a veggie, and she doesn't believe that vegans actually exist."

"Luckily, I'm neither. Carry on, I'll just tuck in when they arrive, you keep talking." Meredith gave her a wink and a warm smile.

"I like you. You're alright for a copper, not bad looking for a granddad either. Is he?" Jody looked at Jo for confirmation.

Jo rolled her eyes. "Don't encourage him, just remember he is old enough to be your granddad."

"Nice as it is to have you two insulting me, shall we get on before any self-esteem I have left disappears?"

"Sorry." Giving Meredith a shrug, Jody continued. "A group of us had been out, we got split up and as my phone was dead I couldn't get hold of them, so I decided to head home. I didn't have enough money for a taxi all the way and I didn't want to wake my parents up for some cash when I got there, because that would have been one row too many. So I decided to walk to the top of Park Street. There'd been a massive punch up on The Centre outside the Hippodrome, and rather than risk passing them to go up Park Street, I thought I'd go up Colston Street and double back along Park Row. That was a mistake on all fronts." Her sigh was heartfelt.

"Something other than the attack happened? What … Oh, hang on, I'll help." Jo jumped to her feet and pulled open the door, allowing Sarah Sampson into the room.

"Help yourselves. I can make more when that lot's gone. Brought brown and red sauce rather than ask and interrupt." Sarah looked around. "I've interrupted, haven't I? I'll sit down, shut up, and let you get on."

Meredith looked at the expression on Jody's face and guessed shutting up might be a tall order for Sarah. "Carry on, Jody. You were going to double back along Park Row."

"There were a few people about, and it was chilly, so it was hands in pockets, head down and get a move on. Then there was some sort of trouble, and this bloke is shouting he's going to kill everyone. He was waving something about, knife, gun, who knows? No one hung around to find out, we all got a move on, ran actually. I was almost at Christmas Steps, and working out which was the best way to go, when I realised I was on my own. Everyone else had obviously run in the other direction. I increased my pace, hoping the nutter had gone, when I heard this grunt. I look up and there's someone on the ground, and this bloke kicked him in the head. It was disgusting. I froze. I didn't know what to do. He was going to kill him if he kicked again, but he was massive. What could I do? Then he pulled out the knife."

Meredith placed his plate on the floor, and gently prised the mug from Jody's trembling hands. The action barely registered, although Jody then wrapped her arms around her torso.

"Did he see you?" Keeping his voice low, Meredith nodded for her to continue.

"Not then. He was saying something to the bloke on the ground. Waving the knife back and forth."

"Saying what?"

"I don't know, he was mumbling, it wasn't clear. Then he dropped to his knees and held the knife above his head. It … Oh my God, I can't believe it happened." Jody covered her face and didn't see Meredith hold up his hand to stop her grandmother from going to her.

"It must have been awful. You're doing really well. Would you like a break?" The last thing Meredith wanted was for Jody to stop talking, but it was clear from the jerking of her shoulders that she was struggling. He smiled when she shook her head. "Do you want to carry on, or shall I ask you questions?"

Jody wiped the drip from her nose with the back of her hand and shrugged. Meredith kept talking.

"What did he do then?"

"He sort of fell forward as he brought the knife down. He was half lying on the man he was attacking. That's when I shouted, or screamed, I don't remember which, it all happened so quickly. But he looked over his shoulder at me."

"So you were behind him. Did you see his face?"

Her eyes closed, Jody shook her head. "Not really. As soon as I saw him turn towards me, I knew I had to get out of there. I had a slight advantage, I was on my feet, he was on his knees. I turned and ran. Fast."

"Judging by the state of her when she got here, she must have run all the way. She could barely breathe." Ignoring Meredith's previous instruction, Sarah went to sit with her

granddaughter, and placing her arm around Jody's shoulders, she pulled her in close. "Horrible, just horrible."

"Which way did you run?"

"Back the way I came." Snorting a laugh, Jody shrugged. "I thought there's the other nutter back this way too, if he follows me, perhaps they'll take each other out. Stupid, I know. I realised that, and I cut back along the road that comes out on Park Row. Once I got there, there was a bit more traffic about, and I tried to flag down cars and taxis, but the taxis all had fares so ignored me, and the rest probably thought I was drunk. There's usually loads of police cars out and about around The Centre. Never saw one, probably all dealing with the earlier punch up. So I crossed the road and went up Woodland Road. Not one car on that road. It was like everyone had decided to stay home last night."

"We can get a map later and you can show us the route you took to get here, but I think it's safe to say he didn't follow you, so your instinct to run was right. Let's go back to the two men. What can you remember about what they were wearing?"

Her head already shaking, Jody held out her hands. "Nothing. I was watching the knife."

"It's obvious that would have held your attention. What was it like?"

"Big. Long, like a bread knife but wider." Jody spread her fingers to show the width of the blade.

"A flat blade or serrated?"

"Um, serrated I think." With her eyes screwed shut, Jody forced the picture back into her mind. "I'm not sure. I didn't see anything else."

"You said you saw the attacker kick the victim in the head. What type of shoes was he wearing? Boots, lace-ups, trainers?"

"Black lace-ups. Old man's shoes," allowing herself a smile, Jody nodded, "and stripy socks. Black and yellow."

"What do old man's shoes look like?" Meredith held up his own foot. He too wore black lace-ups. His were highly polished, Italian leather brogues. "I'm an old man. Were they like these?"

"No. Not shiny, I don't think. More like Doc Marten's but without the bit that goes up the ankle."

"Good, well done. Moving up from the stripy socks, what did he have on his legs, trousers or jeans?"

"Trousers. Not denim."

On realising she had the information in her brain, Jody closed her eyes again and pressed her fingertips to her temple. Meredith finished his sandwich as he watched her forehead wrinkle in concentration. After a few minutes, her mouth fell open, and she looked at Meredith.

"He was wearing overalls. Dark blue ones. I worked my way up from his socks and realised there was no jacket or jumper. The trousers just kept going. Never knew I knew that. Thanks."

"Well done, keep going. Hair or hat, bald or curly?"

Warming to her success, Jody continued. "No hat. Dark hair and although it wasn't long it sort of reached the collar of his overalls. And before you ask, he was white, but I've no idea of his age, unless you go by his shoes."

After trying several more unsuccessful prompts to gather more information on the appearance of the attacker, Meredith moved on to the victim.

"Remind me what drew your attention to the two men."

"I had my hands in my pockets, and head down against the wind. I was freezing. I remember wondering if I would walk into a lamppost. Then I heard the shout, I—"

"You said grunt the first time. What did he shout out, can you remember?" Flipping back through her notes, Jo nodded. "I heard a grunt, and etcetera, was it a name perhaps?"

"No. It was a shouted grunt, he'd just been taken out." Her brow furrowed, Jody looked at Meredith. "If someone had hit you from behind, you wouldn't speak, would you?"

"How do you know he took him from behind if you had your head down?" Meredith winked at her and tapped his temple. "It's all up there, Jody, we're just trying to get it out."

Jody considered this for a while. "Because when I looked up, the victim was on all fours and the bloke with the knife had to walk forward to be side on and kick him in the head. Then the victim fell onto his back. Force of the kick, I expect, it was vicious."

14

Clapping his hands, Meredith's smile was broad. "You're one of the best witnesses I've had in a long time. But what does that tell us?"

Even Jo frowned, not understanding what Meredith was getting at. He let them think about it for a while before explaining.

"You said when the attacker fell on the victim with the knife, he looked over his shoulder at you when you shouted, but to get to get into position to kick the victim he had to move, so at some point he was at least side on to you. Do you understand? Go back to the victim being on all fours. Based on where you were standing, which way was his head facing? Right, left, forward or towards you?"

The questioning went on in this way for another twenty minutes. At the end of it, they had no further description of the attacker, but had established that the victim had been wearing something silver around his wrist, most probably a watch. Jody also confirmed that the victim was wearing a white shirt, dark coloured trousers and a jacket, which didn't match the trousers. Meredith already had the latter

detail but was pleased he'd managed to get so much out of Jody. It proved the case for speaking to a witness as soon after the event as possible.

"Thank you for the sandwiches, Mrs Sampson, very much appreciated. Jody, you've been a star. I'm sure you're on twitter book or whatever it's called, and although I hope to get wide coverage on this, for your own safety I'd ask you not to publicise what you witnessed. First, because you'll have every reporter from here to Edinburgh on to you once the story breaks, but most importantly, until we catch this man, which we will, I don't want him looking for who at the moment is our only witness."

The colour drained from Jody's face, and Meredith smiled reassurance. "We'll get him as quickly as we can, but not sure how long that will be. We've yet to identify the victim. Jo has your number, she'll call you, and someone will come round and get you to sign a statement about what you saw and go through your route with you. I—"

A knock at the door interrupted him.

"That will be your mum and dad. I'll take them through to the kitchen, shall I?" asked Sarah jerking her head towards the door.

"No need, we'll be off now. Thanks again, and Jody, remember next time you're out with your mates, stay with them." Meredith nodded a greeting to Jody's parents before leading the way out into the street.

"She's a nice kid, and we now know that the victim was wearing a watch. We need to find out who he was quickly, and that should help." Jo trotted to keep up with Meredith, adding, "I thought this might have been planned at first, but now I'm not sure. You wouldn't plan to kill someone there, even in the early hours of the morning, there was always going to be someone around, don't you think?"

"I think he planned it, yes. Overalls, big sharp knife, the question is; did the plan involve our victim, or was he simply random and in the wrong place at the wrong time?"

Chapter Three

Patsy looked Meredith up and down as she handed him his dinner on a tray. "You look exhausted, that shower did nothing to wash away your fatigue."

"No. I'll eat this, catch the end of the match and then get to bed. Smells nice, what is it?"

Patsy grinned and cuffed his shoulder. "Beef bourguignon, don't be cheeky. I'll have you know it took me seconds to tear open that packet and add water, not to mention trimming the beef. It tastes nice though. In bed by nine? I doubt that. Fingers crossed though."

As Meredith made himself comfy on the sofa, his phone rang. He pointed the remote control at her. "That was your fault for tempting fate. If I'm called away, I'm blaming you." Frowning as he checked the screen. "Well, that's interesting. It's Mr Duggan … Henry."

The name meant nothing to Patsy, but Meredith was clearly not put out to be speaking to the man. Curiosity made her hover in the doorway. Meredith looked at his watch, nodding.

"Yes, pop round. I'm eating dinner, tray in front of the TV, but it's that or take your chances. We had a nasty murder this morning, not to mention the other cases on the go. No, no, don't apologise, I'm intrigued. Tell me someone else has died and left me money." He laughed at the response and hung up. "That's the match gone out of the window. I'll have to record it. But someone is bound to let the score slip before I get to watch it."

"Am I allowed to know who's coming round? You seemed very pleased to hear from him."

"My solicitor, and has been since I was a teenager and my grandmother popped off. One of his clients has him left a conundrum, and he wanted my advice before, as he put it, he causes an unnecessary fuss. I could do without it, but he's a really nice bloke and I owe him many favours."

"Interesting. How long until he gets here. I might want to eavesdrop."

"Never said. Depends where he's coming from. If it's his office or home, about ten minutes."

"Well, I must get that report finished for Crispins as there's a big balance due in, so I might miss him. However, I shall expect full detail. If it's interesting, of course. I'll be in the kitchen."

Twenty minutes later, she heard the warm welcome offered by Meredith when Duggan arrived. Meredith had few people he would consider he owed favours to, much less ones he would welcome so enthusiastically. Curious, she closed her laptop and went to introduce herself.

"Apologies for the delay in my arrival, although I'm glad I didn't interrupt your dinner, but I thought it easier if I brought this." Henry Duggan waved the dictation machine in his left hand and held up a mask in his right. "Would you prefer I wear one?"

"Not on our account, we're both vaccinated. Only if you want to."

"Splendid, still a lot of cautious people out there, although it seems that, in this country at least, we have downgraded Covid to a flu. We'll all be holding our breath come winter though." The mask was shoved in his pocket, and he tapped the machine. "This will be ten times quicker.

I don't want to bother you unduly; you have a lot on your plate." Smiling at Patsy as she entered the room, he held out his hand. "And you must be Mrs Meredith, I'd heard John had married. Congratulations, lovely to meet you. Look after him, he's a good man."

"Please call me Patsy. I'll do my best, but he's a hard man to control. Some would say impossible. Stubborn, I would say."

"Ha. I think I'd prefer single-minded given the choice."

"Can I get you a drink? Beer, wine, coffee?"

"A coffee would be splendid."

Once Patsy had left the room, Meredith pressed Duggan for the reason he was there.

"It's great to see you, but I can't for the life of me begin to guess why you thought I might be of use to you, so don't keep me waiting. Fire away."

"Still straight to the point I see. Well, here you go, let's hope you don't think I'm an old fool. Amy certainly wasn't, which is really why I'm here." His sigh was heartfelt.

"Amy? Should I know her?"

"No, sorry. From the beginning. Amy was my neighbour, she died recently. With no immediate family, she has left me not an inconsiderable sum in her will. I refused, of course, so she made me call in another solicitor to sort it out. I thought it was all done and dusted, but then she turned up with some envelopes not to be opened until her death. She died last week. And I have to tell you, she's left us with a bit of a puzzle to solve. The first part, I suppose, is finding out if her death was an accident, or if she was, as she suspected she would be, murdered. But it does explain the money. It's going to take some time to work out what, if anything, happened."

He pointed at the sofa as Patsy placed his coffee on the table and smiled. "You can join us, Patsy, if you want to,

that is. This isn't confidential. Unless John thinks there might be some substance to it, then I'm not sure. John?"

Not wanting to be dragged into a wild goose chase due to his fondness for the man, Meredith forced a smile.

"As I don't have the slightest idea what's coming, or what's on that recorder, and the fact that Patsy is ex-job, she can stay if she wants, but I think she has a—"

Patsy jumped in, having caught the tail end of Duggan's explanation, she was keen to hear more. "My reports are all finished. I'll join you." Taking the seat next to Meredith, she smiled at Duggan.

"So, Mr Duggan, start with what was in the additional envelopes."

Meredith relaxed back into the sofa, biting back his smile as Duggan played them the tape, and then told of his own basic investigation.

"I found that in 1979, Jeremy Rossiter, economics student at Bristol University, died instantly when his car hit a wall. The boundary wall of Bristol Zoo as it happens. The inquest concluded that although there was alcohol in his blood, it was not sufficient to conclude that he was drunk. There was no mechanical issue found with the car, and it was recorded as Death by Misadventure."

"But you're not convinced. Have you found something else, or is that based on Amy's request?" Patsy smiled and leaned forward. "Never play poker, Mr Duggan, your face can't hold a secret."

"Really? Never have, perhaps that's why. And it's Henry, please. I know John struggles with that, but no reason you should. As to what I think, I read the whole inquest transcript. What was intimated by the experts, but never stated, was that the most probable cause of collision was intent. There was no reason for the car to leave the road, mount the curb, and travel across a grass verge at that speed, unless the driver swerved to miss something."

"But you don't think that likely?"

Meredith smiled as Patsy pressed on.

"I saw the photographs of the scene. Even if he was driving way too fast, then swerved to miss a fox, as was suggested, having avoided the animal, why didn't he then try to stop? That question was never asked, and I'm guessing that may have something to do with the family not wanting it to be asked."

"His family had a say?" Meredith asked. "Who were his family?"

"The Rossiters were a big name in international finance. From my meagre search I've established that during the last century their fortune dwindled a little, but was still quite considerable at the time of Jeremy Rossiter's death. His aunt confirmed as much, although she is very elderly and a bit ... let's say she kept drifting off."

"You've met his aunt? What else did you find out?"

"Only relative, other than the cousin, I could find alive. His mother died in 1980. I'm afraid I took advantage of the aunt." Another tape was pulled from his pocket, and Duggan slotted it into the machine. "I asked permission and she gave it, as you will hear, but to be honest I'm not convinced she understood what I was saying."

As he fiddled with the machine, Meredith raised his eyebrows at Patsy and asked, "Is she in Bristol, and why did you record her?"

"Oh no, London. The reason I recorded it was twofold. First, and most importantly, if something criminal is going on, I wanted the evidence recorded. Second, as the poor long-suffering Michelle will confirm, my handwriting is nigh on illegible, and I didn't want to forget or miss anything crucial. Shall I?" Duggan held up the recorder, finger poised on the start button.

"Before you start, I need a drink. Are you sure I can't interest you in a beer?"

"No, no. If I start I might get carried away, and then I'll have to mess about getting a taxi, you carry on."

Establishing Patsy would join him in a glass of wine, Meredith headed for the kitchen. He'd been gone seconds when he called Patsy.

"Hodge, I can't find the corkscrew."

Patsy rolled her eyes and excused herself. "Can't look for it he means, it's where it always is. I won't be a moment."

"Why did he call you Hodge?"

"It's my maiden name, and when we first met, I was working for him, so we all used surnames. Now I think, most of the time, he forgets both my first name and the fact that we are actually married."

As she entered the kitchen, Meredith waved the corkscrew at her. Their wine sat poured on the kitchen table.

"A quick yes or no, or we'll be here all night. Don't know what the aunt is going to say, but it doesn't sound like this is a case for the police. I'm going to recommend that if he wants to take it further he should hire

20

some help, he's too old to be chasing ghosts all over the country. Shall I recommend you?"

"Yet."

"Was that a yes?"

"No, it was a *yet*. This isn't a case for the police – yet."

"So, it was a yes. Come on, let's get on with it." Glasses in hand, Meredith headed for the sitting room.

"I didn't say that."

"Yes, you did. It's more interesting than anything else you've got on the go, and you do think it might be a police case. Therefore, if he's interested in hiring you, you can say you told me so if you find anything criminal."

Now at the sitting room door, Patsy couldn't answer, but her smile revealed Meredith was right. They settled down next to each other, and Duggan played the tape for them, forwarding it past pauses and asides which bore no relevance. It was clear he'd listened to it many times.

"Thank you for seeing me. Very much appreciated Mrs Rossiter."

"I was amused. I wanted to know, how a masseuse in Bristol thought she might have something to leave to a Rossiter, did her family have money?"

"No. You misunderstood, and Amy Cleaver was a physiotherapist, quite prominent in her field. There is no bequest."

"Then I misunderstood. I thought you said she'd left something to Jeremy in her will. I assumed she was a masseuse as all the Rossiter men are philanderers. They can't help it, it's in the genes you know. I was lucky, my philanderer died young. Before Jeremy drove into that wall, in fact. Still, every cloud. It meant my boy inherited, so I wasn't sent to the poor house, given that my husband had squandered what little he'd inherited from his father. I don't wholly agree with these modern ways, but I do think they should share family fortunes amongst the siblings, don't you? Seems wrong that one should inherit more because he popped out first."

"I quite agree. As a solicitor I've seen my fair share of family feuds over such matters. Which brings me back to why I came. Amy indicated that if I found out what happened to Jeremy, I would find some mutual friends of hers. Of course, finding Jeremy had died in that terrible accident, I was at a loss, and I thought perhaps his family might be able to point me in the right direction. One of your children, for instance. Were they close to Jeremy?"

"Son. I only had one. And no, they were not close. They were quite the opposite. Two years difference, and they hated the sight of each other, which made little or no

difference you know, as so did their fathers. Also, a family trait. A bunch of philandering grudge bearers." Kathryn giggled. "All in all, I did quite well, don't you think? Mother didn't think so, and said I got second best. But my husband couldn't stand his family, and neither could I, and then he had the decency to have a heart attack in a taxi, no doubt on his way to or from a woman friend, and now my son… hmm, how to describe him? My son is a disappointment in as much as he didn't step up to the mark. On anything really, but luckily, he's not interested in me. I'm settled here, the allowance is enough, especially now I've stopped travelling. I've had such fun. Not being tied to those two, did a bit of philandering myself… once free of course." She giggled. "Now I'm making you blush."

"Quite. What can you tell me about Jeremy? Awful hitting that wall. After swerving to avoid a fox, wasn't it?"

Kathryn spluttered her derision. "If that's what you want to believe. I heard it was following the row with his father. Not convinced he wanted to kill himself, probably wanted to wreck the car he'd been given as a birthday present and messed it up. They're also good at messing things up, the Rossiters. Although, he did like a drink, don't they all, so perhaps he did."

"Row, I've not heard about anything untoward."

"Oh dear man, there were always dramas, rows, and scandals when the Rossiters were involved. I don't know what about on this occasion. My husband had already died, and I had removed myself as far from their clutches as I could. I went to the funeral, of course. It was quite moving."

"How did you know there had been a row on this occasion?"

"Can't remember who told me. That girl Anna, or perhaps it was Bea – both dead now, at least I think they're dead. They were my source of Rossiter gossip. Oh, it could have been Freddie, my son. He'd been to Bristol for the party. Jeremy's birthday, I said, didn't I? Well, he didn't care how he died, of course, it meant he got the money. So, no, I can't remember. Although, saying that, there was the other business… oh, what was I going to say? No, it's gone."

"I see. Is there anything else you can tell me that might help me track down Jeremy's friends from that time?"

"No. Nothing. The old man lasted another four years, then my boy got his inheritance. He is the last of the Rossiters. No children. As mentioned, always been a disappointment. Now, is there anything else? I'm ready for my nap. If you've finished, I'll let you go."

22

The recorder was switched off, and Duggan tapped it on his knee.

"That was it. But here's the thing, Freddie Rossiter did inherit the bulk of his uncle's wealth, despite the old man having two daughters, but that's an aside. I've looked up the will, and it was made two weeks before Jeremy's death. Even if Jeremy hadn't died, Freddie was due to inherit anyway. I pondered this on the train on the way back. What if Freddie knew this? What if Amy knew? What if they told Jeremy, or worse, what if Freddie knew, and concerned it might be changed back was somehow responsible for Jeremy's death? I don't think it was an accident. Not for one moment, but was it murder? And that, John, is why I'm here. Do you think I might be dallying with things that should possibly be part of an official investigation? Should I go to the police? If it was murder, it's a cold case, and I don't think you do those, do you?"

"I'll tell you what I think, Henry, I think that's a lot of what ifs. It's an intriguing story which would probably make a good film, but at this moment in time, from what you've told me and what I've heard from the aunt, there's not enough for the police to go on, not to open an investigation. I think, in fact I know, anything is possible, and much stranger things have happened. Perhaps if Amy had told you why she felt she was in danger, it might have had some impact, but I'm afraid the best I can do for you is check out the driver of the car that killed her. If his name was Rossiter, we might be in business. But I think that's a long shot."

"You think I should forget it?"

"Not if you don't want to."

"But where would I start, do you think? I owe it to Amy to do that much."

"If it were me, I'd track down Freddie and ask if he knew who the four were and take it from there. Have you considered a private investigator?"

"Yes. My first thought. I was going to speak to the aunt, and if I thought it might go somewhere, I was going to hire one. It was only when I realised Freddie was in the will prior to Jeremy's death that I thought I should speak to you first."

"May I recommend Hodge? Her rates are reasonable, she's bloody good, and she already knows what's what."

Duggan looked at Patsy. "You're a private investigator? Well, I would never have believed it." Turning back to Meredith, he wagged his finger. "Stop calling the poor girl Hodge."

"It's her working name. It seems mine wasn't good enough." His lips twitching a smile, Meredith also turned to Patsy. "Are you interested?"

"Of course. Murder or no murder, there is certainly a mystery to be solved, and I don't think Mr Duggan will sleep well until he's done as his friend asked. If you're interested in taking this further, Mr Duggan, shall I come to your office so we can discuss fees and a way forward."

"Absolutely. And it's Henry." Henry got to his feet, but left the recorder and tapes on the arm of the chair. "I'll leave those in your safe-keeping. Here's my card, although I'm not in the office tomorrow, I wasn't sure how long the London trip might take, so I'll be at home." Scribbling his home address on the back of the card, he handed it to Patsy.

"Let's say ten tomorrow morning, that will allow me enough time to go to my office and tie up anything that's required. Nice meeting you, Henry."

Immediately the door had closed behind Duggan, Meredith collected the glasses from the sitting room and switched off the lights. "Bed, Mrs Meredith. Now."

"Don't you want to discuss the—"

"Nope."

Chapter Four

By the time the rest of the team had arrived, Meredith had listed the details of the description provided by Jody on the board. Underneath the photo of the victim, he wrote: Known or Random? He was pondering this when Seaton and Rawlings arrived. They crossed the office to join him, scanning the additional information as they approached.

"The girl came up trumps, then, Gov." Rawlings tapped the board. "Interesting, overalls. Blue-collar worker or going prepared? Possibly both I suppose."

"That's what we've got to find out. Anything interesting come up on the CCTV footage?"

"We've got a few men wandering that way in the half hour or so before, none wearing overalls though, don't think so anyway. I'll get it up and let you have a look."

"Cheers, Dave. Ah, Trump. Better late than never. Did you get the press release out, I didn't catch the local news last night, any joy?"

"Morning, sir. *Crimebusters* website and the Police Facebook page have requests for information. I checked them first thing, there were a few shares, but no useful comments. *ITV* local news did tack it onto a bulletin last night, but promised more this morning. *BBC* asked for an email with details and said they'd see what they could do. I'll check my emails now." Already punching in his password, Trump looked up. "How useful was the witness?"

"Good in as much as she got a good look at the back of him. But that helps with searching through the CCTV. Unless we get any leads in, that's where we need to start. I've got to get that report signed off on the Cummings case. Shout if we get anything. Dave, let me see those clips before I start."

Meredith studied some of the recordings already singled out by his team, doubting the new lot was of any interest, before opening the file he needed off his desk. His team busied themselves with the slow, painful job of looking for the needle they wanted in the ever-growing stack of footage arriving from the surrounding area. With the description of both men in hand, they now had two people to track down, but almost two hours passed without a sighting of either man. Although the footage was still trickling in, they had broken the back of the principal supply.

A few responses were coming in from the media requests, and Meredith assigned Seaton and Hutchins the task of sifting through them to see if anything was worth following up. He also managed to get hold of several uniformed officers to patrol the taxi ranks in the hope of finding someone working in the area that night, although he didn't hold out much hope on that angle, given what Jody had said. It therefore surprised him when Trump appeared in his doorway.

"We might have something, sir. Sounds promising." Trump grinned at him.

"Great. Are you going to share what or is this a parlour game now?"

"One of the PCs working Temple Meads taxi rank, found a chap that was working at the time of the murder, and was in the area. He had a dash cam, and let our man have a look. As luck would have it, he finished two hours after the time of the murder, and—"

"Get to the point, Trump."

"We think we have our chap in overalls coming out of Trenchard Street carpark."

"Wasn't that easy? All the info I needed in a few brief words. When do we get to see the footage?"

"That was a bit of a fight, the driver didn't want to give up the SD card. So he's on his way in with PC Jacks. Not happy about it apparently, means he's not earning. He wanted to come in after work but Jacks was worried that he'd overwrite it."

"What does that mean?"

"The cams record continuously, once the memory is used up, it just dumps the oldest stuff to make room for new material. As he's a taxi driver, that could be any time now."

"Bugger. So vital information could be being dumped from other recorders as we speak, if it hasn't already."

"Afraid so. Depends how big the memory is of course, and how often the car is used. With a taxi—"

"I get it. Consider me educated. Let me know when it arrives."

Meredith closed the file in front of him and placed it in the basket on the floor next to his desk. Another case closed, only three on the go now.

He looked up as Trump called to him and gave him the thumbs up. Scooping up the file, he hurried to catch up with him.

He pointed at the tablet in Trump's hand. "As you've got that with you, I take it that means the recording is here."

"Yes, but the driver won't let it out of his sight. Jacks needs to get back out there, so I said I'd do the honours."

"I'll come with you. I can drop this off on the way."

1.

~ ~ ~

Meredith smiled at the taxi driver and pointed to a seat on the other side of the table. "Take a seat. This shouldn't take long."

The man looked around, he'd become nervous when invited into the interview room.

"I stand." His smile was crooked and lasted seconds.

"Please yourself, you're not in any trouble you know. Quite the opposite."

"Me in trouble, sir. Big trouble."

"Why's that then?" Watching Trump insert the card into a reader attached to the laptop, Meredith barely glanced at the driver.

"My boss will not like this. I am probably sacked."

The driver's sigh was deep, and Meredith turned to look at him. He appeared to be of Ethiopian descent, and his well-worn clothes hung loosely about his body. Meredith doubted it was from weight loss and more likely that they were second-hand.

"Why would your boss sack you for helping the police with a murder inquiry? Has he got something to hide?"

"Oh no, no. I don't know. Not about help, about no money. No driving, no fares. If not the sack, then no pay today."

"Well, that's not good enough. Who is he, your boss, what's his name? I'll have a word."

A look of horror seemed to diminish the man further still, and he shook his head as he spoke.

"You must not. You must not." The driver held his hands as though in prayer and nodded. "I beg you, sir, please, I have a family." Wiping the perspiration from his brow, he looked at Trump. "It is over. I go now. No problem, sir." His hand shot out and Trump dropped the card into it. "I may leave now?"

"You may. I'll walk you out." Pulling his wallet from his pocket, Meredith plucked out several notes. "Trump, help the man out."

"How? Oh, I see. Of course." Adding to the notes in Meredith's hand, Trump tapped the tablet. "Your office, sir?"

"Yep. Give me five minutes." Handing the notes to the driver, he jerked his thumb. "Come on, this way." He flapped his hand to hush the driver's enthusiastic thanks.

Walking the driver through to reception, he opened the door and shook his hand. "I know it's difficult but try to find a job with a better boss."

"I will try. Thank you. May God bless you."

"I doubt he will, but it's a nice thought." Letting the door close behind him, Meredith hurried around the desk. "Is he in the car park, George? If so, get his Hackney number and find out who owns it. His boss needs a visit when I'm not so busy."

"He is. I'll get you some stills and see what I can do. What's his boss been up to?"

"Other than ripping his staff off, I don't know. But if there's anything, I'll find it. Email them over."

Taking the stairs two at a time, Meredith joined Trump and Jo in his office. "Let's hope Jacks was right, and this has something for us."

"Jacks said it was around two am, we'll go straight to it. You do the honours, Jo. You're quicker than I am." Trump passed Jo the tablet. With a few flicks of her finger, she took them to one fifty-five on the morning of the murder.

They watched as the taxi turned off Park Street, navigated through the late-night revellers until pulling over at the rear of The Hippodrome. The view was of the hoardings around the latest building site, and the rear of the Trenchard Street carpark. Several people walked up the steep pavement to enter the carpark, only one vehicle entered, a people carrier with several passengers, and four cars exited before Jo tapped the screen.

"And there he is... or might be. Big man, overalls, granddad shoes. Damn you can't see his face clearly."

"Stop it there. Print that screen. That's two hours before the event, give or take, yes?"

"Yes, I—"

Meredith yelled for Seaton to join them.

Jo placed her hands over her ears. "Bloody hell, Gov, give a girl some warning."

"You bellowed? What've you found?" Leaning forward, Seaton squinted at the screen. "Fits the description, but not very clear, is it? What do you want me to do?"

"Give or take, that was caught two hours before the murder. Get a map, mark up the routes he could have taken on leaving the carpark, find out what cameras are on those routes, make sure we have the footage and find out where he went before he got handy with the knife."

"Will do. He could have gone straight there, of course, lots of doorways to hide in."

"Then prove it. We can't find him after the event, so it might help if we know where he was before it. Jo, that carpark must have CCTV – get it and find out if he was driving, and if he was, what?"

"On it. What do you want done with that printout?"

"Stick it on the board, get one of the techy guys to enhance it. Depending on what turns up in the next few hours, I ... Oh no. What do you reckon I've done now?" Fixing a smile, Meredith held out his hand and strode away. "Morning, or is it afternoon? How are you, sir? To what do we owe the pleasure?"

Chief Superintendent David Brownlow shook Meredith's hand. "I was in the area, heard you had a messy one and thought I'd pop in and see how you were doing."

"Early days, as you know. No ID on the victim, we're checking through all mispers and will get a shout if anyone fitting the bill is reported missing. Good ID on the killer, only from the back, but we think we've spotted him on CCTV in the vicinity two hours before, so we're trying to find out where he was in the interim. Trump has managed to get us airtime on TV and radio, in a nutshell we're firing on all cylinders, but with little to go on. Would you like a tea or coffee, or aren't you stopping?"

Brownlow's lips twitched. "If I didn't know better, I'd think you were trying to get rid of me. But I'm sure that can't be the case." Catching Trump's eye, he saluted, then jerked his thumb towards the door.

Stifling a grin at the grimace from Trump, Meredith headed to his office. "Ah, family business. I'll leave you to it."

"Thank you. And, Meredith, an update as soon as you have anything, don't want to be caught out."

"Of course. As soon as we know anything, I'll get someone to update you."

Fifteen minutes later, Trump reappeared and stuck his head around Meredith's door. "May I steal five minutes of your time, sir? I would have chosen a better moment, but as Uncle David has raised the subject, I thought two birds etcetera."

"That doesn't sound like a conversation I want to have. Are you leaving us, Trump? Has Uncle David found you a better position somewhere else?" Leaning back in his chair, Meredith supported his head in his hands. He knew he was out of order. Neither Trump nor his uncle took advantage of

their connection, but it sounded to him like Trump was on the move, and he didn't want to lose him.

"What? Of course not, and to be quite honest I—"

"Then why didn't you say so? Why the song and dance, what could a visit from Uncle David possibly have to do with me?"

"It's the wedding."

"Ah, the wedding. I'd ask how it's going, but I don't want to know. The best weddings are short and sharp with a good old knees-up somewhere that can put on a decent buffet. All this faffing about with colour schemes, seating arrangements and menus is an unnecessary distraction. What do you need? More time off?"

"Distraction from what?"

"Everything important." Making a point of looking at his watch, Meredith shook his head. "By my reckoning it has distracted you from your job for thirty minutes and distracted me from mine for five and counting."

"Ah, point made. Accepted, but Linda and Uncle—"

"For God's sake, Trump, spit it out, or we'll be here all night."

Stepping into the office, Trump shut the door. "Would you do me the great honour of being my best man?"

Meredith smirked. Not sure what he'd been expecting, he knew it certainly hadn't been that.

"Are you sure? Don't you have a posh friend from school or university that could do a proper job?"

"Don't put yourself down, sir. You have a very quick wit, and you can be sensitive on occasion."

"I wasn't putting myself down. I'd be wonderful at anything I chose to undertake. The question was code for 'Why me?'" Meredith pinched the bridge of his nose. "Look, Trump, cards on the table. I like you, I like Loopy, I think you're good together, and this is a better outcome of what did Uncle David want than I expected, but have you thought it through?"

"In what way? I consider you a friend and confidante, as well as my boss. A good friend at that. Are you looking for compliments? I'm sure I could think of some." Unable to hold back his grin, Trump took a seat. "I won't be offended if you're trying to say no. Hurt, but not offended."

"There really is no one else?"

"Not that I'd like to do the job, no."

"And there you have it. A job. I need more responsibility like a hole in the head." Releasing his head and slapping his hands on the desk, Meredith lifted a finger, which he pointed at Trump. "If I say yes, it's on these conditions: I'm not going somewhere exotic for an extended stag do. A delegate of my choice will arrange any stag do and it will be a one night only affair. My speech will be short. Funny, but short. Oh yes, and I don't suit a top hat, so if you're having tails forget it."

Jumping to his feet, Trump held out his hand. "Deal. Thank you, sir. I'm honoured."

"Well, you shouldn't be. And, Trump, on the day you can call me Meredith."

"Will do. We can iron out the details later. Thank you."

"And I'm not doing any bloody ironing. Simple, keep it simple. Now get out and get on with your job."

Smiling at Trump's retreating back, Meredith flipped open his diary. He loved a knees up as much as the next man, probably more, but he didn't want half the team distracted in the middle of a case. The wedding was four weeks away, and Meredith guessed he'd not been the first choice. That didn't offend him, after all, he wouldn't have chosen himself either.

A little after two o'clock, Meredith received a call from Frankie Callaghan.

"Sherlock, what have you got for me?"

"I think our victim is gay. There are signs of recent sexual activity, might even get some DNA. Thought you'd like to know before the full report gets typed up. And, Meredith, remember I said might be, and DNA results will take a few days."

"Of course I want to know. I also want to know why I'm only just finding out. You've had him for hours."

"I'm going. Believe it or not, I have work to do, I don't have time for your humour."

"Wasn't trying to be funny. I—"

"I stand corrected, I don't think you do funny, do you? That's the lot for now. You'll have to wait for lab results to come back."

"I can be very amusing. Thank you for the update."

"You're welcome. Bye, Meredith."

Clapping his hands, Meredith walked to the centre of the incident room.

"Listen up, Sherlock says our chap is gay. Signs of recent activity but the usual wait to see if there's any DNA that might be useful. Find out how many gay clubs are in the vicinity, and double check the CCTV from around that area. It gives us a probable motive for the killing and the damage to the heart. Could be a jilted lover. That's it, get on with it."

The day dragged on. Nothing new of any consequence came in, and the team scoured hours of CCTV footage. Meredith called the team together a little after six.

"It's been another long day, in the absence of anything worthwhile turning up, let's have a summary of what we have then you can all get out of here. Early start in the morning."

There were several clips in the vicinity of the murder and around the right time, where they believed they spotted their man, but none of them were of real use. They showed a large man moving within the sight of a camera for seconds, and although they were tagged as possible exhibits for when a fuller picture emerged, they raised more questions than they answered.

In one, their suggested target was walking towards Christmas Steps and the scene of the murder, but in another, minutes later, he was walking back towards town. In another, he was carrying a bag, but not in the next. They found no footage with even a slight resemblance to the victim.

Jo Adler switched off the recordings. "That's all we have at the moment, Gov, it might be useful eventually, but no help now. My next job is to get the registration of all the cars entering the carpark. I'm going to start two hours before the taxi's camera picked up our suspect, then work backwards from the sighting. If nothing else, when we catch him, we'll already have that information. And, before you ask, the camera captures every car coming into the building but is focused on the number plates. We won't get a facial. That's it."

Grimacing, Jo returned to her desk, but another thought occurred to her and she remained standing. "We should consider the fact that he might not have parked there, because if he planned this in detail, he might have walked into the Park Row entrance and then down and out onto Trenchard Street to avoid detection. What do you think?"

"Yep, I thought of that. But why? The Park Row entrance is closer to Christmas Steps, or the top of them where the attack took place."

Seaton held his hand up. "Perhaps he didn't plan it, not to get that victim anyway. Maybe he was simply out looking for a victim, hence the zigzagging around the area."

"Possibly, Tom, but why stay in that vicinity? I think it's more likely he knew his target, but didn't know when, or maybe even if, he'd be around. I ... excuse me." Trump held up a finger as he snatched up the receiver of the phone on his desk.

Meredith got to his feet. "And, on that note, that's enough for now, go home. Bright and early in the morning, unless of course something worthwhile comes up."

There was a rustle of papers, and the murmur of conversation as his team packed up. Meredith had almost made it to his office when Trump called out. Turning as the room fell silent, Trump kept his hand over the mouthpiece.

"I believe we may have found the identity of our victim."

Although there were smiles and a few shouts of delight as it appeared the case could now move forward, there were a few groans and disbelieving sighs from the team as they unbuttoned their jackets and pulled out their chairs.

Meredith stepped forward. "As you were. This isn't going to take all of us. Let's hear what Trump has to say, then the majority of you can go home, although you'll get a call if we need you."

The room fell silent as Trump completed the call and hung up.

"Central has taken a call from a Mrs Kentish. She lives in Cheltenham, her husband lives in Bristol, and she's been unable to get hold of him for over twenty-four hours. She wondered if we could go to his apartment and make sure he's okay. He's been ill. Central took a description and believe it fits our man."

"Cheltenham is just up the road. Why didn't she come down herself, and why call the police? Twenty-four hours isn't long if you're not living together. I assume they're not. Particularly if he also has an interest in men."

Walking to Trump's desk, Meredith looked down at the few words Trump had jotted down.

"She doesn't have a key, so knew one way or another someone would have to break in. He still lists her as his next of kin, and as mentioned he's ill, but didn't turn up for his hospital appointment." Ignoring the few comments of gallows humour about understatements, Trump continued, "The oncology unit at the BRI has been trying to get hold of him and called her to make sure all was well. She didn't have a clue, not spoken to him for a few weeks, but felt she should do something. Her something was to call us once she couldn't reach him by phone."

"And she described him? Why?"

"No idea. Perhaps Central asked for a description. The details are being emailed across."

"Go on then, have a look."

The email had arrived and Trump read out the basic description, concluding, "It certainly sounds like Christopher Kentish could be our man. He lives in Clifton."

"Okay, as this might be a wild goose chase, I want two volunteers for a bit of overtime. Check out the home, and if we find it is our man, get off to see the wife in Cheltenham." Meredith raised his own hand. "Make that one, you'll have the pleasure of my company."

They agreed that Jo would accompany Meredith, as it would be preferable having a female officer available if it was necessary to see the wife.

"The rest of you go home but keep your phones on. You never know what this might turn up. If you're not called in, seven o'clock in the morning. Adler, make your excuses to Aaron, then get hold of someone who can get us into the house, I'll get hold of Sherlock and see if he can shed any light on the oncology angle."

Chapter Five

Patsy looked around the overly furnished sitting room, shaking her head in disbelief.

"Wow, I thought you were exaggerating. I don't think I've ever seen so much stuff in one room. I suppose it's a bonus that it's so neat and tidy. How are you ever going to go through it all?"

"That's the thing. I don't think I can. I'll do the obvious stuff like her dressing table, and take a cursory look through the drawers, pulling out anything of real value, then I'll have to get a house clearance firm in and if there's anything of real value they'll have a bonus."

Henry Duggan held out his hands. "What else can I do? It would take far too long doing it for a couple of hours here and there, which is all I'm able to give. The saddest thing, of course, is not so much someone might find a wad of cash or a secret stash of valuable gems, which could have gone to the beneficiaries, but the memories that will just disappear." He pointed at a collage of photographs in a frame on the mantel. "Look how happy she seems. Particularly the skiing one, I don't know any of those pictured with her. That will end up in landfill, or if they keep the frame, perhaps recycled. Gone. Sad."

"You're right. It is sad, but then I suppose it's what happens even if you have a family. They will keep bits that are important to them, but unless they are also hoarders,

they'd have to get rid of most of this stuff too, one way or another at least. What would anyone do with things that weren't memories for them and have no value, sentimental or otherwise?"

"True. I wouldn't expect anyone to keep any of the junk I hold dear. Not even the wife. I probably should talk to her about having a clear-out at home before we pop our clogs. Our son will be stuck with it otherwise. Mind you, she'll tell me I'm being morbid, might send her over to see what I mean."

"Do that, because I have to say, Henry, I'm daunted by this task, I'm going to bring a couple of colleagues in to help, and if we find anything that seems to be of value I'll set it to one side. I also think you should sell some of the individual pieces of furniture. I don't know much about antiques, but the dining room suite, the piano, and that sideboard all look as though they shouldn't just be chucked in the back of a van."

"You're probably right, but I'm not sure I have the time or inclination. Call in whoever you like to help you, Patsy, it's a lot of paperwork to go through, with little prospect of success, or why would she not just have given me the detail I needed?"

"Who knows? But there are clues here, Henry, it's how much time you want us to take looking for them. Let me call the office now and see how much help I can get. I'll get some black bags out, and we'll bag any irrelevant paperwork ready for shredding and recycling. Box up the not sures and take anything we believe is relevant to the case. How does that sound?"

"Absolutely perfect."

"It will put up the daily rate, but I'll keep it as low as I can."

"Charge me the going rate, Patsy. You are not a charity, I know you won't ask for more than is due, and that's good enough for me. Poor old Amy must have known clearing this house would eat into her estate, and yet look at it." Throwing his arm towards the two glass-fronted cabinets, full to bursting point with books, documents and bric-a-brac, he gave a twitch of the shoulders. "No, Amy would understand the necessity." His eyes strayed to the attractive walnut clock on the sideboard. "Now, are you happy for me to leave you to it? I have a call to make in about half an hour, and I want to run through the file before I do."

"I'll be fine, thank you, Henry."

Once he'd left, Patsy walked through the house again, although she was unsure why. Every available storage space was stuffed to the brim. Even the meter cupboard had several plastic boxes of odds and ends balanced precariously on top of the meter. She pulled out her phone and called the office. Sharon Grainger, Patsy's late partner's wife, answered the phone.

Patsy explained her predicament.

"Let me have a look at the diary. How long do you reckon it will take?"

"Ooh, I don't know, a month or two. Sharon, seriously I have no idea. Could be a full week, but less if we get stuck in soon. I'll need to keep Linda focused and not off down memory lane with someone else's stuff, but most of this isn't going to be of use. We'll know that quite quickly."

36

"Linda is needed here for the next couple of days, she has to get that system sorted for Jenson before we distract her further. Although it would be a welcome break from the wedding plans. I'd offer to help myself, but to be honest I can't face it, I still haven't sorted through all Chris's stuff, so doing it for a stranger ain't going to happen. I'll send Angel round in about an hour. You'll probably get more done with her. Linda would only get side-tracked by the intrigue."

"You're probably right. Anything else I need to know about before I get started?"

"Nope, all under control."

~ ~ ~

Patsy searched the kitchen and found a roll of bin liners and took them through to the dining room. She tore several off, and going back into the sitting room, she opened one of the cupboards built into an alcove on each side of the fireplace. Lifting the nearest pile of documents and pamphlets, she took them to the dining room and began the laborious process of going through each document. By the time Angel appeared an hour later, she'd almost completed the left-hand cupboard.

Patsy found nothing of interest to the investigation: an old building society passbook, which she'd placed to one side for Henry Duggan, she'd put a pile of ten or so books to the left of the dining room door, and was on her sixth bin liner with paperwork to be shredded.

Grateful for the break she put the kettle on, explained why they were there, and the system she had in place.

Drink in hand, Angel sipped her tea as she walked through the house. When she returned to Patsy in the dining room, she drummed her fingers on the table. "Do you mind if I take my own approach for an hour or two? Because it's clear there's money in this house, and if your bloke wants to maximise what he gets you need to sell some of this stuff, not get clearance in."

"Yes, I realise that, but Henry doesn't have the time or inclination and I've got an investigation to get going. I

haven't got time to be haggling with people on stuff I know little or nothing about."

"I'll do it. During one of the brief periods my dad was actually working, he did house clearances and sometimes took me with him, and the bloke he was working for said something like, on fifty per cent of jobs we earn more from what we can't see, to what we get for the rest."

"I'm sure, but we don't have the time, Angel. Henry will pop in later you can speak to him, but I can't see he'd want to pay for it."

"What's he got to lose? He will make more money, I guarantee it."

"Okay, but what I don't get, is even if that's true and we do it your way, why? Why do you care?"

"Because we know something is hidden here, I've had a lifetime of my family hiding things – in one way or another. You'll remember when we met, I had stolen money, and all sorts of bits and bobs that were valuable to someone hidden below the floor in the cupboard under my stairs."

"Yes, you did. Go on then, you have until I have the second cupboard done. Anything of interest goes on this table, all shreddable rubbish in a black bag, the rest the house clearance people can deal with." Holding out a black bag, Patsy jerked her thumb towards the sitting room. "Start in there, I want to see you at work."

Patsy was impressed at how quickly Angel worked, it was as though she'd been trained. Starting with the various couches and chairs, Angel checked down the sides before turning them upside down, then content there was nothing more to find than the four pounds sixty in loose change, and a pair of silver earrings, she moved on to the bookcase. The books were removed one shelf at a time, and Angel leafed through them looking for documents, removed dust jackets, and checked the first few pages for any notes, before

replacing the books on the shelf she'd taken them from. The result was four postcards of varying ages, several photographs, the copy of a birth certificate, and fifty pounds in ten pound notes. She placed this stash on the dining room table.

"Let me call a friend who deals in second-hand books, by the time we finish we'll have half a shop full. I'll get you a decent price."

"Feel free, I didn't know there was a market for second-hand books, not unless you count charity shops."

"Yep, I know a man who knows a man who runs a second-hand book shop. He takes what he wants and donates the remainder to charities and hostels. I'm moving on to the sideboard."

The pair worked in silence, making a collection of things which may be useful or valuable. Patsy had almost finished the second floor to ceiling cupboard when Angel called out triumphantly.

"Yes! Oh, sorry, that might have been a little over the top. You did say late seventies, didn't you?"

"I did. What have you got?"

Angel counted the photographs she was holding. "Nine photographs, in a blank envelope apart from the date 1978." Looking at the photographs, she gave a shrug. "No names, don't know how we'll find out who's who in these groups, looks like they're all having a good time though. My granny used to have a dress like that, one of the few photographs I've got of her."

Patsy took the photographs and leafed through them. "All taken in the same place by the look of it. A bar of some description. If I'm not mistaken, the girl in the red skirt is Amy. Look."

Walking to the mantel, Patsy held one photograph against the collage Henry had pointed out earlier. "What do you think?"

"You're right. Is the woman next to her this girl? Hair is a different colour but look at the nose."

"Could be. Pop them back in the envelope and add them to the pile. Keep going, Amy. You might be on a roll."

By a little after two o'clock, the pair had worked their way through both the dining room and sitting room. They had found a small amount of jewellery, mainly odd earrings, over seventy pounds in cash, a birth certificate, an old passport, and a selection of photographs. Patsy had set aside a handful of journals from various years, the oldest being 1983 and the most recent 2010. In amongst the things Patsy had put in the bags for shredding were numerous medical publications, and periodicals. Angel had fished them all out, insisting they would have value, if only to university students.

"Great timing, we have thirty minutes before Bill the Book gets here. Help me collect the books from the rest of the house. He might not have to make a second journey."

"Okay, but we haven't even thought about the loft. There could be more."

"If we get a move on, we'll find out, and then he can wait, or help." Angel was already walking into the sunroom. "I'll finish down here, and you do the master bedroom. There were quite a few in there."

Patsy saluted. "Yes, boss."

By the time they'd finished, Patsy estimated they had around four hundred books. Angel had set aside a birthday card which had in it what appeared to be a cryptic note, or it was to her, but they hadn't discovered anything else of interest. Angel had just filled the kettle when the doorbell rang.

"I'll get it. You finish making the tea. I'll ask him if he wants one." Leaving Patsy to it, she went to open the door. "Oh hello. We weren't expecting you, Patsy's just making tea."

"Good, because I've bought cakes." Handing Angel a bag from a local patisserie, Linda Callow removed her coat. "The cavalry has arrived. Get an extra cup out," she called as she peeped into the sitting room. "Delightful house, I expect there's carpet under all that furniture somewhere."

Before she reached the kitchen, the doorbell rang again.

"Go on through, it's Bill the Book."

"Ooh, are we dealing with that sort now?"

"What sort, I–" The bell rang again, this time for a little longer. "Linda, shut up." Pulling open the door, Angel smiled. "Hi, Bill, thanks for coming, you're going to like this. Before we start, would you like a drink?"

Linda looked at the young man on the doorstep. At least his face was youthful, as was the mop of blond hair that fell over one eye. His clothes, however, looked as though he should teach geography in a classroom and one which still had a blackboard and inkwells in the desks. Smiling at him, Linda took his order and wandered along the hall to find Patsy.

"I thought I heard you. Sharon gave me the impression you were indispensable. Tea or coffee?"

"Two teas, a bloke called Bill has arrived. Three in mine, none in his, and for the record I am indispensable. Client is procrastinating as several employees have asked for tweaks on the system if, and I quote, someone is mucking about with it. Don't worry, I controlled my response, but I explained it would be cheaper if he got a list so I could do it all in one go. So, here I am. With cake."

"Ah, you wanted to come and have a nose around and found a get out of jail card. Should I expect Sharon too?"

"Nah. Sharon had her nails done yesterday and has an appointment with a boutique somewhere. Hey, good news about the skipper. I got so fed up waiting for Louie, I almost did it myself."

Much to his irritation, Linda had christened Meredith the skipper when he became a partner in the firm.

"What news? What's Meredith done now? And you almost did what?" Patsy watched Linda's face fall.

"He hasn't told you, has he? Well, I hope that doesn't mean he's undecided. I've got enough on my plate."

"Linda! Told me what?"

"He's agreed to be Louie's best man. Louie was naturally delighted, as was I, but I was also relieved that it was one more item to cross off the list. You see?"

"I can see that Meredith has agreed to be Louie's best man, and I'm delighted too, but when did all this happen, and why might he be having second thoughts? Linda, you usually supply too much information, why are you being so evasive?"

"I'm not. Louie asked the skipper this morning, it's now afternoon, I know they're busy, but I'd have thought he'd at least have texted you, if he was excited."

"I'm not sure Meredith does excited, he usually just wears a smug smile. I'm sure he'll be saving it for when he sees me. How long have I got you for? We've done two and a bit of the five rooms on this floor, although to be honest I doubt we'll find anything in the kitchen."

A smile lit up Linda's face. "Yes, you're right. I forgot how the skipper likes to tease. It's this wedding, I'm my normal super-efficient self when I'm dealing with anything else, but never, EVER, did I imagine organising such a small wedding would be so irritating. I've almost called it off twice. There's a lot to be said for taking the cheap route, like the skipper did. And, for the rest of the day, maybe into tomorrow, it depends how long they take to decide what extras they want. The rest of it is completed."

"Great, and for the record, don't tell Meredith we had a cheap wedding, he did it to avoid the stress you are experiencing. By the look of it, he was right. Grab that tea and come through here and I'll explain the system we've been using."

When she entered the dining room, Angel grinned and waved a photo at her. "It's only a picture, but it's a good one. It might help. Bob found it stuck between two pages. Not sure which one of us missed it, but the book is valuable too. First edition, and I was right, he does want the medical publications, the students buy them."

Giving Bob his tea and a quick hello, Patsy returned her attention to Angel. "That's all splendid news. Why is the photograph a good one?"

"Because as you will see, Jeremy Rossiter, or I hope he's that Jeremy, is in it."

Taking the photograph, Patsy looked at the names on the back, smiling she flipped it over to study the faces.

"A black tie event. They don't look much like students, do they? Linda, write these names down, please. Andrew, Claire, Amy, Jeremy, Pen, Chris, Sue and Bea." Turning to study the faces again, she mused, "I wonder if they are in the right order? We know that's Amy, and if they are, this, ladies, is Jeremy. Handsome, wasn't he?" Patsy tapped the man standing next to Amy and stood back to allow the others to look.

"Working on the basis that this is him, the others might be some or all of the four. I can't wait to find out what they did that got them killed. Shall I make a start?" Linda looked around.

"Got them killed? What exactly are you working on? Is this some sort of insurance fraud, killed for the pay-out?"

Book still in hand, Bill wandered over and tried to take another look at the photograph.

"An insurance job?"

With a laugh, Angel patted him on the shoulder. "Sorry, Bill, I should have said, I'm working for a private investigator at the moment, and ..." Looking at Patsy, she asked, "Can I give him an outline?"

"Of course. They're all dead, and I don't think he did it. How do you two know each other?"

"Don't change the subject, that's boring. What are you working on? May I?" Lifting the photo, Bill squinted at it while Patsy gave him an abridged version on why they were there. "Wow. Cool. I can have a look through some year books, they still did them back then. But unless you know the names, won't be much more use than this photo."

"Your turn. How do you two know each other?"

"I went to uni with Dan, her bloke, well I did until I dropped out. I was left a bookshop. My uncle owned Bill's Books on Park Row. It was because of him I was studying English, specialising in ... too much information! Anyway, he got really ill, cancer, and I was virtually running the shop for much of my second year. When he died, he left it to me, and I thought, it's got to be better than teaching, which is probably what I'd have ended up doing, not having any sort of vocation, et voila! I became Bill."

"Is that not your name then?" Linda grinned as he shook his head. "You see, PHPI, not everyone has to use their own name."

"Paul. Paul's papers didn't have the same ring, but to be honest it's because when people find out I'm the proprietor they make assumptions and call me Bill."

"And you make enough to make a living, I thought bookshops were struggling."

"Linda, that's a bit personal. Sorry, Bill ... Paul. Linda doesn't do subtle, and interesting as this all is, we really need to get on. We haven't even looked to see what delights the loft holds yet."

"I'll pop up and look if you like. I'm nearly done here, you've got a couple I'll pay you for individually, but the rest are worthless."

"Unless you run a second-hand bookshop."

"Of course. But you want rid, and I'm not ripping you off on the good stuff. Shall I?" Bill pointed to the ceiling.

"Yes, I'll come with you. You can get rid of the cobwebs. Is that okay, Patsy?"

42

"Of course. I'll get Linda started."

Thirty minutes later, Linda had almost finished going through the contents of the sunroom, and Bill had assisted Angel in lugging all the items from the loft down into the box room at the front of the house. They had added a further twenty or so books to the pile.

Bill found Patsy emptying a drawer in the hall table as he added the last two books to the now considerable pile. "I'm done. Do I speak to you about money? By the way, if you want rid of this furniture, I know someone that will give you a fair price."

"No, not me, hang on, I'll get the chap you need."

After a quick phone call to Henry, Patsy went to put the kettle on, knowing he'd want an update once he'd agreed on a price. There was little to show for their efforts connected to the case. They had a jewellery pile with a bracelet and two further earrings, the card, and a pile of photographs. The ever-growing pile of stuffed bin liners showed that their clearance efforts were bearing more fruit.

It took less than ten minutes for Henry to agree on a price for the books. When Bill went off to collect some
boxes from his car, Henry took a seat at the kitchen table with Patsy.

"I have to say, even though you have found nothing of use to the investigation, and I suppose that's a good thing in a way, I'm most impressed with how much rubbish you've cleared. I'll load the car up first thing and take the bags for shredding. I wasn't expecting to make any money on the books, that was a bonus. Thank you. Oh, yes, while I think about it, I thought I should get things moving, and I've arranged for a couple of estate agents to come around tomorrow, one at ten thirty, the other at two o'clock, I can be here for the first one, but have an appointment in the afternoon, would you mind showing him around, my wife can pop over if it's not possible, so don't feel obligated."

"I can do both if it will help, they hardly need handholding. It's no… blimey, what's got her excited?"

Linda had yelled, and then started speaking so quickly it was difficult to understand her. She came running into the room as Patsy got to her feet.

"I've only found something crucial. The problem is this!" Waving what looked like a plant catalogue at them, she placed a ruled sheet of paper carefully on the table. "First read that."

Henry Duggan and Patsy stood shoulder to shoulder to do as instructed, and Angel came running down the stairs to see what all the excitement was about.

"What? What's happened?"

"I think you're right, Linda." Turning to Angel, Patsy lifted the sheet and read it to her.

And so, my dear friend, please be on guard. I honestly believe I'm right. Poor old Andrew, he was so scared. I was like you and told him he was mistaken, exaggerating even, but now he's dead. DEAD, Amy, gone. Our lovely Andrew never hurt a soul in his life.

Ignore me if you will, but please, be careful, and please keep in touch. I couldn't bear to lose you too – and to whom? Why did Andrew tell me to be careful, but not why? It makes little sense, but it seems he was right. If anything happens to me, I meant what I said, you must go to the police so they can protect you. I know you are rolling your eyes and asking why I don't go to the police myself, but I have no proof. Only a distraught conversation with an old friend which made no sense, although his fears became reality. We both know that it wasn't an accident and it certainly wasn't intentional. Not Andrew. BUT if I get bumped off too, you must go to the police.

Have to go now, I have a patient coming any minute, but I will call you tonight. I'm only writing this because then you will have evidence with which to go to the police.

Take care,
Sue x

"I believe that's Susan, one of Amy's friends. I met her a couple of times, but a few years back now. Is there a date?" Looking at Linda, he pointed at the item she was still holding aloft.

"Probably. There's also an address, but it's well and truly stuck to this seed catalogue." Placing the catalogue on the table, Linda explained, "It was sticking to the back of the bookshelf beneath the window in the sunroom. I don't know if there was a leak, or it was condensation, but I'm guessing Amy put it at the back of the books for safe keeping, I mean who would hide a seed catalogue?"

Henry picked up the offending catalogue and peered at the first sheet of the letter which, barring one corner, was stuck written side down to the catalogue. Although Susan had a neat flowing hand, it was impossible to work out what she had written.

"Well, that's a blow. This was probably what Amy was hoping I'd find. Poor Susan. I'm not prone to flights of fancy, you know. I like things neat, tidy and explainable. But I knew Amy too well to let her down, and having read this, I'm beginning to think she was right."

"All is not lost, not definitely, anyway. I know a man that might be able to help. What do you know about Susan? She mentions a patient, was she a doctor?"

"Psychiatrist, I believe. Most of Amy's friends, those I met anyway, were in the medical profession in some way. I believe she lived in Chippenham, or did when I met her, she'd brought Amy a basket full of goods from the Farmers' market, and … sorry, none of that's relevant."

"Where she lives might be." Patsy patted his hand. "I'm glad you took it seriously, now I also think she was right to alert you."

Picking up the photo of the black-tie event, Angel handed it to Henry. "Is that the Susan you met, and I'm guessing if so, that's Andrew. Where are the address books, diaries, and stuff that old people keep?"

"Yes, that's her. Oh, and Amy wasn't old, she was only sixty." Henry knew from the twitch of Angel's lips that she considered sixty to be old. Grinning, he shook his head. "Not to me, anyway. Right, I'd better get back. Good work, ladies. Let me know when you leave, a text will do, even us oldies do texts."

Lifting a large envelope from the table, Patsy slid in the catalogue and the end of the letter. "Another hour, ladies, and we'll call it a day. I have Peggy coming round for dinner and I have to shop first, and …" She paused as the doorbell rang. "That must be Bill, Angel, I'll leave you to sort him out, Linda, finish the sunroom. I'll give Frankie a ring and see whether he thinks he can unstick the other page from the catalogue and tell us what we're missing."

Unable to reach Frankie, Patsy placed the envelope next to the one containing the photographs and card, she'd take them home and although it was a long shot, she'd try to find something on Google while dinner was cooking.

Working without a break for the next hour they found nothing further of use but had managed to go through all but a row of cupboards in the kitchen. Washing up the cups, Patsy explained her plans for the next day.

"Not sure when I'll speak to Frankie, but whatever happens I think the best plan of attack is for one of us to finish the kitchen, and the other two to start on the stuff brought down from the loft. Hopefully, as that's much older, it might bear more fruit. Having had a cursory glance around the bedrooms, and now all the books have gone, there's not much there to search. You two get off, I'll see you in the morning."

"I'll bring coffee and cakes. What time, eight thirty?" Pulling on her coat, Linda pointed at Patsy. "Don't forget to let me know what

Meredith says. Or does, if it's only going to be a smug grin. I don't want the worry overnight."

"Linda, he said yes. Go home, dream sweet dreams." Putting on her own coat, Patsy ushered them down the hall and locked the door behind them.

~ ~ ~

Patsy had just finished loading the shopping into her car when her phone rang. Suppressing a sigh, she knew Meredith would be late for dinner.

"Husband, I'm in a rush, just tell me what time."

"Charming I'm sure, but I have no idea. There's a possibility our victim has been identified, if that's the case, I'll be going up to Cheltenham to see the wife. Could be a late one. Apologise to Peggy for me."

"Hmm, I suppose that's a half decent excuse. I don't suppose any of your team were available, so despite having a dinner engagement it had to be you."

Despite her words, Meredith heard the amusement in her voice.

"It's only Peggy. Although don't tell her I said that. He had a weird set up, so I want to see first-hand."

"I can't even be bothered to go there. I must get on myself. With you not turning up Peggy won't be best pleased if dinner isn't even cooking when she arrives. Bye, Meredith, good luck."

"Thank you. How did things go with Henry Duggan's case by the way?"

"Nothing to report of any consequence other than the fact that I'm covered in dust and need a shower."

"Shame. Jo's here, I have to go. Bye."

Dropping her phone into her bag, Patsy headed for home. She tried to call Frankie several times, but knew he too must be working, as the answer service picked up each call. Finally, she left a brief message.

On arriving home, she found Peggy sipping wine at the kitchen table. Peggy had been a witness Meredith met on a previous case and had become the self-appointed matriarch of the small family.

"Ah, the wanderer returns. What time do you call this? And where's Merewinkle?" Frowning, Peggy cocked her head. "You look pale. Are you feeling okay?"

46

"Yes, fine, thank you. Just a long day and I'm covered in dust. I'll get dinner sorted and jump in the shower. I'm sure we can find you something to keep you occupied."

"Amanda's in the shower. She let me in." Peggy made a show of turning to look at the clock. "I'm sure we said seven thirty, and you haven't told me where Merewinkle is."

"We did indeed." Unloading the shopping, Patsy pointed a cucumber at Peggy. "It's only five past seven, so you're early. As for Meredith, he's working on a nasty murder case, and hopefully they've just discovered the identity of the victim. He sends his apologies and says he'll get home as soon as he can."

"Typical. He always gets a juicy case when he should be entertaining me. But don't sidetrack. You said seven thirty, so I got here on time. Seven for seven thirty, time for canapés and cocktails before the main event."

"In which case it was seven thirty for eight, and you know it. If I'd meant any different, I would have said. I have an excellent teacher in saying what you mean. Were you bored, Peggy?"

"Enough to start banging my head against the wall. I shall deny it if you tell anyone, but I miss Antony when he's not around. But they've finally decided his mother will come and live over here, they're going to rent first, then find somewhere to buy. They get back tomorrow. But at least they will be living in Bristol, and I'll get to see more of Pablo. He's almost three, you know, such a bright lad." Peggy's eyes twinkled. "Fluent in two languages by the time you're three. That's impressive, although, of course, he has me to thank for his English."

Antony was Spanish and training to be a solicitor, He had a brief fling with Meredith's late ex-wife leaving her pregnant. She died shortly after the birth, and Antony took their son to live with him. While he was searching for a permanent home, he lived with Peggy.

"Oh dear. I hope they find something close, Antony's mum depends on you, not having any other friends over here. How's her English coming along?"

"Not as good as her grandson. On the other hand, my Spanish repertoire has grown, I even know a few curses, can't wait to use them on Merewinkle."

Pulling a chopping board from the drawer, Patsy laughed. "He'll ignore insults in any language, you'd be wasting your time. Chicken and chorizo pasta okay for you?"

"Is there anything else?"

"Nope. Not if you want to eat tonight."

"Then it will have to be. Move over, what can I do?"

"None for me, I'm not stopping." Amanda, Meredith's daughter appeared. "I came home to pack the last of my stuff up and needed a shower."

"I'm guessing you're seeing Frankie? I've been trying to get hold of him for a couple of hours with no joy. I have no idea why you are taking on a property when you'll hardly be there."

Amanda didn't reply, and the two women turned to look at her. It was Peggy that spoke.

"What? What aren't you saying? Come on, Amanda, you can speak freely in front of us. Merewinkle isn't here."

"I'm not. I'm not going to live in it, I mean. I'm still buying it, but I'm going to let it out. Frankie and I have decided, that, as you pointed out, it would be pointless and unnecessarily expensive, but the flat will still be a wonderful investment."

"Oh. When are you going to tell your father, I'll make sure I'm out?" Patsy held out her arms and hugged Amanda. "What I mean is congratulations."

"I'll have one of those," Peggy pulled Amanda away from Patsy, and hugged her tight, and in a theatrical whisper, asked, "You're not pregnant, are you? That would be a good reason for changing your plans."

Patsy's hand flew to her mouth. "I didn't think of that. Are you?"

Amanda flushed and shook her head. "I am not. Although had a bit of a panic over that last month, false alarm. So now, like the educated woman of medicine I am, I've sorted that out."

"Ah shame, we could do with more young blood, but remember, when it does happen, I have to be in the room when you tell Merewinkle he's going to be a grandfather." Hooting her familiar laugh, Peggy turned back to the chopping board. "Let me get on with this, or I'll die of starvation. Patsy, get in that shower."

A relieved Patsy squeezed Amanda's hand. "That was almost a shock. Now, I'd better do as I'm told. Have a lovely evening."

Halfway up the stairs, Patsy remembered the catalogue and called to Amanda. "Would you do me a favour? In my bag are two envelopes, one has some photographs, the other a seed catalogue with a rather crucial piece of writing paper stuck to it. Would you give it to Frankie and tell him I'll email him?"

"Will do."

When Patsy returned, Amanda had left, dinner was almost ready, and Peggy waved a photograph at her.

"I know them. What have they done?"

48

Chapter Six

Smiling, Jo watched Meredith jog back across the road. He waved the bag he was carrying as he approached. Back in the car, he handed her a wad of napkins.

"Five more minutes won't hurt. We don't know if we're on a wild goose chase yet, and I can't do any chasing on an empty stomach. Haven't had fried chicken for months." Pulling a box from the bag, he handed it to Jo before opening his own and selecting a large piece of chicken. They ate in silence for a few moments.

"I feel so guilty, it's curry night and Aaron cooks, and he will put one up for me. I'll never manage both. This is lovely though, good shout, Gov."

"And your problem is what? This isn't a real meal, not you and your two pieces, anyway. You can have the curry for supper. Me? I know Patsy will have done something healthy. Tasty but healthy. Never quite takes the edge off the hunger."

"I obviously don't have your appetite."

"Then stick it in the fridge and bring it in for me tomorrow. He'll never know it wasn't you." Selecting the last piece of chicken, Meredith waved it at her. "This will be a des res. Expensive clothes, Sion Hill address, wife lives in Cheltenham, and it's called an apartment. Did you find anything on him?"

"I did, but des res?"

"Desirable residence. Where have you been living?" Dropping the stripped bone back into the box, he shoved it in the bag and wiped his hands. "Go on, tell me what you found before we get there."

Starting the engine, Meredith headed for the Downs. Jo read through her notes.

"Assuming this is our bloke, because the photograph on Google is old and the bloke in it has lots of hair, we are on our way to the home of Christopher Kentish, born Cheltenham nineteenth of June 1961. The eldest son of Edward Kentish, jeweller to royalty and the stars. Inherited the family business in 1988 a year after marrying Beatrix Holmes. No children that I could find."

"Good work, we're here."

Indicating, Meredith cursed as he slowed to find a parking space. "Might be a des res, but there's still no bloody parking. Don't know why anyone wants to live in Clifton, it's a nightmare." Reaching the end of the parking rank, and the property he wanted, Meredith parked on the double yellow lines on the bend in the road. "I doubt we'll be long."

Exiting the car first, Jo pointed at the Clifton Suspension Bridge. "There's your answer. What a view to wake up to every morning."

Turning, Meredith agreed. The iconic bridge looked stunning when lit up at night. "Yes, I suppose it's better than a brick wall. This one." Climbing the few steps which led to the front door, he peered at the bell. "Only one." Looking over the railings to his left, he jerked his thumb. "That is the basement flat, this is the rest. It's not an apartment, it's a house." Waving his hand up towards its facade, he shook his head. "Not what I'd call an apartment."

Placing his hand against the door, he gave a shove. Nothing happened, and he bent to peer through the letterbox. The hall was so dark there was nothing to see.

"Let's ask the neighbours, would be a shame to damage this door."

"I'll go." Skipping down the steps, Jo rang the bell of the basement flat. An old man appeared after a few minutes.

"Yes, madam, how may I assist?"

Jo pulled out her ID. "DC Jo Adler. We've been asked to check on your neighbour above. His wife is concerned about him, she's not been able to get hold of him for a few days and has asked us to pop in. There doesn't seem to be anyone at home. I don't suppose you've seen him or have a key, do you?"

"His wife!" The old man was visibly shocked. "I didn't know such a creature existed. He's lived there, must be fifteen years now, and I've never seen or heard of a wife. Mind you, he's not always home. Chaos when he first moved in, and the noise the builders made—"

"I'm sure, so you haven't seen him recently?"

Meredith came to join Jo in the tiny courtyard. "Evening, sir, DCI Meredith. Do you have a key?"

"DCI? What's he done? Yes, come on in. No one has asked for it for years, I'm sure I know where it is though."

Baring his teeth at Jo as the old man turned his back, Meredith gave Jo a push, and they followed him into a surprisingly elegant apartment.

50

"This is nice. Have you been here long?" Meredith looked around the spacious kitchen as the man searched a drawer in the floor to ceiling dresser.

"Thirty years or more. We moved in, that is me and my wife, she's been gone seven years now. She didn't much like him."

"Mr Kentish? Why's that?"

"Because he didn't speak. Pleasantries, of course, but never conversation. Maureen liked a good chat."

"How did you end up with a key? If he wasn't friendly, seems an odd thing to do." Desperate to take over the search, Meredith pulled out a chair at the small kitchen table.

"Plumbers. They had to turn the water off when they put the heating system in. Something was wrong with what they did, and..." Turning to face Meredith, the man rubbed his balding head. "Do you know, I can't remember. But we needed to let them in if we were to get our water back on. Never took it back. I've no idea if that was an arrangement, or omission. But I know I have it because I saw it last week, or perhaps the week before. Labelled upstairs, which is probably not very safe. Not that we've ever been burgled, but you never know."

Giving a laugh, Jo stepped forward. "I doubt they'd ever find it. You seem to have a lot of stuff. Are you sure it was in there?"

"One of these. I was looking for the pliers, can't remember why, but I do remember seeing it and tucking it in... That's where it is." Walking to the end of the dresser, he opened the glazed cabinet above. It housed a bone china dinner service, and lifting the lid of a delicate looking sugar bowl he produced a key with a cardboard label. He gave it to Jo. "There, I knew it."

Getting to his feet, Meredith took the key. "Thank you, much appreciated. We might keep hold of it if that's alright with you."

"Oh, I don't know about that. Not without Christopher's permission. Wouldn't seem right. Although I suppose you could give me a receipt."

"Jo will do that for you while I pop upstairs. When was the last time you saw him?"

"A couple of nights ago. Probably... No, I don't know for sure. But Helen, my cleaner, had been so it would have been Tuesday or Thursday, because that's when she comes. He was arguing with someone. A man. I say arguing, the man was shouting, Christopher was reserved, showed restraint and just kept saying no until he went in and closed the door. The language that man used was disgusting. I'm surprised he didn't have the entire street out."

"Where were you when all this was happening? Did you see the man?"

"Only his legs. I'd come out to put the mop back in the cupboard in the courtyard, Helen had forgotten to do it. At first I thought it was drunks passing by, but then I saw his legs pacing back and forth and heard Christopher. You see?"

Exchanging a glance with Jo, Meredith smiled. "I do. Jo is going to stay here and take a statement from you. Remember everything as best you can, and I'll be back down."

"A statement? Has something happened to him? Was that man involved? Goodness me."

"That's what we're trying to find out. I won't be long."

Inserting the key in the lock, Meredith crossed his fingers that there wasn't an alarm, he hadn't thought to ask, and didn't want to go back down. Pushing the door open, he waited a few seconds. No alarm. Stepping over the threshold, he paused, calling out before going any further.

"Mr Kentish? It's the police. Do not be alarmed, I'm coming in."

He waited only seconds, and having found the light switch, he knew there was no one there who would worry about the police. Pulling his phone from his pocket, he called the station.

"DCI Meredith. I'm at the home of Christopher Kentish. Full details on the system. It's been turned over. Get me a forensic team here as soon as you can. I'm going to do a walk through to make sure no one's here. I'll call an ambulance if necessary, just get me forensics."

Stepping around the upturned hall table, he pushed open the nearest door with his elbow. It was the kitchen. A few drawers had been opened, but other than that it was clear. Moving along the hall, he pulled on some gloves, found the light switches and checked the dining room, utility room, downstairs toilet, and a bedroom. All the rooms had been searched, the damage in some worse than others.

On reaching the next floor, he realised why there had been a bedroom on the ground floor. The sitting room was the width of the house and the three windows overlooked the bridge. It was a spectacular view. Turning away, a smudge on the door caught his attention. He could see it was blood. His eyes skimmed the room. There were no other marks that he could see. Exiting the room he entered the bathroom. Other than the cabinet above the sink being open there was nothing to see. They had caused minimal damage in the single bedroom, but when he entered the master bedroom, he knew the killer had been there. He stepped into the room and took photographs with his phone.

Above the bed was what he believed to be the word 'GUILTY' written in the same dirty brown red colour he'd seen on the door. To one side of

52

the bed, a large oil painting was propped up with a hole kicked through the middle of it. Meredith tilted his head to look at what remained of the picture the correct way up, but he didn't know what the composition was, nor who the artist might have been. Everything about the property screamed money, so he guessed it had been worth something.

But what he was most interested in was the lump of flesh sitting on the crumpled bedspread. Although it would need to be confirmed, he guessed it was the remainder of Christopher Kentish's heart. Noting the trail of tiny red dots, he followed them to a door on the other side of the room. He pushed it open with his foot. They had left the seat of the ensuite toilet up, and blood smeared over the taps above the basin. On closer inspection, the basin had some red staining around the plug, as did the towel hung on the holder next to it.

Allowing himself a brief smile, Meredith hoped that some of the killer's blood was also left there. Leaving the room, he took the last flight of stairs. He found two further bedrooms, one had been barely touched, the other had considerable damage to the door of a built-in cupboard where a substantial safe was bolted to its base. It was locked. Stepping back, Meredith examined the door, and guessed it had been kicked in from frustration by the person who had been unable to open the safe.

Leaving the room, Meredith hurried back down the stairs. He checked the key was in his pocket before closing the front door behind him. Jo called her goodbyes and reached the top of the steps as Meredith pulled his gloves off.

"Nothing there I take it? What Mr Thomas told me might be of use. We'll need to do a door to door."

"We will. Look." Meredith handed her his phone.

"Shit. Who are you calling in? I take it you don't want to wait until tomorrow."

"You're absolutely right. Call Trump, he'll moan the least. Give me the phone. I need to make sure the wife is going to be there. And get hold of Sherlock."

His first call was unsuccessful. Beatrix Kentish had not been at home when she made the call but in London, staying with friends. She would travel home the next day.

"Is this about Christopher, is that why you're calling? I'm with friends, you can tell me over the phone. Is he dead?"

"I think so, yes. But I'd rather speak to you in person. Can we meet tomorrow?"

"Oh dear, poor Christopher." There was silence for a moment while Beatrix Kentish composed herself. "I feared as much, and yes. Shall I come to you?"

To Meredith's delight she agreed to get off the train at Templemeads station. That meant he wouldn't have to waste time driving to her. He gave her his number.

"If I can't be there myself, someone will pick you up and we'll get you back to Cheltenham once we're done. Wait by the flower stall at the entrance. You have my number, call me if you have any delays."

"Of course, I won't have to see him, will I?"

"I'm afraid so. We need a formal identification. We can do it by photograph if you don't want to see him. I'm sorry for your loss, Mrs Kentish. I'll make this as painless as possible."

"Loss? Oh, yes. Thank you. Thank you for being so kind, I'll see you tomorrow." With a gulp of air to hold back the tears, Beatrix Kentish hung up.

Getting hold of Frankie Callaghan on the second attempt, Meredith tried charm as his first offensive.

"Evening, Sherlock. I hope I'm not disturbing you."

"It's eight o'clock in the evening, I'm in a restaurant, so yes, you are. But thank you for asking, it's never bothered you before."

Hearing the amusement, Meredith tutted. "I was doing polite because I think I just found the last piece of your puzzle."

"Oh, I didn't know I was looking for one. Cut to the chase, Meredith, our food will be here any minute."

"Are you with my daughter? If so, I think it would only be polite to humour me. I've found the heart. Or to be more accurate, the bit you're missing. If you're out gallivanting, what do you want me to do with it?"

"Where? Don't touch it. I'll send someone to deal with it. Is it damaged?"

"It's not beating if that's what you mean. And I think it was used to paint a wall. Not the whole thing, just the word 'Guilty'."

"Very droll. Where is it?"

"On a bed in the victim's house. I've got our forensic team going over now. Just need to tell them where to get it to you and. But I'm guessing you're not going to give up your dinner to look at it."

"No, Meredith, I'm not. Let me make a phone call. I'll get back to you."

"Thank you. Enjoy your meal, don't worry about me, not eaten since breakfast." He hung up with a smile as Frankie suggested, with much amusement, that would never be the case.

54

As he finished the call, Trump arrived, and he beckoned him over.
"False alarm, sort of."

"It's not the heart or …" Trump looked bewildered.

"No, it is the heart, but I don't have to hightail it to Cheltenham with Adler, so you don't need to oversee the forensic team. The wife is in London, she's coming into Bristol Templemeads around mid-day tomorrow. I've arranged to see her then. Talk of the devils."

A dark van pulled up and Meredith returned the salute from the senior officer. He walked over and as they put on the shoe protectors and lifted various pieces of equipment out of the van he explained the situation.

"Hello, Phil. Our victim lived in this house and as Jo probably told you part of his heart is missing. I think it was used to leave a message on the bedroom wall, and left on the bed. There's a trail of blood from the bed to the ensuite where there's further staining. The place has also been ransacked. I'm guessing there's little left of any value that was easily transportable. Other than the assumed killer, I'm the only one to have been in there, and yes, I had gloves on. It's four beds, how long do you think it will take?"

"I haven't got that piece of string with me, Meredith, but every surface will need doing, so we'll be here all night. Are you staying?"

"Good. Because he's got a key. Trump, arrange to have the locks changed and for a uniform to stand guard." Returning his attention to the forensics officer, Meredith held out his hand. "I'll be back first thing. Call me if you find anything I might want to know about, and Frankie Callaghan will send someone over to deal with the remains of the heart."

"Will do. Now get out of the way and let us get on."

Hearing Jo's voice, Meredith looked over the railing and saw her speaking to Mr Thomas. He looked troubled, and Meredith felt sorry for him. He went down the stairs to join them.

"You've been a great help already, Mr Thomas, but you could do me one more favour. Who should we speak to first, if we want to know if anyone saw who was arguing with Mr Kentish? Who's the nosiest?"

"Well, when she was alive, that would have been my wife. But these days, I'm not sure. Although I'm guessing
with all this going on, you simply need to cross the street and look to see who's looking out. This is a nasty business, DCI Meredith, and no mistake."

"It is. But sleep soundly, Mr Thomas. Whoever killed Christopher Kentish stole his keys and have taken what they wanted. There will be a police presence for a couple of days, and by the time we're gone the locks will have been changed."

"I'll start using the chain, I think. Is there anything else you need? I think a tot of brandy might be in order. Will you join me?"

"On duty, and no, we don't need you, go in and put your feet up. Have an extra one for me." Meredith winked and received a chuckle in return. Following Jo up the stairs, he took her elbow. "Come on then. You look left, I'll look right, and we'll see who the nosey ones are."

To Jo's surprise it paid dividends. Three doors up, a couple stood on their doorstep, and in the first-floor window of the house two doors up, a woman beckoned to them. Jo crossed the road and waited for her to come down and unlock the door, while Meredith went to speak to the couple.

Beverley Moon had not only seen the argument with Christopher Kentish, she'd also had a word with the man causing the commotion.

"It had taken me over an hour to get the children to sleep, and I'd just put our dinner on when there was this disturbance. We get the odd drunk wandering past here, so I ignored it at first, but when it carried on, and then Harry came down, I lost my patience. My husband told me not to of course, but … do you have children? If you do, you'll know what I mean. All we want is a little time to relax before we're back on the wheel making everything happen."

Casting a glance back towards her front door, she lowered her voice further. "He has no idea what it's like, not an inkling. When I told him to put Tom back to bed, you'd think I'd asked him to paint the bloody bridge."

"I know what you mean. What did you say to him? I mean the man causing the trouble, not your husband."

"Well, I shocked him because such was his tirade, he hadn't realised I was there. I tapped him on the shoulder, and he quite literally jumped. His feet left the floor." Beverley Moon giggled. "Like a cartoon. With hindsight quite amusing, but at the time I had steam coming out of my ears. I asked him what he thought he was doing, and did he realise this was a residential street where young children were trying to sleep, and if he didn't shut up, I'd call the police."

"How did he respond?"

"First, he appeared angry and half raised his fist. Then said something like, 'He has something of mine, and I'd like it back, but I'm sure we don't need the police.' He then looked up to the door, and the man slammed it shut. I'm sorry I don't know his name."

"And then he left?"

"He did. Apologised as well."

56

"Sounds like you got a good look at him. Do you think you could describe him?"

"Oh blimey, I'm rubbish at that. It was dusk, so around eight thirty, maybe nine. He was tall. At least six feet, and slim to average build. Dark hair that looked wet, or I suppose it could have been greasy, blue jeans and a dark jacket. An ordinary face. I can't remember anything about his face, although I'd know him if I saw him again. I'm not much use, am I? He walked back up this way." Beverley pointed up the street. "If he got as far as Princess Victoria Street, they have cameras I think. There might also be one

by the crossing. Oh I am sorry, this isn't much good. What do you think he's done? What's going on down there, is it serious?"

"Quite serious, yes. May I take your details please, I think we'll need to have another chat with you, possibly even do an E-Fit with a police artist, you'll be surprised how much you remember when you see it taking shape."

"Oh my goodness. I was only complaining half an hour ago that I had a boring life. I drop the children off to nursery about nine o'clock and have to pick them up by one or I'm charged an extra hour, so I'm free tomorrow morning."

Taking down her contact details, Jo agreed to call her early the next morning to arrange taking a formal statement and to do an E-Fit. Meredith waited until Beverley had closed her door and went to join her.

"I got nothing from those two, never heard anything, never saw anything, only noticed what was going on tonight because the wife had popped down to the supermarket. I take it this one was useful."

"Very. At least six feet tall, dark hair, skinny and he went back up towards The Mall pub. And, as she pointed out, there are cameras up there, if he went the right way. She's coming in tomorrow to give a statement and E-Fit." Frowning, she turned to Meredith. "You don't seem very impressed. He also said words to the effect that our victim had taken something from him."

"On the face of it, it's good. But the man Jody Sampson saw, and the man we've been trying to trace from Trenchard Street, wasn't skinny. Get the E-Fit sorted and then get it around to Jody. Where's Trump gone? I think we've done enough for today, we'll let the others take over until the morning. I might get lucky and still get a meal."

He checked the time. "Yep, don't forget your curry has my name on it though."

Leaving Trump to sort out the door-to-door enquiries and search for CCTV footage, Meredith drove Jo home. It was only when he pulled into the drive he remembered Peggy might still be there. He saw her coat on the newel post as he stepped into the hall. Fixing a smile, he pushed open the sitting room door.

"Merewinkle! Don't you ever call? My taxi is on the way now, I'd have stayed if I'd known you were on your way."

"Oh bugger, that's a shame, Peg. We'll have to arrange it again for next week, can't risk this week as we're in the middle of a big case."

"So I hear. You two seem to have a lot going on."

A horn sounded, and Meredith helped her to her feet. "Why didn't you drive, not car trouble, I hope?"

"No. I'm getting old, Merewinkle, don't enjoy driving at night, and I fancied a drink. I too have had a bit of a week of it, but not interesting enough for anyone to care. I will accept your renewed invitation. Let's say Tuesday, seven for seven thirty, and you can assign one of your minions to cover for you." The horn sounded again as she buttoned her coat. "Impatient devil isn't he? Will you see me out, good? Bye, Patsy, it's been interesting, next week you can cook. I'll see you tomorrow all being well." Taking Meredith's elbow, she allowed him to escort her to the taxi and open the door. As he pecked her on the cheek, she smiled. "Bye, Merewinkle. See you next week. I'll let Patsy tell you about Amanda."

"What about her?"

"The meter's running, Meredith, do you think I'm made of money? And you know I don't gossip."

Pulling a face, Meredith slammed the door and waved her off. Back in the house, he called to Patsy.

"I'm knackered. I'm starving and I think I might smell. I'll jump in the shower first."

Patsy appeared in the doorway to the kitchen. "First before what? Have you got designs on me, Mr Meredith?"

"Possibly, we'll see how it goes, but first, before you tell me about Amanda, pour me a drink and feed me."

Allowing her chin to fall to her chest, Patsy groaned. "I'm going to kill Peggy."

"You can do it next Tuesday, she'll be here seven for seven thirty. You have five minutes to soften the blow." Without awaiting further comment, he took the stairs two at a time.

A few hours later, Patsy climbed into bed where Meredith was already half asleep.

"Night, Meredith."

"Night. Oh, one thing you didn't tell me, is why are you seeing Peggy tomorrow? You're not planning on moving her back in when Amanda goes, are you? Because the answer is no."

"No, as we already know it's a very small world. Not only does she know one of Amy Cleaver's friends, but Antony is also looking to buy a house so is after some decent second-hand furniture. She's bringing him round to see Henry tomorrow. At least that's the plan if he's free."

"Stop talking, Hodge. I thought it might be interesting. Glad to know young Paul is going to be staying in this country though. We don't see enough of him."

"He's mainly Pablo now. I'll invite them around next weekend. Do you think you might actually be here?"

"Good point. Night, Hodge."

"Night, Meredith."

Chapter Seven

I t was a little after eight when Patsy arrived at Amy's house to meet with Henry Duggan before he left for work. She put the kettle on and was soon lost in thought. Henry's arrival startled her.

"Oh, my goodness. Sorry, Henry, I was miles away. I'm not sure who scared who the most."

"You certainly were. I did call from the hall. Is something troubling you? You were frowning."

"No, no. Trying to work out the best plan of attack. I've had another look at what's left to do, and I'm happy to deal with both the estate agents for you. No need for you to come back if you don't have to. Antony, the chap that might be interested in some of this furniture will be coming in around midday. By the way he's a recently qualified solicitor, finding his feet at a place in town. It's a big practice, and I got the impression it wasn't what he was expecting, but I must have been wrong because he's looking to buy in Bristol, hence the need for some furniture."

"It can be quite intimidating when you first start out. Partners strutting around snapping orders, a pile of files that never seems to diminish, and of course the overwhelming fear that you'll either miss something or put a comma in the wrong place and cost the firm millions." Henry laughed. "I hated my first job too, but I was lucky. My uncle had his own business, which I joined once I'd found my feet, and eventually took over. He'll get there if he's bright enough."

"I'll tell him you said so. I'll make a list of anything he's interested in, and what he's prepared to offer, then once you've had a chance to consider it, I'll leave you to the bartering."

"Quite right too. You've got enough on your plate." Pulling a folded sheet of paper from his pocket, Henry handed it to Patsy. "Names and addresses of the beneficiaries. I haven't got phone numbers, although I'm expecting them to start contacting me today as even with our current postal service they should have received my letter. I'd rather you didn't contact them before I've told them the news. I have no idea if they were close or not, and although I've put an obituary notice in several places, local and national, I'm not sure if they know Amy has passed."

"That's no problem. I will see if I can find out anything about them beforehand, I think age will eliminate those that won't be a help to the investigation. Would you like a cup of tea? I was just about to make one."

"No, thank you. I'm ready to leave for the office. I'll grab a couple more bags for shredding on my way out. I have a few appointments today but do feel free to call if you need me."

Before he'd reached the door the bell rang, and he was greeted by an exuberant Linda.

"I come bearing gifts, and better still they're straight out of the oven." She shook a paper bag at him. "Oh sorry, I was expecting Patsy. Still, you're very welcome to join us. Angel is parking, so we can have a powwow before we get off and running."

"A powwow? Much as I'd love to join you, duty calls. Have a fruitful day." Making good his escape, Henry called a similar greeting to Angel, who also seemed to be carrying food.

"Lasagne. Not exactly a salad, but better than letting Linda buy me more bread and cakes. I've been putting on so much weight. Have a good day too."

"Do we need a powwow?" Patsy asked, as she joined Linda in the dining room.

"We start with a meeting every morning, why should being here be any different? Come on, Patsy, don't let standards slip just because you're wearing jeans. Recap on what we have, plan on what we will do, and go over possible outcomes."

Patsy looked at Angel and held out her hands. "Am I right, or am I right?"

"What I think you mean, is a quick gossip so you can drink your coffee while it's still hot." Shrugging off her coat, Angel pulled the bag towards her. "What have we got?"

Over coffee they came up with a plan of attack, and Patsy updated them on the discovery, that not only did Peggy know exactly where the photographs of Amy and her friends celebrating in a bar were taken, but she had been acquainted with them, although not closely.

Patsy placed two photographs on the table and lay Peggy's list next to them.

"From the left. Susan James, Amy, Chris and she believes the girl who you can't see properly is Julia Ellsworth, hence the question mark. And in this one, our man Jeremy Rossiter, Chris – she can't remember his

62

surname, and Beatrix Holmes. They were taken in a nightclub on Colston Street called Capones. Peggy's husband was at university with them. He was a little older than them, but they went to a few of the same parties, and Peggy never forgets a name. She said Jeremy was a charmer, and both he and Christopher, who was very shy, were from privileged backgrounds, and not shy of throwing their money about to ensure their friends could be where they wanted to be. The girls were great fun. They lost touch once her husband graduated. It was a short conversation because as you know she doesn't like talking about her husband.

"But what's interesting," continued Patsy, "is that Henry gave me the list of beneficiaries this morning, and one of them is a Marcus Ellsworth. Maybe a connection, we'll know more when, hopefully, he gets in touch with Henry."

"Who are the others?" Linda held her hand out for the list. "I can try to track them down."

Patsy passed her the list and repeated Henry's request. "The big money goes to charities, but there are decent bequests to four individuals. But because they might not know about Amy's death yet, Henry has asked that we hold off contacting anyone until he's heard from them. Although, if they don't because they could have moved, we'll have to. I've brought my laptop so we can make a start."

"James Clark, Harry Swinton, Susan Clarkson and Marcus Ellsworth. It's interesting that they're mainly men, don't you think?"

"Why?"

"I don't know. For some reason I was expecting it to be all female. Odd how you do things like that, isn't it?"

"Linda, everything you do is odd. Now the powwow has been completed shall we get on?"

Patsy set up her laptop, ready to begin the search once they'd completed the ground floor. It took them a little over an hour with little success, apart from Linda setting aside a waffle maker which she had her eye on. That completed,
they went upstairs and took a bedroom each. Angel gave a shout after ten minutes.

"And I found it. You were right, Linda."

Linda hurried from the box room and leaned against the doorway of the room Angel was in.

"I always am, but about what?"

"This!" Angel held up a laptop. "It was in the drawer under the bed. Odd place to keep it."

"What's all the excitement about? Nothing in the back bedroom, other than a rather full jewellery box that I think Henry needs to keep elsewhere."

"I said yesterday that it was odd there was no computer. She was a professional, intelligent woman, so she would have had one. Want me to look at it?"

"Of course. I'll put the kettle on. This is an exciting development. Do your worst ,Wizkid."

The three traipsed downstairs, and Linda set the laptop up next to Patsy's. As expected, they needed a password to open the system. Aided by Patsy's notes, the passport, and what they knew about Amy, Linda's fingers worked quickly, and she listed everything she had tried on her notepad. After ten minutes, the others left her to it and set about finishing the bedrooms.

The first estate agent arrived fifteen minutes late, and when he realised Patsy didn't need convincing to use his agency, his visit took less than fifteen minutes. He agreed he would email Henry his valuation and fees. Patsy heard Linda calling for her after she'd shown him out.

"I don't like to admit defeat, but I haven't got the equipment to do this without a password. I hate to say it, but I'm going to have to call Trev."

"Oh."

Trevor Baines was a digital wizard with a complex. He believed he was being watched by various secret organisations, having spent some time in prison for cybercrimes. Although his business was now, for the best part, legitimate, he still spent his life looking over his shoulder, and had several escape plans if they ever got too close. He was also smitten with Linda.

"Yes oh. Of all the men blinded by my charms, he's the one I could do without fawning over me." An involuntary shiver ran up Linda's spine as she lifted her phone. "Do you mind him coming here, or would you like me to go to the office?"

"Depends what time he's coming. If it's soon, do it here or I'll lose you for too long. If not perhaps the office, but make sure Sharon will be around, that way she can get rid of him for you."

Linda agreed, closed the laptop, and left a message for Trevor, who never answered a call without first hearing the message. She stood and went to help Angel. Patsy took Linda's seat and began her search for information on the beneficiaries of Amy Cleaver's will. She'd not got far when the doorbell rang again. It was Peggy and Antony. Ushering them through, she smiled at Antony.

"Hello. Good to see you again, I'm glad you are staying in Bristol as is Meredith, who is missing Pablo."

"He is strange, your Meredith. But the affection I think is mutual, Pablo calls him… um…" Clicking his fingers, he tried to remember the toddler's interpretation.

"Winkle." Peggy let out her familiar cackle. "Don't know where he got that from." She looked around at the piles of paper and stuffed black bags and shook her head. "I can see you've got your work cut out for you. Have you found anything that helps?"

"Yes, well, we hope so anyway. We have her laptop. Waiting for a man that can. Other than that, just a pile of photographs." Sweeping her arm around the room, she added, "Anyway, feel free to wander and have a look, if you're interested in anything, make a note and speak to Henry. Oh, hang on." She lifted her handbag from the floor, pulled out the card Henry had given her at their first meeting, and handed it to Antony. "Here, take this, I don't need it anymore."

"Ah. Also a solicitor. It is as Peggy keeps reminding me, a small world."

"And getting smaller by the day. I'd start in there, it's good quality stuff, and I'm sure Henry will give you a fair price."

"I hope so. Even with the sale of our home in Spain, it is going to be difficult. Prices in Bristol are so high. I will go and see now."

Watching him wander away, Patsy turned back to Peggy. "I was expecting Antony's mother to be with you. Doesn't she want a say?"

"Pablo is off colour, she looks exhausted from the travelling, and decided she could trust him. Between you and me, I think I'm going to be a regular visitor. I'm not sure she can cope on her own with five days of nonstop Pablo while Antony is at work."

"Ha. How heartbroken you must be."

"Don't be cheeky, it doesn't suit you." Peggy looked down at the group photograph. "I was thinking about them after I left you last night. Almost got brave enough to get the photos out of the loft, I thought there might be a few of us together, but I couldn't face it and another pile of photos wouldn't get you any further."

Peggy's daughter had died in a car accident, her father was driving, and unable to live with the loss and his all-consuming guilt, he had taken his own life.

Knowing how painful the memories were, Patsy nodded. "And you'd be right. You've already given us quite a bit to go on. Here's something though, one beneficiary was called Marcus Ellsworth, I don't suppose you knew him too, did you?"

"Nope, only Julia. Could be her brother, I suppose. I know she had one, but I never met him." Peggy picked up the photograph of some of the group in black tie. "Still difficult to believe he killed himself. He was generous, I'll give him that, but he was also very sure of himself. Arrogant I think, and sarcastic." Hooting a laugh, she nudged Patsy. "He told me once I was the only person, other than his father, that could take him on. Although I don't know what he meant. Look at the time, I'd better see what Antony's up to, and let you get on."

"It's okay, I'll wait till you've gone. I really should be with the girls checking the boxes upstairs, but I can spare twenty minutes."

They found Antony bouncing on the seat of the armchair.

"I like this, it is big and comfortable. I think my mother will too."

"Ooh! My grandmother had one of those. That's worth a few bob. How many secret compartments does it have?" Peggy went over to the ornate bureau, which sat behind the door.

"Secret compartments? It got little cubby holes and drawers inside if that's what you mean."

"It's a good job I came. I suppose they are all a little different, but this was my favourite."

Pulling open the door to the cupboard below the writing table, Peggy leaned in and ran her hand along the underneath of the table. She grinned as she released the catch. A narrow drawer slid out, lined with felt, split into three compartments and empty.

"Well, that's disappointing. Let's see what else is here." Snapping the drawer back into its support position, Peggy lowered the writing table. "I love these don't you?"

"Yes, particularly if they bear fruit. Keep going, how many are there? Although, I suppose there's always a chance Amy was as ignorant as I am."

"Well, you see this upright here … "Peggy ran her finger down a strip of wood separating the two sets of cubbyholes before pushing the middle. The wood moved forward a little, and with Antony's help they slid it open. The reason it hadn't moved smoothly was because inside there was a slim book stuffed so full of loose pieces of paper it had restricted the mechanism. Antony handed it to Patsy.

"Bingo. An address book. We knew she must have had one, that's the laptop and the address book this morning, we're on a roll. Thank you, Peggy, carry on. How many more are there?"

"Two to my knowledge, although this one isn't really secret, you can see it."

The lid of the bureau which lowered to become the writing table had an inset, engraved piece of leather. It was old, cracked and lifting in places, revealing a tiny gap which indicated that the wood it was stuck to was not fixed. Peggy pushed and tapped around the corners, and when this was unsuccessful took hold of a piece of leather which had curled back on itself and pulled hard. The inner lid lifted away. The compartment beneath which was so small it could hide hardly anything had, however, a folded piece of newspaper. Peggy opened it.

"Oh. I must have missed this one." It was *The Times* obituary page from the nineteenth of May 1979. In the centre was the death announcement and the funeral arrangements for Rossiter, Jeremy Edward. "I had no idea he had died until you told me." Handing the paper to Patsy, Peggy returned her attention to the bureau. "The only other one I remember should be behind these cubbyholes."

Gripping the righthand section of separators, Peggy wiggled it about and slowly slid it forward. It revealed a small wooden door with the tiniest of brass hinges and a central handle. "Shall I?"

"Yes!" Patsy groaned when the pristine interior revealed that it was unlikely the little hidey-hole had ever been used. "That was an anti-climax. But at least I have this address book. If you'll excuse me I'll leave you to it and have a read."

Returning to the dining room, Patsy took a seat at the table and began the task by removing all the loose notes and cards that were stored there. For the time being they meant nothing, and other than a few thank you notes, she slid them into an envelope and labelled it.

The address book had many notes and scribbles written in the pages up to the first page of A, and she skimmed them. The only one which gave her pause for thought was one for a dentist appointment. It simply said: Dentist – Thursday 2.30. It caught her attention because they had found no form of diary. Being a hoarder of everything else, Patsy found it hard to believe that Amy didn't also store birthdays, thoughts, and most importantly appointments. After all, at the time of her death, she had been a practising physiotherapist as well as teaching it,. Flipping to a new sheet in her notebook, she started a list of 'to-dos' and started it with an entry to check if Henry could collect any personal belongings from Amy's workplace.

Returning to the address book, she ran her finger down the names. It surprised her that Amy had made some entries because the surname began with an A, and others because the first name did. Jotting down the telephone number for Susan, who it appeared had moved three times since Amy had started the book, she ploughed on until Peggy appeared in the doorway.

"We're done. Antony will ring Henry as soon as we get home." Lowering her voice, she added, "I think he wants to bring his mother round to make sure she likes it. Hopefully you'll be finished by then."

Getting to her feet, Patsy smiled. "It's not a problem. I'll just leave them to it, like I did you today. I think Henry would like it sorted sooner rather than later, and although I have to see how far the girls have got, we surely can't have much more to do."

"They're surrounded by bags of rubbish, so they must be getting somewhere, and Linda only mentioned the wedding twice. Don't work too hard. You're looking peaky again. Are you sure you're okay?"

"Yes, I'm fine, but makeup-less, so thanks for pointing out I need to enhance my features just to look healthy."

Having shown them out, Patsy called up to the others.

"Time is galloping on, and the next estate agent is due at two. Shall I put the lasagne on?"

They carried on working until the timer told them their meal was ready. Carrying her plate through to the dining room, Linda continued a running commentary on what they'd found. "And do you know she has a box in the loft just full of cards. It's unbelievable. Even the cheap Christmas cards, which say no more than, 'best wishes, Ant and Dec.' I'm only halfway through. I suppose I have to look at every one or we might miss something. Oh, talking of which, Trev will be here about two. He's probably outside driving up and down looking for spooks. By the way, what did Meredith say?"

"Blimey, you've paused for breath. About what?" Seeing the look of utter horror on Linda's face, Patsy tried to recover her position. "Just kidding, he's really pleased."

"Not thrilled?"

"Okay, he's thrilled."

"Now I know you're lying. It's too late. Pleased is not thrilled. And another—"

"Saved by the bell. I'll get that, you eat."

It surprised Patsy to find a rather smart looking Trevor smiling at her. His usual attire was trainers, jeans and a sweatshirt that looked in need of a wash, as did his hair, but today he had on a shirt, trousers, and polished shoes. His hair had been cut short.

"Miss Hodge. Here to help again. How are you?" He walked into the house, not waiting for an invitation, and sniffed. "Something smells good."

68

"Lasagne. There's some left over if you want to join us. Trevor, don't be offended, but have you got an interview or something, you look very smart."

"Not for me, I have a lunch date, and no interview, just a date." His smile was almost charming.

"Well, good for you. Who's the lucky lady? This way."

"Charlotte, or Lotte as she keeps reminding me. Our fourth date. We met quite by chance, on Saturday."

"Saturday? That will be four dates in less than a week. Blimey, you two must be smitten."

Trevor's cheeks flushed, and he raised his eyebrows.

"Hello, Linda, change of plan. I have a date so I came early. I wasn't expecting her to ask, but she did. Where is it then? I need to be out of here by two."

"Hi, Trev. I'm fine, thanks for asking, and that's only an hour. Do you think you can do it in an hour?"

"Ha, ha. Hilarious. Ten minutes tops."

Looking him up and down, Linda pointed to the laptop on the other side of the table.

"That one. You look smart, I've not ever seen you look smart before. She must be very special."

"Oh, she is." Taking a seat in front of the laptop, he pulled from his pocket what looked like a storage device and plugged it in. Lifting the lid, he hit the on button. Then his fingers moved so quickly, and such was her angle, Linda couldn't see what he'd done.

"What did you just do?"

"In layman's terms, I asked the laptop to let me in."

"I know that much, but how?"

Trevor tapped the black shiny box, and a series of lights flashed along the side. "This can detect how many characters they used for the password, it also picks up whether they are numerals or alphabetical, or symbols of course. But here's what makes it so clever, I told it that it was a personal home computer, so it knows it will be sim … here we go. I'm in."

Linda hurried around the table as Trevor got to his feet. "Can I buy one of those?"

"No. Do you want an invoice, or is it going to be cash?"

"What? Trevor, what's happened to you? You don't do traceable money, you only do cash."

"Lotte explained that—"

"Who's Lotte?"

"His girlfriend. Linda, let the man go. He has a date. How much do we owe you, Trevor?"

"Let's call it fifty."

"For five minutes work?" It was Angel's turn to question him.

"I can always shut it off." Trevor took hold of the lid.

Pulling the notes from her purse, Patsy held them out. "No need of that. Thank you."

"No worries." He nodded at Angel. "Teach her some manners." And I know you should know this, Linda, but change the password before you do anything else."

Linda twitched a smile and dropped into the chair he had vacated. "Enjoy your date, Trev. I can take it from here."

Once he had gone, she scanned the desktop. Other than the usual shortcuts, there were two documents saved there. One called 'Words', the other 'What next?'

She opened 'Words' and grinned. "You will never believe this, Amy has made a document with all her passwords, including the one for the laptop. We shouldn't have any problems getting into anything else. Guess what her password for the laptop is?"

"Password?" Angel suggested, collecting their plates. "I'll do the washing up and get on."

"Not far off. SecretWordOne. I think we can remember that. Now for 'What Next?'"

Patsy came to stand behind her and clapped her hands as she scanned the document. "Bingo. This should help."

The document named 'What Next?' was a list of dates and names, most now known to the three women, and a lot of question marks. "What I really don't understand, and I know we have to decipher this, is why she didn't give Henry chapter and verse, up to the point she made the tape anyway. That's another thing that's not here. The recorder, perhaps she did it at work."

"Buggeration!" Linda cursed. "Anyone seen the power cable? There's only two per cent battery left. Patsy let me have a look at yours, we might get lucky." She shook her head as Patsy held up her connection. "Nope. There must have been one. No one has a laptop without a charger. Think, and quickly. I don't know how fast this will power down."

"There were a few wires in the sideboard, but not attached to a plug. It must be upstairs where the laptop was. I'll go and look."

"One per cent. Oh, who's that now?"

"Probably the other estate agent. I'll go."

"I'd better get upstairs and look then." Rolling her eyes, Linda hurried past Patsy. "I don't know why I'm running, it'll be dead before I get back."

They failed to find the power cable. The second estate agent took his time, dictating features as he moved from room to room, constantly trying to engage the women in conversation.

When he left, Linda made a suggestion. "I think you two should carry on with the search, I'll go and buy a cable, and get started on this. What do you think?"

"I think we should complete the search first. I feel as frustrated as you, but if we get sidetracked with what we find on there, we'll never get the search finished, or we will but it will drag on and on." Holding up her hand to halt Linda's protest, Patsy pulled her phone from her pocket. "I'm going to order one online, and get it delivered to the office. If we crack on now, we'll get the search finished today, then we can start work on the beneficiaries, the laptop, and this address book."

"Sounds like a plan," Angel agreed. "I've just found a folder containing some insurance policies, and some building society passbooks. There is still more to find."

"Well, I don't agree. But you're the boss, and wrong, but still the boss."

"I am. Come on."

They worked solidly for the next three hours. They found nothing of any use. Patsy wasn't convinced they had found everything of value to the investigation, but knew they had to move the investigation forward.

"I'll meet you at the office tomorrow. We'll have a meet ... powwow, and then get on. Linda, your first job will be to track down Freddie Rossiter. If we know who the four were, we'll save ourselves a lot of time, and he should be able to help us. Grab some of these bags, it will save ... oh, talk of the devil."

Henry called out a greeting, and waited in the hall until the women had forced their way down with bulging bags of paperwork.

"We're all done, Henry. Something is bound to have been missed, but I think we need to move this on. Oh, and while I think about it can you arrange for me to collect Amy's personal belongings from her work please?"

"No need, they're sending it over. Never said when though."

"I'd rather go. I might see something they think is unimportant."

"As you think best. Let me move these bags. I'm meeting your friend and his mother here in ten minutes."

"In which case we'll leave you to it."

Collecting what they needed, the women left. Patsy waved to Peggy as they passed at the end of the road, glad she hadn't been held up talking to them. For once, she wasn't hoping Meredith would be home on time as, despite her words to Linda, she was keen to start working through what they'd discovered that day.

Chapter Eight

Meredith took the image and studied it for a moment before handing it back to Jo.

"And she's happy that this is a good likeness?"

"She is, she was working with Harry, and he told me she got quite excited when he changed the eyebrows. He thinks it's as good as her memory is, so that's as good as it gets."

"Get a copy round to Jody Sampson, but take a couple of others with similar colouring, see if she picks it out. Then get over to Clifton village and see if anyone there recognises him. I doubt he's local, but if he is our man, there's a good chance he would have been following Kentish. Take Hutchins. Also—" Meredith read a text on his phone. "Got a report in from Sherlock, says it's important. But apparently, he's too important to speak to me directly these days. You get on, call me if you get anything."

Turning his attention to his computer, Meredith opened the email.

Hello Meredith and team.

I'm up to my ears this morning, but I've had some results you'll want to know about – and before you start shouting Meredith, I'm banging out a quick email to keep you in the picture. A full formal report is being prepared.

Pending the DNA confirmation, the tissue found on the bed in Clifton, although badly damaged, appears to be a section of Christopher Kentish's heart. It seems your killer did indeed take his keys.

Results back on the anal swab. It was semen, and I have run a DNA test. Guess what – he's in the system. Michael Janus DOB 30.6.1989 – he has a criminal record, but I can't access that from here.

Other than that, all other tests came back belonging to the victim, who, although he had a serious head injury, I'm guessing by hitting the pavement with some force due to the pattern of the fracture, death was caused by bleeding out. The initial wound severed the superior vena cava, then the hacking of the chest area with a curved serrated blade also severed the right coronary artery. Death would not have taken long.

I've checked his medical records and although you probably know this by now, he had lymphoma, and he was being treated at the BRI. Prognosis was good as they caught it early.

That's probably all you need for now, report to follow.

Frankie

Scanning the incident room, Meredith spotted Seaton standing by the printer and called to him.

Holding up a finger, Seaton replied, "On it. I got it too, printing it off as we speak."

Meredith went out to join him. Lifting the charge sheet as it left the printer, he scanned it quickly.

Michael (Mikey) Janus has been arrested twice, one charge of soliciting had been dropped, but a second of ABH (actual bodily harm), and causing an affray had been upheld, and he'd received a three-month sentence, suspended for two years, and one hundred and twenty hours of community service. Both incidents had taken place in 2010.

Seaton lifted the photograph. "I don't think he's our man though. Too small. Five foot seven, and seventy-six kilos."

"Remind me what that is in English?"

"About twelve stone. And he doesn't fit the bloke Jody saw, nor the image of the one arguing with him from this morning." Seaton pointed at the image Jo had affixed to the board. "Not even close."

"Bring him in. Regardless of whether he did the deed, he was with him sometime that day."

Trump came back into the room. "Back in 2015 there had been a spate of what turned out to be homophobic crimes. Two men were left permanently disabled. There was a rumour in the community that the witness descriptions resembled a punter who liked to get rough. Several of the attacks included rape, so some of the gay community came forward to be eliminated from the inquiry."

"Why?" Seaton looked at the picture of Mikey Janus again. "Just as I don't have him for Kentish, I can't see he'd be able to overpower a grown man."

"Promiscuity. Those selling sex knew there was always a chance it could happen to someone they'd been with." Handing Meredith the file he'd collected, Trump looked at the photograph of Mikey. "But I do see what you mean."

74

"What happened to safe sex?" Turning back to his office, Meredith glanced at the clock. "You two pick him up. I've got the widow coming in, so I'd better be here."

"You do realise that you can get DNA from other stuff too, don't you? It doesn't need to be sex."

"Get on with it, Seaton."

~ ~ ~

Beatrix Kentish was an attractive, well-dressed, well-spoken woman but without any airs or graces. She answered Meredith's questions with what appeared to be an open honesty. Meredith liked her, although as he showed her out, he wondered if she had chosen such a life for the reasons she gave, or if she too had something to hide.

Collecting the tape of the interview, he handed it to Rawlings. Watch this and tell me if she's lying, or perhaps more accurately, omitting something."

"Really?"

"Yes, really. Or why would I ask?"

"What happened to that gut instinct which keeps getting you in trouble?" Rawlings grinned as Meredith punched his arm.

"My gut instinct tells me she is. If I'm right, she's an accomplished liar. Watch the bloody tape. I'll be in my office."

Grabbing a coffee and taking the tape to one of the interview rooms, Rawlings made himself comfortable before hitting the play button. He smiled when he saw Meredith's eyebrows rise as they showed Beatrix Kentish into the room.

Getting to his feet, Meredith held out his hand.

"Mrs Kentish, thank you for coming in. I'm DCI Meredith. Please take a seat. Can I get you any refreshments?"

"No thank you. How could I not come in? How did Christopher die?"

"He was stabbed. His murderer then stole his keys, and I'm guessing other items such as wallet, jewellery and any other valuables he had with him. As I mentioned during our telephone conversation last night, his flat has also been burgled."

Placing her hand over her mouth while she composed herself, Beatrix nodded.

"I should tell you that this interview is being recorded and a transcript will be typed up for you. I understand that when asked, you said you didn't want your solicitor present."

"Not so much didn't want, as couldn't see the point. I wasn't in Bristol yesterday, I haven't been in Bristol for a few weeks, maybe a month, so unless you are suggesting I'm lying, what would be the point? I have nothing to hide, Detective Chief Inspector."

"That's a mouthful, please call me Meredith. But, as this is a serious crime with no known motive as yet, I'm going to caution you. Are you sure you wouldn't like legal representation?"

"No need."

As Meredith proceeded with the caution, Rawlings noticed a flicker of amusement from Beatrix, and noted the time. As was normally the case when interviewing, Meredith held her gaze as he delivered the caution, his voice slow and calm. Beatrix never averted her eyes as was usual when one was under scrutiny from Meredith. Caution complete, Meredith got straight to the point.

"Mrs Kentish, is this your husband?" Lifting the cover of the file in front of him, Meredith revealed a photograph.

"It is, yes. That's Christopher. Where did you get that photograph from, I don't recognise it?"

"A website. I'm sorry that was necessary."

"Of course. Now, how can I help?"

"You have unusual living arrangements for a married couple, some of these questions may seem too personal, but I assure you they are necessary. I—"

"Shall I help you out, Chief … Meredith? It might save a lot of messing about. I would rather you were out searching for his killer than attempting not to offend me."

"Please." The twinkle in Meredith's eye was reciprocated. Rawlings noted the time and wrote 'flirting' in his notes.

"Christopher and I met many years ago. Here in Bristol, in fact. We had the same group of friends, and we hit it off immediately, shared a flat for many years. His family had money, lots of it, it was a nice flat." For a moment, Beatrix faltered. Looking into her lap, she blinked furiously, and there was a huskiness to her voice when she continued. "He was a good man. He was my best friend. Then, and now."

"But…" Meredith coaxed.

"But nothing." Looking irritated, Beatrix lay her perfectly manicured hands on the table. "It's obvious you already know my husband was gay. And as fate would have it, and fate is a cruel mistress, we fell in love with the same man. It was awful for a while, you know, when we realised this. But luckily for us, I suppose, fate decided he would love another. We were heartbroken then, and again later when he died. We made a pact never to do that again, and to always look after each other. Christopher recovered quicker than I and used me as a willing accomplice to fend off any awkward questions from his family about his sexuality. He was convinced his father would cut him off, even though Christopher was a great jeweller."

Seeing Meredith's eyes travel to her hands, she tapped her wedding finger. "He designed this ring. Chose the diamonds himself, made the heads and the band, although he wouldn't trust himself to cut it. But he could have. He also had a good head for business. It delighted his parents when we married, he became the golden boy, that light dimmed a little when we didn't produce children, but one can't have it all."

"Why did you marry him? Didn't you want a more … fulfilling relationship?"

"Because I loved him in a way that one should be loved. As an equal, and unconditionally. When we took our vows, I meant nearly every word."

"There would be no forsaking others, I'm guessing." Meredith's lips twitched.

"No, we were going to get it dropped, but that would have kicked up a storm given that his uncle was marrying us, so we crossed our fingers at that bit." Beatrix grinned and her face lit up. "It was such fun. And as should be the case for a bride, it's a day I shall never forget."

"Did you live together in the beginning?"

"We live together now … Oh. We still lived together. Oh gosh. This is very difficult." She retrieved a tissue from her handbag and dabbed her eyes. "I promised him I'd be brave."

"Promised who?"

A mirthless smile appeared. "Christopher. Apologies, I didn't sleep much last night. I promised Christopher I would protect his reputation as a good man, because he was, and that I'd deal with this with my head high, and shoulders back. I would not become a jabbering wreck." Tilting her chin, she sniffed. "And I won't. My husband and I still lived together, at least six months of the year. We holidayed together, we spent Christmas and birthdays together, and although we both had independent romantic interests, they were never more important than our devotion to each other. Odd to a man like you, I'm sure. But that's the way it was."

"A man like me?" Meredith queried.

"Yes, like you. I know you know what I mean, and I won't entertain you by justifying that remark. What else do you want to know?"

"I wasn't after entertainment. Many women have thought they knew what a man like me was like. Few got it right. It was genuine interest. But perhaps that's a conversation for another time. Explain your living arrangements, when you called the police to voice your concern about Christopher, you stated you didn't have a key for his home in Sion Hill."

"No, I don't. Our home is in Cheltenham, Christopher retained his affection for Bristol, and has a thriving business here. It was sensible he had a home here too. On the occasion I had to be here, I chose to go home to Cheltenham, it's not far, as you know. I also have my little cottage in Bournemouth, and we have a flat in London. It's where I was when you called."

"Who benefits from Christopher's death?"

"Me. Is that what you want to hear?"

"No, I'm guessing there's a lot of money and that it won't all come to you."

"I don't know for sure, but I know he would have made sure I was comfortable. His sister and niece, his mother, although she is independently wealthy. He was patron to many charitable causes, I'm sure he will have left them something. I don't know, it's not something we ever discussed, I haven't even made a will. I was happy for him to have everything when I died. But he gave me all I have. I was a lucky woman, Meredith."

"It certainly appears that way."

Beatrix's eyes narrowed, she knew Meredith didn't mean that, but she let it drop.

"Is there anything I can tell you that might actually help?" Irritation was showing, and her head tilted a little higher.

"Would you be able to tell if anything was missing from his home? Was there any jewellery he wore all the time? Do you know if his wallet was distinctive in any way? Anything at all that might tell us what his murderer was after."

"Of course, some of that. But surely it was the other way around? You are implying they killed him for a reason. I was under the belief that he was killed during a robbery. Was my husband targeted? Is that what you are telling me?" When Beatrix raised her tissue, the tremor in her hand was noticeable. "Because he was a jeweller, do you think?"

"We don't know. We only found out who he was last night. Your husband was murdered in the early hours of the morning of the fourteenth. Now we know who he is, we can try to work out why. Because, yes, I believe he was known to his murderer."

"Why? What else do you know?"

"We know he had sex in the hours before he was murdered, and we know who with, we're bringing him in now. There was a witness to the attack who believes the attacker said something to your husband. Because of the nature of the injuries, and some evidence found at Sion Hill, we believe the attack was personal. How personal we don't know. Has your husband ever expressed any concerns about being followed or blackmailed, any concerns for his safety in any way at all?"

"No. He's always been concerned about security and safety at the retail outlets, of course. But a security company deals with them now. He never personally transported any stock or cash – not that much cash changes hands these days. As to blackmail – for what? The only reason one assumes someone might think they could do that would have been the fact that he was gay and married to me. Although Christopher would have hated for me to be embarrassed, and I assure you, I wouldn't have been, since his father is long gone, he had nothing to fear. I also think that had anyone tried such a thing, he would have told me about it. Christopher was awful at keeping secrets. I really don't think blackmail was the cause."

"And yet he carried off the perfect deceit. Perhaps he was better at hiding things than you think? Perhaps he was trying to protect you."

"Perfect deceit? What do you mean?" Piqued, Beatrix leaned forward. "Please do not attempt to soil my husband's name because you don't understand our love for each other. He was a good man."

"I wasn't. But to the outside world, you are the perfect married couple, and yet ..." Meredith allowed the sentence to drift away.

Tapping her fingernail on the chipped table sitting between them, Beatrix smiled. There was no amusement, and her eyes revealed her resolve. "Because, Inspector, we had the perfect marriage. Ha! How do you like them apples? As the Americans would say. I loved him, he loved me, we were wealthy, and until a few months ago, healthy. My husband had cancer. It was treatable. He was being treated. We wanted for nothing. We were blessed that we found each other, neither of us wanted a different life. Are you married, Mr Meredith? I'm guessing yes, and more than once, because you don't seem like a man who wants perfect. You seem like a man who likes risk. Christopher was neither."

"I seem to have hit a nerve. I'm sorry, I had no intention of upsetting you, but you must understand that these questions are necessary if we are to apprehend your husband's murderer quickly."

"You have not, as you put it, touched a nerve. I'm simply trying to make you understand that everyone is different, and few are as lucky as we were."

"You demoted me twice. I went from DCI to inspector, and then down to lowly mister. No offence taken, but something I said caused that. And I am far from perfect, and yes, I am married, currently hoping it's third time lucky. But everyone wishes something in their life had been different, however insignificant, or perhaps in your case significant."

Knowing Meredith was being genuine, Beatrix's features relaxed. "I apologise, your demotion was unintentional. What significant difference would that have been?"

"Your love of the same man. Unrequited for both, heartbreaking for both. If it hadn't been for his lack of interest you may not have had a perfect marriage. I find it difficult to believe neither of you wondered 'what if?', a safe dream to have given his death. But what if he was still alive, would either of you ever have given up the dream? I don't know, it's not relevant. But I am an observer of people, and I have yet to meet anyone who was perfect. Good. Great, even, but not perfect. Indeed, I'm sure the man you both loved wasn't perfect, and yet he captivated both of you, leaving you both heartbroken. I am not trying to be unkind, Mrs Kentish, merely trying to establish if whoever killed your husband got what he wanted, or if he's still looking. If the latter is the case, you may be in danger."

Pulling her head back as though he had slapped her, Beatrix's nostrils flared. "Thank you for that insight. Let's hope he did because I can think of nothing that someone could want that either of us could supply, except for money.

I am a housewife, not a career woman or heiress. I have nothing but what my husband provided. Now, is there anything else I can help you with? Much as I'd like to sit and listen to you analyse the human mind, I have things to do, not least speak to Christopher's mother."

Rawlings made a note.

"Of course. On to missing items." With a total change of direction, Meredith listed the personal items Kentish may have had with him on the night he was killed. All should be found either at their home or his flat if they had not been stolen. Before he ended the interview, Meredith got out the E-Fit of the man Kentish had been arguing with.

"Finally, can I ask if you know this man? He was seen arguing with your husband a week or so ago outside his home."

Leaning forward, Beatrix inclined her head, her lips pursed. "No, I don't think I do. But he's got a very average face, don't you think? There's something about the eyes, but no, I don't think I've seen him before."

"Bane of a copper's life, men looking average. Average height, average build, average looks."

80

Returning the E-Fit to its folder and closing his pad, Meredith got to his feet. "Thank you, Mrs Kentish. If there's anything you need, don't hesitate to contact me. I'll arrange for someone to take you wherever you need to go." He passed her his card. "I know you don't like me, but for what it's worth Christopher would have been proud of you. You protected him, you didn't become a jabbering wreck, and you were almost looking at the ceiling. This way."

Tilting her head, Beatrix looked at him, a quizzical expression on her face. "You have a remarkable memory, Chief Inspector, and thank you, I did my best."

"I do, it's what makes me brilliant, that and being able to hear things that don't get said. And to know when people tilt their head when they are trying to remember something. This way."

Closing her eyes for a moment, Beatrix nodded. "Please keep me informed of your progress. Am I required to identify Christopher?"

"No. You did that with the photograph, and we have DNA. But if you would like to see him, I can arrange that."

"No, thank you. Although, I don't know Chief Inspector, I really don't know."

~ ~ ~

They left the room, and Dave Rawlings stopped the tape. Finishing his coffee, he retrieved the tape and went to find Meredith. He found him holding an impromptu briefing.

"I want all the usual fences notified to keep an eye out for these items. I want someone on the internet selling sites. We're looking for a gold Cartier watch, white gold engraved wedding band, gold signet ring with the jeweller's crest – you'll get that from the website. Brown leather Hugo Boss wallet. Oh, and the laptop, but she couldn't remember the make. The two rings were the only jewellery he wore, apart from wrist watches. He loved watches, but they made outings only on special occasions. For everyday use, it was the Cartier. To be sure of that we'll need to get into the safe. Not much to go on. She didn't recognise the bloke he was arguing with outside the house. That's it. Anyone heard from Trump or Seaton? Have they found him?" Jerking his thumb over his shoulder, he walked towards Rawlings. "Has Jody Sampson seen this? Someone tell me something is happening, anything will do. What did you reckon, Dave? Was I right, or was I right?"

"Almost right. I think there's something she's not saying. I'm not convinced it's anything that will help us though. Maybe too embarrassed or something."

"No. She doesn't do embarrassed. I believe everything she told us was the truth, but not all of it. Damned irritating, I might leave it a couple of days and try again. Give Seaton a call and find out if they've tracked Mikey whatsit down. I'd better put the report in before I've got Uncle David on the blower."

Meredith's phone rang as he entered his office. "Adler, what news?"

"Jody said he had the right look whatever that means, but that she couldn't say one hundred percent. I'm in Clifton now. No one remembers seeing him as yet, but the barmaid in The Mall said her boss had an exchange with someone who kicked over an outside chair and he looked like the E-Fit. Being inside at the time she couldn't swear to it, but thinks it was that night. She's going to call me when he gets back, about half an hour. In the meantime, I'm collecting another batch of CCTV from other businesses on that road. How did it go with the widow?"

"Not bad, she's not saying something, who knows what, but nothing to go on, although we know what was stolen from the body now. I'm waiting for Trump and Seaton to bring in the victim's lover. Let's hope the landlord of the pub bears some fruit. Keep me informed."

It was over an hour before Seaton and Trump reappeared. Having settled Mikey Janus in an interview room. Seaton put his head around Meredith's door.

"We've got him, Gov. Shall we get on with it?"

"Yep, I'll watch from next door. Make sure you find out what personal belongings Kentish had on him. The widow has given us what he should have had, but of course she didn't see him that day."

"Will do. Give us five, he's a wreck, Louie's gone to get coffee."

"Why is he a wreck? What did you say to spook him?"

"Nothing, other than we needed help with our inquiries, and no, it couldn't be when he finished work. He's got a job selling mobile phones now, his boss wasn't pleasant. We were very nice too. He talked nonstop on the way back, even Louie's patience was tried."

"Going to be a long interview then. Carry on."

By the time Meredith had settled himself, Seaton was finishing the caution. Mikey Janus was of slight build and immaculate. His shirt was pressed, his tie knotted perfectly. The suit he wore was well cut, and although his blond hair had been allowed to grow long enough to curl, it was clean and tidy. In Meredith's opinion, the only thing that let him down was the tattoo on his neck which showed above his collar. On his pinky finger he wore a gold signet ring. Although Meredith couldn't see the detail, he guessed it was identical to the one Beatrix Kentish had described."

"I know all that but how do I know if I need a solicitor if I don't know what you think I've done?" Mikey gave a half sob. "I've probably lost my job over this. The manager doesn't like me because I'm gay, and because I'm better at selling than he is, but mainly because I don't give him anything to flex his muscle over. He's a bastard and always docking the others' bonuses for one reason and another. Never caught me yet, I need the money."

"So you've stopped your other work then?" Seaton asked.

"Am I still on the game, you mean? No. Would I be putting up with that prick if I was earning real money? Is that why I'm here, has someone said that I am, because I'm not. Too many macho men, too many hidings. I rent a nice little flat off Park Street, small but perfectly presented, much like myself." Mikey held his hands up. "So, please, please, tell me why I'm here. Actually, I can't mess about like this anymore, yes, I want a solicitor. You're obviously going to string this out."

In the next room, Meredith rapped on the desk in frustration. That would take at least another hour. It was going to be another long day."

"No problem. I'll give the duty sergeant a call, but first, because it might not be worth the bother, do you know Christopher Kentish?"

The colour drained from Mikey's face. "He's dead, isn't he? The bastard got him. Oh my God, oh my God. Please tell me he's not dead, please tell me that."

"Calm down, Mikey, old chap. Let's get a solicitor first." Getting to his feet, Trump opened the door.

"How long will that take?"

"I don't know, usually an hour or so."

"Then I don't want one. Tell me what's happened." Wiping away tears with the back of his hand, Mikey leaned towards the recorder. "I do not want a solicitor."

Retaking his seat, Trump smiled. "Would you like me to get you some tissues, this is clearly going to be upsetting."

"For fuck's sake. Will you just tell me!" Mikey jumped to his feet but sat down again when Seaton pointed at him.

"Christopher Kentish has been murdered. It was a violent death, after which he was robbed. Things taken included his house keys. His property was searched and vandalised. Tell me about your relationship with Mr Kentish, and the last time you saw him."

Dropping his head on to his arms, Mikey wept. He was saying something, but it was impossible to decipher through the sobs. Trump suspended the interview.

"Interview suspended at four fifteen." Turning to Mikey, he added, "I'll get you some tissues, and water. Do you want me to ask for a solicitor?"

"No, hurry up."

Switching off the machine, Trump left the room. Meredith met him in the corridor.

"Be quick about it. Let him talk, he'll like that. Seaton was right, I don't think he's our man, but find out about the ring he's wearing, is it the victim's or an identical one?"

Once he'd calmed down and the interview had recommenced, Meredith was right: Mikey didn't stop talking.

Mikey had first met Christopher Kentish five years before in a gay bar. Mikey was in a bad way, he'd come off the game, and was sharing a flat, where his room was little more than a cupboard. Money was tight, and Mikey was at the end of his tether. He'd been drunk, and when Christopher had started talking to him, he'd told him in no uncertain terms to go away. When Christopher asked if he'd eaten, as he'd been let down on a dinner date, Mikey, who was starving, changed his mind. It was the beginning of a regular relationship.

Christopher was married and loved his wife. He wouldn't move in with Mikey although he professed to love him too, but he bought a little flat which Mikey was allowed to decorate and furnish as he wanted. He gave Mikey a lease for a peppercorn rent. Although Mikey knew Christopher had a property in Clifton somewhere, they always met at his flat. Christopher was generous with gifts, outings and holidays, but he never gave Mikey cash, telling him he needed to find some self-esteem and pay his own way in life. Because in the future Christopher might not be around, and Mikey would need to fend for himself. And it worked.

When asked about the ring, Mikey became very animated. He'd suggested the design to Christopher, and within weeks he'd had two made. One for each of them. Christopher had been with Mikey on the night he was

murdered. They'd been together most of the day as Mikey wasn't working. After lunch they went to an art exhibition at the Museum, then to a bookshop on Queens Road to collect some books Christopher had ordered. They went back to Mikey's after dinner, and he'd been planning to stay the night. Before they retired for the night, he checked his emails and cursed.

84

"'Fuck off', he shouted. Christopher never swore, ever. He always said the English language provided more than enough words for one to express oneself accurately. So it made me laugh. I teased him. He didn't see the funny side. To be honest, I don't think I've ever seen him mad before, and when he got up and said he was leaving, I was worried. I even followed him into the bathroom when he showered. He didn't tell me much, but he said something like, the past never lets us go, however much we want it to. I asked what that meant, and he told me someone connected with his past thought Christopher owed him. He assured me he didn't, but initially he had felt sorry for this man, because Christopher was like that. Nice. Kind."

The tears returned, and Mikey took a while to compose himself.

"What happened after he'd tried being nice?" Seaton prompted.

"I don't know. He didn't give me any detail. 'I tried to be kind, but he's an obnoxious piece of work. I won't be threatened.' That's what he said. I got all dramatic and asked if he was in danger, and he shrugged. Said he doubted it, it was probably all talk. Wagged his finger at me and said, 'You can't blackmail someone who hasn't done anything wrong. He's an idiot.' I tried to find out more, and of course why he was leaving, but he said we shouldn't give it substance by discussing it. He'd been going to leave in the morning anyway, he had appointments the next day.

And that's another thing, he never had *'appointments'* but the last few months he'd used that excuse to leave quite often. I asked him where he was going, and when I would see him again, and he said it might be a week or so as he was going to see Beatrix. But not where he was going then, so I assumed it was home."

"What did he check his emails on, phone or laptop?"

"His phone. I've never seen him with a laptop."

"I told you earlier that he'd been robbed, can you tell me what personal effects he would have had on him when he left?" Turning to a blank page, Trump smiled encouragement.

"His ring," Mikey twisted the signet ring on his finger, "and his wedding ring of course, his watch, and his phone."

"Do you know what make?"

"iPhone, I upgraded it for him. Do you want his number?"

"We have it, thank you, and the watch?"

"Oh a Cartier, gold. Beatrix gave him it as an anniversary present. He loves it. Sometimes wears others, but not often. And that was it, oh, and he had his wallet. Brown leather Hugo Boss. I bought him it for Christmas a few years back. He loved it but was cross because it was too expensive. But … Oh my God. I can't get my head around this. He's not coming back, is he? He always came back."

Mikey broke down again, and catching Trump's eye, Seaton wound his finger in circles.

"Nearly done, Mikey. What time did he leave?" Trump smiled at Mikey, although Mikey's face was covered by his hands. They dropped away suddenly.

"Oh my God. Does Beatrix know? That poor woman, they've been together for ever. Have you told her? Can I have her number?"

"I don't think that would be appropriate. What time did Christopher leave?"

"Of course it's appropriate. She'll need someone who understands. Please, please ask her if I can call her. She knows about me, she has her own … friend."

"Okay, I'll ask. What time did he leave?"

"I don't know. We'd watched a film on Netflix, I had a shower, he was checking his emails, then I wanted to know what was going on. Half one, maybe two? I don't know, he wasn't rushing, just determined to leave. I only ever asked him to stay once, he doesn't like it if I press him, and I hate him telling me I know the rules. You will ask her, won't you?"

"I will, yes. Interview terminated at five thirty." Hitting the button, Trump got to his feet. "Come on, I'll get someone to give you a lift home. I'm guessing you don't want to go back to work."

"No. Don't want to go back there ever. But I will, for Christopher. I won't let him down now."

"You could always look for another job."

"I know. I will now."

~ ~ ~

While Trump arranged for Mikey to be taken home, Meredith and Seaton pored over a map of the area, trying to guess the route Kentish would have taken from Mikey's flat on Great George Street to get to Christmas Steps.

"If he'd gone down Park Street and along Frogmore, he would've had to pass Trenchard Street, and the car park. We've got all the CCTV from there, so it must have been up Park Street and along Park Row," Seaton argued.

"Yep, but we've already got that footage too." Meredith clicked his fingers. "Unless, he didn't go straight there. What if he jumped in a taxi, went somewhere, probably, possibly his home and then went out? Mikey was vague about the time. He had time." Shoving his hands in his pockets, Meredith nodded in agreement with himself. "That's my best guess. And his phone records show no calls in or out, have we checked his home number? He could have gone home and got a call. We need to get into his emails, any luck there?"

"Don't know. And before you shout, I'll check on all of it."

"Good man. Once we know that, let's start work on the taxi front. He probably went to Park Street and flagged one down. Actually, find out who's taking Mikey home, and get them to ask him if he knows how Kentish would normally get home from his. It's walkable if you're fit and like walking. Oh shit, why didn't I think about that? Out of Great George Street, up Park Street, cut through Richmond Hill, choose a route into Clifton Village and then where? We need CCTV from there. Ask Mikey, check the home number, more CCTV to collect."

~ ~ ~

An hour later they had established that Kentish did walk home on occasion, it depended on the weather, if it was raining he'd get a taxi. He also had a land-line at home, and they were waiting for an itemisation of his account. Jo had got a positive ID on the photofit from the landlord of The Mall, who had an exchange of words with the man when he kicked over a chair set out on the pavement. He didn't appear drunk, he was tall and skinny, and he didn't notice any form of accent. The man had doubled back on himself and flagged down a taxi. Jo had also acquired more CCTV footage.

At a little after seven, Meredith called it a day.

"Get off home, we've got a lot to get through tomorrow. Hutchins and Bailey are covering the incident line until eleven, then it will flip through to the front desk. We'll get a call if anything of interest arises. Bright and early tomorrow. Have a good evening." Saluting them, Meredith turned back to his office.

Trump put his head around the door on his way out. "Are you not going home, sir?"

"I am. But I've got to call Beatrix Kentish first. Mikey is awaiting a call too. Just wondering how much she knows, and if it's not much, how discreet he'll be. She'll agree to talk to him, I know that much."

"Good luck."

"Thanks."

~ ~ ~

"And she did, although she took his number and said she would call when she felt the time was right. Funny old set-up, but he's not our man. And that, Mrs Meredith, is all you're getting. You are welcome to talk about your day, but I've had enough. I think an early night is in order. I take it Amanda has abandoned us for Sherlock?"

"No, she's on nights, she told us yesterday. I don't think you listen to a word we say." Leaving the table, Patsy carried the stack of crockery to the dishwasher and began loading it. "My day was bitty, some good bits, some frustrating bits, we found Amy's laptop, managed to get into it and then it ran out of battery. Tomorrow should bear more fruit. Although I did a little work once I got home, and I've got an appointment to meet with Jeremy's cousin tomorrow. That means a trip to London, but there's plenty for the girls to get on with." Closing the dishwasher, Patsy yawned. "I think an early night is a good idea, I'm dead on my feet."

"Oh, I wasn't planning on sleeping."

"Then you'd better make a move now. I'll go on up, don't forget to lock the back door."

Another yawn escaped and Meredith grabbed her arm.

"Are you okay? You look a little pale."

"That's what Peggy said the other day. I'm going to have to start putting my makeup on with a trowel. I'm fine, move your arse though, or I really might be asleep."

Reaching behind her, Meredith hit the light switch, plunging them into darkness.

"Oh, you are keen. But not the kitchen table, and you haven't locked the door." Patsy pulled away from him with a giggle.

"I'll see you up there, Mrs MOUCH! I think I've broken my toe."

"That's what you get when you fumble in the dark."

"I can't remember much fumbling." Turning the key, Meredith slid the lock home. "Bed."

"Of course."

Chapter Nine

Patsy dropped the paperwork and some of the photographs she'd taken home into the office, then waited for her taxi to take her to the station. A cheaper option than parking the car at the station. Hopefully, she should be back by mid-afternoon. Her meeting was at ten. She locked her car, checked the time, and smiled as a taxi pulled into the carpark. She would make the seven thirty train. The train had almost reached London when she had a call from Henry Duggan. She got to her feet, slung the strap of her bag over her shoulder and left the carriage.

"Hi, Henry, I'm on a train. My signal is intermittent. Off to meet with Freddie Rossiter."

"Oh, how interesting. I won't keep you, just to say one of the beneficiaries has called, I've broken the news, although he'll have to wait until the reading to find out how much he's been bequeathed, but he's agreed to see you. He seemed genuinely intrigued."

"Wonderful. Would you email me his details, as I'll have a couple of hours to kill on the way back?"

"Will do. By the way, your friends were very interested in quite a lot of stuff. The house will be empty in no time."

"That is good news, I … I'm sure you heard that, we're arriving at Paddington. I'll speak to you later."

Glad she was at the head of the scrum of people seemingly desperate to disembark, Patsy dropped her phone into her bag. Once off, she headed for the Hammersmith & City tube that would take her to Liverpool Street Station. Despite the crowded platform, a chill wind whipped her hair from its band, and she pushed her hands deep into her pockets, only to remove them as the crowd surged forward as the tube arrived. She remembered why she didn't like London.

Patsy arrived at her destination thirty minutes before she was due and went into a café a little up the road and bought a coffee. She sipped it as she checked her emails and jotted down the telephone number of Marcus Ellsworth, deciding to call when she'd finished with Rossiter.

Freddie Rossiter's offices were sleek and sophisticated. The staff were immaculately presented and seemed to glide silently about their business. She watched the clock tick round to ten o'clock When the second hand passed the hour Freddie Rossiter's PA got to her feet and held her out her hand. "Mrs Hodge, this way."

Patsy was momentarily thrown, but realised it was because she was wearing her wedding ring, and smiling, she followed her down the corridor to a set of double doors. The PA knocked once and pushed open a door.

"Mrs Hodge for you." She closed the door as Patsy entered.

Freddie Rossiter stood and held out his hand. "Punctual. Well done. Take a seat please. I understand you wish to speak to me about my cousin Jeremy, and I'm intrigued, he's been dead for donkey's years, so I have no idea what this is about." Waiting for Patsy to sit in one of the chairs, he sat on the sofa opposite, draping his arm along the back rest. "Fire away."

"Thank you for seeing me so promptly, I—"

"As I said, I'm intrigued. But time is money, so let's not preamble. Straight to the point, I have another appointment this morning."

"No problem. I've been retained by Henry Duggan, a solicitor, to investigate claims in the will of one of his deceased clients, Amy Cleaver." Noticing the lines appear on Rossiter's forehead, Patsy paused, but when he didn't speak, she resumed. "Amy believes that she may have been murdered, and that if she has, then it is linked to the death of your cousin Jeremy."

Again, she paused, knowing this information would normally evoke some form of response. Rossiter merely raised his eyebrows "Amy," Patsy continued, "asked my client to investigate and mentioned that there were four people key to the investigation. Four people who knew your cousin and also attended his funeral." Patsy stopped speaking.

Realising she wasn't going to continue, Freddie shrugged. "And? You haven't actually asked me anything. I'm still none the wiser."

"I thought you might want to pass comment on what I've told you so far."

"No. Carry on."

"Okay. I would therefore be grateful if you could tell me what you remember about the last few days of your cousin's life. Whether you believe he committed suicide or had an unfortunate accident. Provide me with the names of his close friends, identify some people in a series of photographs I have with me, and confirm whether or not they were at his funeral."

"You don't want much, do you? So, from the beginning. The name Amy Cleaver rings a bell, although I can't place her. But I'm assuming she wasn't murdered, or the police would be here investigating and not you. On that basis, and for some reason I can only guess at, your client has decided to plough on with this charade, and here you are bothering me. Is that accurate?"

"I apologise, I didn't—"

"Let me finish. I didn't much like my cousin. He was vain and arrogant. And as I was younger than him we did not have the same group of friends. I will, however, look at your photographs to see if there is anyone I recognise. There were many people at his funeral. But apart from family, I have no idea who they were. I took little notice, to be honest, couldn't wait to have done my duty and got on with something far more interesting." He grinned at the look on Patsy's face. "Don't be shocked. Had it been the other way around he'd have thought the same. In fact, I'm sure he would've come up with an excuse not to attend at all. The dislike was mutual."

"You have an excellent memory, you've addressed all my questions, however you didn't say whether you think the crash that took his life was deliberate or an accident."

"That's because I'm not sure. Credit where credit is due, Jeremy was a skilful driver, and this notion of there being some form of wildlife causing him to swerve is nonsense. Jeremy would have hit the animal, although there is the train of thought that he didn't want to damage his new car. But he could have been hitting back at my uncle who bought the car for Jeremy, but had earlier that evening told Jeremy he wouldn't be getting his inheritance, so yes, I suppose he could have wanted to damage the car and that little ploy didn't work, or he could have been so upset, angry, call it what you will, that he decided to end it all. I don't err on the side of the latter. Jeremy was a man of action, a go-getter, he would have waited for the old man to pop off and challenged me over the will. I'm not sure if any of that helps. But it's all I have."

"I wasn't aware that Jeremy knew he wouldn't inherit before he died. Did you know?"

"Of course."

"Did your mother know this? When my client spoke—"

"You've been to see Mother! How dare you? She's an elderly lady, dementia is setting in. That is totally out of order. Who is this client of yours? I'd like a word."

"I'll leave you his details. He only asked the same questions I've asked you, but unfortunately your mother couldn't remember much. I believe she said she had removed herself from the family's clutches, so was no longer in the know."

"Which I could have told you, had you had the decency to ask. As you are investigating something to do with Jeremy, you would know who I was, and how you could contact me. You bloody people drive me mad. Are we finished?"

"Not really. Would you mind looking at these photographs?" Patsy pulled the envelope from her bag, shuffled through the pictures and placed two on the table. Tapping one, she said, "The girl in the middle is Amy Cleaver, our deceased client. Do you know the names of the others?"

Freddie Rossiter lifted the photograph and squinted at it. "I vaguely recognise them. They were at the party. I remember him shouting at them. And before you ask, I don't know what it was about. The girl on the end had a thing with Jeremy. Julie or Juliet, I caught them at it once."

Laughing, Freddie picked up the other photograph. His smile got wider. "These are the same people, except for him, I don't know his name, but he was also my cousin's lover. Pretty boy, isn't he?"

Patsy accepted the photograph and studied it. "The blond one?"

"Yes. Jeremy liked, as he called it, to 'spread the love', although I don't think there was much love involved, it was a power drive. He liked to have power. He learned the hard way, and possibly with his life, that batting for both sides doesn't always pay dividends. Ha! How apt."

"Are you saying his father disinherited him because he was bisexual?"

"Something like that."

"Can you expand, please? If I can find out what happened to Jeremy, I might have a greater understanding of what Amy thought was going on. It's clear you're not upset by his death, so I'd be grateful if you would give me a little more detail."

"Upset? Why would I be upset? Even if the old man hadn't changed his will, it meant I inherited. My father was dead. I was the spare, as Jeremy was also an only child, and when the wheel came off, I was needed."

"If it wasn't his sexuality, what was it that caused his disinheritance?"

"I'm sure Mother waxed lyrical about the Rossiter men, and to be fair she's not exaggerating. We are achievers. We get things done, but only what we want to be done. Be that money, property, wine, women or song. If we want it, we get it. And so it has been for many generations."

"What did Jeremy's father want from him that he didn't get? I'm guessing that's what you're alluding to." Patsy didn't bother to hide her

92

distaste, or her dislike of the man in the tone she used. She guessed he wouldn't care one way or the other, and she was right.

"Oh dear. Are you a delicate soul? You women are so emotional." His smirk irritated Patsy even more, but she tried to keep her expression neutral. "It's not what you do, it's how you hide it. Philip Rossiter, Jeremy's father, had no problem with anything any of us did. Including his wife. He'd probably done worse, but what had to be upheld was the family name, the pretence that there was some substance to us, a respectability. Do you see?"

"Not really, no. Why? If he was all powerful, surely it was for him to call the shots."

"My dear girl, you really are naïve. We work with money, larger sums than you can imagine. We have royals amongst our clients, and not only in this country. Some clients are delicate about who their names are associated with, and what they get up to. Therefore, the only Rossiter rule was: what you do, you do behind closed doors. Jeremy broke that rule, or at least allowed it to be broken. His father hit the roof, and when Jeremy refused to accept his wrath, he pulled the plug. I couldn't believe my luck."

"You were there?"

"Oh yes. The party was wonderful. The toasts had been made, the food consumed, and although alcohol still flowed freely, he summoned Jeremy and me to a meeting. It wasn't unusual for his father to do that. Only the month before he'd called my father back from the Riviera over something trivial. Power. My dear girl, unless you come from money, or had it and lost it, or lost it and recovered it, you will never understand. Money is power. Simple as that."

"What happened at the meeting?"

"We entered his suite, he was staying at the Grand, but he wasn't there, so Jeremy helped himself to a drink. His father entered as he was sipping it. He smashed the file he was carrying into Jeremy's face, it split his lip against the glass, and Jeremy cursed. He was told that was the least of his worries, and that if he couldn't pay for it, he shouldn't touch it. Even I thought that was odd. Jeremy demanded to know what that meant, and his father told him he was out on his ear as he didn't know how to behave. Again, came the demand for information, only Jeremy showed no respect in his demands, he'd had too much to drink and had forgotten his place. Me, I was cowering by the window, hoping not to get noticed. Philip Rossiter was a mean bastard. I knew to keep well away."

"So he'd called you there to tell Jeremy he was out, and you were in."

"Not quite, I don't think. He called us there to make Jeremy grovel and to allow me to witness it. Jeremy demanded again to know what he'd done, and his father listed off numerous misdemeanours, going back years, but eventually he got to the point. He walked to the desk and pulled out a pile of photographs and threw them at Jeremy one by one."

"Photographs of a sexual nature?"

"Well they weren't family portraits." Rossiter's smirk was back.

"And what happened next? In what way did Jeremy refuse to accept his father's wrath, is how you put it I think?"

"Jeremy collected up the photographs, had a quick flip through and smirked. 'It was once.' He laughed at his father. Well, I knew from blondie there," Freddie pointed at the photograph, "that wasn't the case. But Jeremy persisted. 'You can see that from the room. I was high, it was offered, I didn't refuse. Don't worry, Father, I will take myself a wife and produce an heir.'"

Rossiter glanced at his watch and gave a shake of his head. "Look, to get to the heart of it, because quite frankly I'm bored and, as mentioned, I do have another appointment, Philip Rossiter had been sent the photographs by a well-wisher. His anger was not about what Jeremy was doing, but who he was doing it to. I'd tell you, but I too don't want that little nugget to backfire on me."

"Someone important?"

"No, not really, not then, but enough that his family wouldn't want those photographs being seen, let alone published. I still have a copy of one. Insurance policy, you see. Not had to make a claim yet. But back to what happened. Jeremy was told he would go to see the father of the poor chap with him in the photographs, tell him how they got drunk, and how Jeremy had seduced him. He would then announce his engagement to the dreary girl his father had lined up for him, get his head down and finish university, and then come back here to London and start earning his keep. Jeremy refused. Said there was no seducing involved, and if his father would like to go with him, they could find the man in a similar situation at that very moment, but what he absolutely refused to do was marry the girl.

"More threats ensued, and Jeremy offered a compromise. He said there was a girl he would marry, one he could make a half decent fist of a marriage with, but that was all he was prepared to offer. My God, if I wasn't already scared enough, I hid when the old man flew at him. Beat him and kicked him like a dog. To give Jeremy his due he managed to land a rather spectacular punch, which shocked the old man into halting the attack. I don't think anyone, least of all Jeremy, had ever stood up to him before. He told Jeremy to get out, that I would inherit the business. The response, as I recall, was with pleasure. He could keep the effing business, and his effing money, because Jeremy didn't want it. And then he left. I was dismissed and told to keep my mouth shut. And I did. I was in as much shock as Jeremy. The next morning, I woke to the news that Jeremy had died." Forcing a smile, Rossiter got to his feet. "And that, as you say, is that."

Patsy remained seated. "Going back to my photographs, you don't recall any of the names?"

"I don't."

"Do you know who sent the photographs to Jeremy's father?"

"I do."

"But you won't tell me?"

"I won't."

"Do you know the name of the girl he wanted Jeremy to marry?"

"Oh yes. They were one and the same."

"Are you telling me that someone who wanted to marry Jeremy was attempting to do so by blackmail?"

"Indeed. Women are far more devious than we poor men. Of course, my uncle's failure with Jeremy was passed on to me. Now, I had thought this was going to be far more interesting, and I do have to get on. It's been a pleasure, Ms Hodge."

"Your uncle forced you to marry her?" Patsy couldn't help herself.

"I didn't say that, did I?"

"Okay, I can see I've outstayed my welcome, but I'm afraid I have two more questions of a personal nature, you are after all an intriguing man." Patsy gave what she hoped was a convincing smile but could immediately see her attempt at flattery hadn't worked.

"You may ask, whether I choose to answer is a different matter."

"You didn't ask why we thought Amy might have been murdered, or indeed how she died. Why?"

"Because, my dear girl, I don't care. Next? Ask as we walk." He took Patsy's arm and steered her towards the door.

"As far as we know from your mother, you don't have an heir. Who will you leave your fortune to? Are there other family members we could speak to?"

"I don't have children with my wife, Ms Hodge, and why would I? That doesn't mean I don't have an heir. Safe journey back to Bristol." Pulling open the door, he smiled a charmless smile. "I doubt our paths will cross again."

"Wouldn't you like to know if Jeremy's death had any connection to Amy's demise?"

"Not really. I'm sorry. My interest in Jeremy died with him. Now, I really must dash."

"Understood. Goodbye."

Patsy found a table in the corner of a cafe and completed her notes. It seemed that Freddie Rossiter had married the girl intended for Jeremy, and she had been the one to force Jeremy's father's hand by obtaining compromising photographs. Jeremy had been a philanderer, who possibly did take his own life after refusing to agree to his father's demands, and consequently losing his fortune. A nasty bunch.

Patsy had been surprised at the amount of information Freddie Rossiter had shared, but she knew something was being held back. Why had he been annoyed that they'd spoken to his mother? Patsy closed her notebook as she ordered her coffee. Did it matter? For the life of her, she couldn't see how any of it was connected to Amy, and she believed that had Freddie known the names of the people in the photographs he would have said so. It wasn't yet eleven, and trains out of Paddington ran every hour. Scrolling through her phone, Patsy decided to call Ellsworth and get an appointment booked in.

Ellsworth agreed to an appointment late that afternoon and was pleasant and accommodating in a way that Freddie Rossiter could never be, unless, of course, he was courting money. Once back on the train she exchanged a series of texts with Linda as to the progress made and was pleased to find that another of the beneficiaries had been in touch with Henry, and she asked Linda to get her an appointment as soon as possible.

When she asked about the laptop she instantly regretted it as the power cable had yet to turn up. Linda was not pleased and reminded Patsy that she had offered to buy one. Patsy placated her by giving her a job that Patsy knew had little value to the case, but it was something that intrigued her. She stood to one side as passengers swarmed into Paddington and called Linda.

"A bit of intrigue for you. Rossiter told me that Jeremy's father wanted him to marry someone, and when Jeremy refused it meant giving up his fortune. Rossiter described her as dreary, but later implied that having inherited the fortune, he also inherited a wife, and one that wasn't averse to blackmail. Find out who she is, and dig up whatever background you can on her, particularly around the time that Jeremy died."

"That's more like it. What was she using to blackmail him with?"

"Not Jeremy, his father, although it was with photographs of Jeremy in a compromising situation with a young man."

"Ooh. The plot thickens. Do we know who?"

"No. Although someone with lots of money, I'm guessing European royalty. I doubt it was our royal family, but who knows?"

"Already on it, and I have to say I thought this one was going to be boring, but it's shaping up nicely now. See you later, unless I find something juicy, in which case I'll call."

Call over, Patsy had to run to catch the train preparing to leave platform four. Finding a seat halfway through the last carriage, she dropped into it with a sigh. She had intended going through her emails but instead picked up a copy of *The Metro*. It held little news that interested her, and the crossword took her less than five minutes. By the time the train had picked up speed towards Reading, she'd leaned her head against the window and nodded off. To her surprise, she woke up as they approached Swindon, amazed that she'd slept through the two previous stations. But refreshed, she pulled out her phone and scrolled through her emails.

She left Linda's until last and dealt with those she was able to before she opened the one from Linda. As expected it was long. As she read through it, she at first smiled but then frowned. Taking the photographs from her bag, she activated the camera on her phone, took a shot of both and sent them to Linda, wondering if Angel was imagining things. Going back to the email, she was relieved that although the picture was building, there was nothing that required her attention, and she'd be able to go home once she'd met with Marcus Ellsworth.

The train arrived back in Bristol on time, and Patsy jumped into a cab. Her meeting with Ellsworth was for four o'clock at Broad Street's Grand Hotel. Patsy thought it apt, given Jeremy's last meeting there. She arrived ten minutes early, so took a seat in the bar and ordered a coffee.

Ellsworth arrived before her coffee, and strode towards her with confidence, he had almost reached her table when he hesitated.

Patsy smiled at him. "Marcus?"

"Ah, it is you, yes. Nice to meet you."

His smile was warm as he held out his hand, Patsy watched his eyes flick from her shoes to her eyes. As she stood to shake his hand, she did much the same. He was smart in an understated way. No jacket or tie, but his clothes were immaculate, and his shoes well-polished. Not handsome in the conventional sense, but he had a look about him, one that made you relax.

Patsy gestured to the chair. "Please, take a seat. Thank you for seeing me at such short notice."

"No problem. I had an appointment cancel on me, so you're saving me from an afternoon of boredom. I'm used to being busy. And, quite apart from anything else, it intrigued me. First the letter from the solicitor, then a call from a private investigator. Tell me more, I've gone through a thousand different scenarios in my mind since your call, and I'm sure all of them are wrong."

The waitress arrived with Patsy's coffee, and they ordered another. While waiting for her to leave, Patsy placed the envelope with the photographs on the table.

"This is going to seem an odd tale, but if I may I'd like to ask you some questions before I tell you why."

"Of course. Does this mean I have to qualify for my inheritance, whatever that is, before I get it? I'll try to get top marks." His smile was easy, and he relaxed back into his chair.

"No, nothing like that. But Amy Cleaver not only left a will but she left her solicitor the task of sorting something out from her past. That's why I'm here."

"Oh. I think this will be a short meeting then. Amy was my mother's friend, I only met her a handful of times. I don't think I'm going to be able to help."

"Just finding someone who remembers her is a start." Pulling the photographs from the envelope, Patsy handed him the first one. "Do you know any of the people in this photograph? We have a few first names, but no more than that."

Ellsworth studied it and nodded. "A couple yes. The girl on the end, not looking at the camera, is my mother Julia Ellsworth. That's Amy Cleaver in the middle. I only know one man, Jeremy Rossiter. My father. Although I never met him, he died before I was born."

"Your father!" Unable to contain her surprise, Patsy leaned forward. "Your mother told you this?"

"Repeatedly. She spoke of him as though he were still alive. You must work hard at school, Daddy was very clever and you will be too. Daddy would be so proud of you, Daddy wouldn't like that, and so on. I actually believed the man was alive until I was about eleven. It's very sad, but I think it was her way of coping."

"Is it possible to speak to your mother? Then I won't have to waste your time."

"Afraid not. She died when I was sixteen."

"I'm sorry. That must have been a shock, I also lost my mother when I wasn't much older than that."

"It was, yes, sadly an overdose. When I think about it, it was always on the cards. She wasn't a strong woman but she would never ask anyone for help. I tried to persuade her, but she wouldn't have it. Wouldn't speak to her friends, the doctor, what little family we had. It was quite hopeless. Although, she was an excellent actress. On the rare occasion we had visitors, she would be chirpy and ..." He waved his hand in circles, trying to find the right word. "Efficient. That's the word. The house was always immaculate, she was always flawless, and she talked a good talk. But when we were alone, she would get lost in herself. I had to fend for myself."

He looked away from Patsy and stared at his cup for a while before shrugging. "But there are others who had it worse than me. I have a good job, a nice home, and I'm seeing someone that I think is pretty special, who knows where that might lead?"

"That's good to hear. Tell me how you met Amy?"

"The first time I remember meeting her was at my mother's funeral. But she'd told me I'd grown into a handsome young man, so I'd met her before that but I didn't remember it. She was very generous, gave me what seemed like an enormous sum of money to a boy of sixteen, and now she's left me something in her will. Such a kind lady. Do you know what she left me? Her solicitor wouldn't tell me."

"I don't I'm afraid. All I can say is that it will probably be money. Henry Duggan is in the process of liquidating the estate to enable him to act in accordance with her instructions. He might not know himself until it's all sold. I also know he's still waiting to be contacted by some of the other beneficiaries."

"Ah, I see. Whatever it is will be welcome, every little helps. How many of us are there?"

"Four I believe, and a few charities."

"Kind to the end. Bless her."

"You said you met Amy a few times, when was the last time you met her?"

"A while ago, maybe a year. Literally bumped into her in the supermarket, or rather she did to me. I thought she'd broken my ankle with the trolley. I didn't recognise her, but she knew me. We had a brief chat, work, the weather, and she told me I had the look of my father about me, and that was that. I'm surprised she's remembered me in her will. Such a gracious lady." He lifted the photograph again, flipped it over, and held it against his chest. "Do you think I look like him? I can't see it, not at all."

"Um. Not really, no. But you're a little older than he was there, and I never knew him. Your colouring is the same, your mannerisms might be too. Have you ever met your father's family?"

Ellsworth's demeanour changed, his jaw set, and his eyes narrowed.

"I'm guessing what you really want to ask is do they know about me? Am I right?"

"Isn't that the same thing?" Worried that this change might cause him to stop speaking, Patsy gave him a reassuring smile. "I ask because I met Freddie Rossiter yesterday, he would be your uncle."

"I know who he is. The Rossiters weren't interested. They had already disowned my father, why would they want me?" Ellsworth closed his eyes, when he opened them his amiable side reappeared. "I'm sorry. I hate talking about them. I've never met any of them, they made it quite clear to my mother that her bastard was of no concern to them. It broke her, I think. It doesn't worry me, but it makes me so bloody angry that they could have helped her and chose not to. Had they done so she might have been alive today. Although I said I don't enjoy talking about them, you've got me interested. What did Uncle Freddie have to say?" He delivered his final sentence in a sarcastic tone, and folding his arms across his chest, he leaned back in the chair. "Was he of any help?"

"None. He didn't recognise anyone in the photographs except your mother, he remembered her name too. He had no interest in any of his family history, I felt like I was interrupting him doing something far more interesting."

"Sounds like him from what my mother told me. They were her favourite topic of conversation, none of them had time for anyone but themselves. My father was the exception. You know he asked her to marry him, about an hour before he died. You can understand why she was so bitter. I wonder if he's happy. Freddie Rossiter, I mean. I'm not sure how anyone can be happy if their only interest is themselves. Sad life, I would have thought. Was there anything else you wanted to know?"

"Did your mother ever mention any other events that happened around the time of your father's death? I hadn't realised he'd proposed to her."

"She'd only known him a year, then got pregnant, then he proposed making all her dreams come true, and then he died. It was the pivotal part of her life. Was there anything in particular?"

100

"I don't know. Amy's assumption was that something happened around that time which has since caused others to lose their lives. And she wanted it stopped."

"To die? Really! How?" Ellsworth now paid full attention. He leaned forward with his elbows on the table.

"I don't know. That's why I was hired. To find out why, and more importantly, who?"

"Who what?" A grin lit up Ellsworth's features. "It sounds like you're hunting for a murderer."

"I hope not, but it's what Amy thought might be possible."

Ellsworth covered his face with one hand, clearly amused. When he dropped it, his smile remained. "If that were true, and of course I have nothing to make a judgement on, why on earth would a private investigator be involved? Surely it would be a matter for the police. Although, I'm guessing it's a nice little earner." Waving his hand, he apologised. "I'm sorry that was rude and uncalled for. But if you look at it from my point of view. Why?"

"Why what?" Understanding his amusement, Patsy took no offence.

"Why a private investigator, why not go to the police? I think they'd be my first port of call."

"And they were Henry Duggan's. But with so little to go on, no evidence, no names, not even a clue as to what had happened, the police felt there was little they could do. That said, I'm on strict instructions to hand over the case if I get even an inkling there may be some truth to it."

"Instructions from whom?" Ellsworth scratched his head. "Do you know this conversation is becoming quite surreal. If someone had told me at nine o'clock this morning that I would have had the conversations I've had today, I'd have thought they were crazy."

"It is all a bit odd, and at the moment I'm thinking it's all going to be a wild goose chase. But I used to be a police officer and if there is any chance at all that there's been foul play I'll be handing over my files. My husband is a senior police officer. The public won't be in danger." Patsy sought to reassure him.

"Quite right too. Now, is there anything else because I do have a date tonight?"

"No, thank you, although I'd be grateful if you would glance at those photographs again. Did your mother keep any documents or photographs from that time?"

"Yes an entire box full. The contents of which I took great delight in burning when she died, they'd caused her ... us, nothing but grief."

Ellsworth lifted the photographs again and studied them. "No one but my father and Amy Cleaver. Sorry. He looks a charmer though, doesn't he, shame I never knew him." He laughed. "I understand Freddie Rossiter doesn't have children, perhaps I'll get an inheritance from him. And then again, pigs might fly, and Bristol Rovers might get into the Premiership."

"I'm afraid that's unlikely. One of the few things he did say to me was that although he didn't have children with his wife it didn't mean he didn't have an heir. I got the impression that he'd been pushed into a loveless marriage for some reason, and he quite possibly has a family he keeps private. I've found out that putting on a front and keeping the family name pristine is quite important to the Rossiters." Putting the photographs back into her bag, Patsy shook his hand. "Thank you for your time, I hope you're pleased with whatever Amy has left you."

Patsy wondered if it was disappointment which had, just for a moment, frozen Ellsworth's features, and if it was who could blame him, it sounded like he'd had a rough time of it in the past. He recovered his composure.

"Oh, I will be, after all, it's more than I had before. I'll get going, bye."

"Bye, nice meeting you. It's a shame you never met Sue, I'll be meeting her soon."

"Who's Sue?"

"One of the girls in that photograph. A woman now of course. I mustn't keep you, and I need to find a taxi."

"Can I give you a lift somewhere?"

"No, thank you. I have some notes to make first."

As he walked away, Patsy was glad she had finished for the day, her head ached, her eyes were sore and she believed, if she remained stationary any longer, she'd fall asleep again. She groaned as she remembered she had to go to the office to pick up her car. Making a decision, she called Linda.

"Hi, Linda, I'm not going to bother coming in for my car, I'm knackered. Can you pick me up in the morning?"

"Why haven't you checked your messages or your emails. Blimey, Patsy, anything could have happened. I'm not impressed!"

"Why what's happened?"

"Well apart from your next day delivery not working so I've still not got into the laptop, I'm going to buy one on the way home. I—"

"Linda, I'm not in the mood. I'll chase them. Was there anything else, and can you pick me up in the morning?"

"Yes, and yes."

"What? Yes, you can pick me up, and there is something else?"

"There is. Do you really want to know? Because from here it sounds like you've lost interest in this case, and just when it was getting juicy. If we're only working office hours, I'll tell you about it in the morning."

Patsy smiled, she knew it was unlikely to be something juicy, but was impressed that Linda was holding it back anyway. "Juicy you say, then I'd better not clock off, I'll stay here so you can tell all. Two seconds."

The waitress had appeared to clear the cups away and asked if she wanted anything else. The coffee hadn't been up to much, too bitter, so Patsy ordered a small glass of wine.

"Are you out gallivanting while we're in here slaving away? What's the occasion?"

"There is no occasion, I'm not driving, the coffee here is awful, and I thought it might give me a boost, either that or help me sleep through Meredith's snoring later. Now give me your juicy findings."

"First, I've found out who Freddie Rossiter was married to, she's in some of the photographs, and second, Mrs Clarkson is keen to meet with you and will be in Bristol tomorrow."

"Who's Mrs Clarkson?"

"Patsy, where is your brain? Susan Clarkson, the other beneficiary. I'd tell you off for forgetting, but this is the juicy bit and I can't wait. Susan Clarkson is scared. She lives in a remote cottage in North Wales, and now this has happened to Amy, she's too frightened to stay there."

"How much did you say? You did emphasise it could have been an accident, didn't you?"

"I'm not stupid. I said nothing. And I didn't need to call her, she called us. Henry wasn't in but had left instructions if any of the beneficiaries should call. They gave Susan our number."

"I apologise, I'm sure you said nothing. What did she say?"

"Was Amy murdered, is this why I have to call you, why not the police?"

"Ellsworth said something similar."

"I only said Amy wanted Jeremy Rossiter's death investigated, and she went quiet. When I prompted her, she said, 'My cottage is remote. I'm not safe here, Amy is right. I'm coming to Bristol I'll see you tomorrow." Then she hung up. I tried to call back, but it was engaged. I can't wait to hear what she has to say."

"Me neither. So who is Rossiter's wife, and what have you found out about her?"

"Her name is Penelope Rossiter, nee Vickery. Older than him, but same age as … you've guessed it, Jeremy. The got married in eighty-three, neither of them looked that happy in the photograph I found, and it was Angel, not me, who noticed that it was one of the girls from some of the photographs. We only have one here with her in it, and she doesn't look thrilled to be in that either."

"I wonder if she's in any of the ones of got? I'll have a look in a minute. Anything else?"

"No. Other than two little snippets, one in the obituary for Jeremy's father, and one in a piece the financial times ran on Freddie. It says she lived in France. I can find quite a bit on Freddie, all of it boring, but not a word on her. If she uses social media, it's under an alias. Hubby goes to a lot of posh functions, there are a few photographs of him with the great and the good, but not one of her, and most of the time not much of a mention."

"Thanks, Linda. Good work. I'm going to head home now. I'll be ready for you from eight." Hanging up, Patsy lifted the wine and took a small sip, her nose wrinkled, and she pushed the glass away. She must be going down with something, everything tasted odd today.

~ ~ ~

It was almost six thirty by the time the taxi dropped her home. It surprised Patsy to find Meredith's car on the drive. She called to him as she entered the house.

"Has something happened? You're home exceptionally early."

He didn't answer, and hearing running water coming from above, she kicked off her shoes, dropped her bag on the hall floor and crept upstairs. Stripping off on the landing, she went into the bathroom and pulled back the shower curtain, Meredith dropped the bottle of shampoo he was holding.

"I'm not that well insured. Bringing on a heart attack will not do you any good."

"I'm sorry, I thought you'd be pleased to see me, I'll leave you to it." Squealing as he pulled her into the shower, Patsy turned to face him. "You're home early. Are you going out again? Never before eight when you're working a murder case like this one."

"Because it's ground to a halt. Absolutely nothing new. Hours and hours and hours of footage, but both men have clearly got hold of that thing they used on *Star Trek*, they've been beaming up and down all over the place, and nowhere near a camera. Everyone is working their nuts off, but nothing new as yet. Haven't even got into his safe yet. I came home before I blew a gasket. Did you get in here to speak about work? If you did, perhaps I will go out."

104

"No, stay here. I've had a good day, but I'll keep it to myself. Pass me the shampoo."

"You can do that later. Come here."

Chapter Ten

By the time Patsy arrived at the office, Linda had been there for two hours and was on her third coffee and getting more hyper by the minute.

"I can't believe you forgot me. Couldn't you sleep?"

"No. The thought of what I hadn't yet found kept me awake, so I gave in and got up with Louie, and forgot all about picking you up. Sorry again."

"Did you find what you hadn't?" Slipping her jacket off, Patsy hung it on the back of the chair in front of Linda's desk. "Coffee?"

"Don't think I should. I've already had three. Sit down, you're going to like this ... sort of."

"What does that mean - sort of?" Perching on the edge of the chair, Patsy nodded. "Go on, spit it out, I won't get anything done, even a coffee, until you have."

"Thank you. I don't think there is anything on her laptop that is of any use to us. I can access her work diary, which is much as you'd expect. I've checked every folder, her browsing history, and then finally her emails. You won't believe how much junk mail she gets. I have no idea why she didn't unsubscribe. Anyway, I set up a load of files to move them into, just in case we do have to go back, and—"

"Can we get to the bit I'm going to like 'sort of'? If not, I'll make a coffee and get myself comfortable." Patsy pushed herself to her feet.

"Have you had a row with Meredith? You seem very irritated. I thought Louie said they were making progress."

"I have not, and they are. As a total aside, and although it's none of your business, Meredith has been very calm since we got married. It's quite spooky. Not as calm and accommodating as normal people, but for Meredith ... anyway, I digress. Am I getting coffee, or are you getting to the point?"

"I've waited this long, five minutes more won't hurt. I'll have tea though."

"You know tea has caffeine in too, don't you?"

"Of course. I also know it goes much nicer with Belgian buns, of which I have a fresh bag. Hurry up and choose your poison and I might just let you have one."

Ten minutes later Patsy leaned back in the chair, and before taking a bite of her bun, said, "Fire away. Short, sharp to the point, and then I can ask questions."

"Finally. So, Amy's emails are quite boring, even the personal ones until I found one in drafts, which was never sent." Raising her eyebrows knowingly, Linda grinned as Patsy rolled her eyes. "And it confirms what she said in her instruction to Henry."

"Which was… this is not short or sharp so far."

"She thinks she was going to be killed, but she was more worried about someone called Scotty because of what she said."

"So help me, I'm going to punch you in a minute. Said what to whom, and do we know who Scotty is?"

"I was getting there. If you haven't rowed with Meredith, who, by the way, has relaxed because you're all his now, then something is irritating you. Are you ill? You've not finished your cake either. Shall I just read you the email?"

"I was savouring it. Yes, please do, that would be so much more efficient. By the way, I'm going to ask Meredith about your theory. I'll let you know what he says." Laughing at the look on Linda's face, Patsy rapped on the desk when Linda pulled a sheet from the file. "You had it printed? All you had to do was it hand to me!" Holding out her hand, Patsy shook her other fist at Linda.

"No, I'll read it. Why are you so grouchy? I might have a word with the skipper myself." Before Patsy could respond, she began to read the email penned by Amy Cleaver two days before her death.

"Don't say anything, just listen.

My Dearest Sue,

I hope you are well, and you are enjoying your retirement. I'd threaten to join you, but I know I'd be climbing the walls within a month.

Get a strong drink! Are you sitting comfortably? I hope so because I'm about to share a theory with you, and it's shocking, but I fear true. So, no beating about the bush:

108

I think those of us who were there on the night Jeremy died are being bumped off.

There. Even though I've put it in print, it doesn't sound ridiculous. But I can hear your giggle and see the roll of the eyes but think about it.

Who was there when we confronted Jeremy? Julia, of course, DEAD. Poor old Andrew, DEAD. Miriam DEAD. It was Miriam who made the connection, perhaps she knew she was next. But she said it as a sort of sick joke, then two weeks later she was dead. People with serious nut allergies do not accidentally eat homemade cake with nuts in. Who made the bloody cake? That's the question.

That only leaves me and Scotty. I'm on my guard, but I don't know how to tell Scotty. I didn't say much that night, just agreed with the others, but you'll remember Scotty was really vocal. Poor old Scotty. She's had so much to deal with, just got herself back on her feet, and although they're not out of the woods, she seemed so much happier when I saw her last week, and now this. That's where you come in. I think if we go and see her together, I'll have the courage to warn her, and you were always her favourite.

And before you say it, I know that: 1) You and Chris were also there, but you stayed up on the steps, do you remember? 2) They all appeared to be accidents or suicide. But they weren't. Just like Jeremy's wasn't. You know what he said when he jumped into that bloody car. We all knew as soon as the news broke that it wasn't an accident.

Anyway, have a think, and I'll call you this evening once you've had time to mull it over. To confirm how serious I am about this, I've included a note for my solicitor to get the police involved should I die suddenly without a decent medical reason, and I'm clearing the house! Yes, really. Can you imagine some poor soul having to deal with it? But that proves I am taking this seriously. I'll call tonight. If I go first, I'll need you to look out for Scotty.

I'll call you after…

"And there it ends. It's not signed, not sent. I don't know about you, Patsy, but I think she was on to something. Shame she never got round to clearing at least one room though."

"You could be right. This is the Susan I'm seeing today? Please say yes, because then we have somewhere to go with this."

"It is. One and the same. Can I sit in on it? She sounded anxious yesterday, I think she has more to tell."

"No, I need you back concentrating on tracking down the other beneficiaries. And yes, you're right. She can tell us what happened the night Jeremy died for a start." Grabbing her jacket from the back of the chair, Patsy headed to her office. "I'm not due to see her until eleven. I can get a couple of hours of paperwork done."

~ ~ ~

Susan Clarkson arrived fifteen minutes early. Tall and attractive, the only thing that marred her otherwise perfect appearance was the frown which left deep creases across her forehead. Now Patsy was free, Linda took her straight through.

"Ms Clarkson," she announced formally. "I'll bring some tea, or would you prefer coffee?"

"Nothing, thank you. I've been up for hours, one more drink and I might explode." Shaking Patsy's hand, she pointed to the chair in front of her desk. "Shall I sit here, or can I collapse on that rather comfy looking sofa?"

"Please." Holding out her hand towards the informal seating area, Patsy nodded at Linda. "Thank you, Linda, I'll let you know if we need anything." Holding back the smile as Linda reluctantly left them to it, she collected her pad and took the seat opposite Susan Clarkson, who started speaking before she'd even settled herself.

"I'm devastated. I didn't really take her seriously. You do know about her theory? Anyway, we'll get to that. When I heard from the solicitor, I was beside myself, but at least I didn't have to go to the police with what, to those who didn't know her, seems like a fantastic story. Perhaps it might be, but I'm here now. We can work that out. How can I help?"

"Amy believed that something which happened on the night Jeremy Rossiter died has caused someone to kill a number of those who were there that night. In her message to her solicitor, she says there were four of them, and from an email she was writing to you, she mentions the names of three people who have already died, Julia, Andrew and Miriam. If she was right and assuming none of the deaths were accidental including Amy's that's four, but she was very concerned about someone called Scotty. So that would be the fifth person there, and my assistant Linda tells me that you seemed concerned for your own safety, so you would be the sixth. I am therefore confused. But it's clear that this all stems from what happened on the night Jeremy died. I know his father had cut him out of his will shortly before his death, but there was clearly something else. You were there, so to start with can you tell me what happened that night, and we'll take it from there."

110

"Of course. Jeremy would love this, you know, being the centre of attention, causing all these fireworks even though he's not around. Where to begin? Shall I just ramble, and you stop me when I go off course?"

"Whatever works for you. Would you mind if I record this, then I'll only need to make notes on what I want to follow up on?"

"Feel free. Whatever it takes."

Setting up the recorder on the coffee table which separated them, Patsy nodded.

"Start with the night Jeremy died."

"There were a group of us that hooked up at university. That fluctuated in number, and we were all from different backgrounds, although all of us, except Julia I suppose, came from very comfortable backgrounds, and we were bright. The world was out there waiting for us to take it on. In the centre of our group was Jeremy Rossiter. Handsome, charismatic, charming most of the time, amusing, and a bit of an arrogant bastard. Although that didn't matter if you weren't in love with him. A bit like royalty, I suppose, he was just used to doing what he wanted, when he wanted. Provided he worked at his studies and pulled in the grades, his parents kept the cash flowing. We were not living on Pot Noodles and pasta, as the student myth suggests, we were going to nice restaurants and nightclubs. We worked hard, and we played harder. They were good days. Despite all the bad things one could say about Jeremy, he wasn't a snob, and he didn't judge others. He simply enjoyed being him. When Julia fluttered into our group, he was smitten for a while, followed her around like a lapdog. Julia fell for him, hook, line and sinker. We did warn her not to get too involved, we knew Jeremy had a roving eye. But they lasted right up until that awful night. Not that he was faithful as we've since found out, but apart from that, which none of us knew, he treated her well." Susan fell silent as her mind took her back.

"Did he argue with her that night?"

"He argued with everyone. Anyone that tried to reason with him. We thought his father might change his mind."

"Ah, so you saw him after he'd been cast aside. Start from there."

~ ~ ~

Mopping the blood from his mouth, Jeremy Rossiter stormed into the lobby of the hotel. He could hear the babble of merrymaking coming from the bar, and he wasn't sure if he was pleased his friends had waited for him. Spitting blood onto the glistening marble tiles, and ignoring the shout from the receptionist, he went to find support.

There was a cheer as he arrived, and Scotty lifted a tray of small glasses.

"Good timing. You want to try these, I promise you'll love them." Walking gracefully to the table, she waited until empty glasses had been pushed to one side and placed the tray down. "Remember the order, red, amber—"

Her final word was lost as Julia returned from the cloakroom.

"Jeremy! What the hell happened to you? Are you alright?"

Bumping Miriam out of the way, she ran to Jeremy and placed her hands on his shoulders, staring up at his face. The group fell silent as they took in the split lip, the red marks on Jeremy's face, and the ripped shirt.

"Have you been mugged? I thought you were going to see your father. You're going to have a fabulous black eye. Come and sit down. You look like you need a drink." Amy jumped up from her stool at the table to make room for him.

Taking her seat, Jeremy picked up a shot and knocked it back.

"Naughty, Jeremy, that was an amber one. You were supposed to start with red." Scotty laughed and held out the sickly red liquor.

Pointing his finger, his teeth clenched, Jeremy hissed, "Don't."

"What? Don't what Jeremy?"

Gripping the table, Jeremy looked Scotty in the eye. "Don't tell me what to fucking do. I'm done with that. My father just tried it, and as you can see he didn't like me telling him no. So, DON'T tell me what to do."

Without warning, Jeremy got to his feet, tipping over the table as he did so. There were shouts and yelps from the others as the glasses and alcohol showered them.

Andrew stepped forward and placed an arm on Jeremy's shoulder.

"Your father did this to you? No wonder you're pissed off. Now, stay calm long enough to decide what you want to do. Would you like to go home, and we'll spend the night trashing controlling parents, or go to a club and party, or shall we just get something to eat?"

Moving carefully between the glasses, Penny grabbed his arm. "Security is coming, let's get out of here. You don't want any more trouble from your father. I'm sure he'll calm down."

Shaking off her hand, Jeremy looked her up and down like she was contaminated in some way. "Get your hands off of me. He can do what he wants. We're done, I'm discarded, replaced by my darling cousin. A nightclub is the answer. I feel like dancing."

Grabbing his arm once more, Penny halted his progress. "What do mean discarded? He can't discard you, you're his son."

Jeremy rounded on her, causing her to stumble as he jerked his arm free. "I won't tell you again. Don't touch me. I don't even want to look

112

at you. Fuck off. You are … I can't find the words to tell you what I think, but so help me, if you touch me again I won't be held responsible for my actions."

"Steady on, Jeremy. Whatever happened it's not Penny's fault." Andrew smiled. "Perhaps we should all just go home."

"Good idea, mate. You have a minute to clear the premises or we're calling the police and pressing charges." The security guard placed his hand on Andrew's shoulder. "Door's that way."

Shoving him forward, the guard looked around the group. The vein in his temple was throbbing, and his shoulders were pulled back his fists clenched. "Anyone fancy letting me try out a citizen's arrest?"

Andrew grabbed Scotty's hand as Julia and Amy each took hold of an arm and pulled Jeremy forward. They managed to clear the foyer before he stopped dead.

Looking back over his shoulder, he smirked. "Do you know I might just try him, would someone call the press, I'd love Papa to see this over the front pages."

"Calm down, Jer. You've had a bad enough night, don't make it worse." Miriam leaned against the car. "I know you've had a shock, but it doesn't give you the right—"

Cutting Miriam off, Julia pleaded, "Don't, please, Jeremy. I need to speak to you." She cast her eyes around the group. "In private. Now. Please."

Jeremy cupped her chin. "You are so sweet. You don't deserve me, you could do so much better for yourself."

The group stilled. Jeremy had never, not once, admitted he was anything but perfect. With Amy's help Julia pulled him down the last few steps, stopping on the pavement where the car Julia now leaned against blocked their path. With a nervous smile for Amy, Julia stood very close to him and almost whispered her news.

"I'm pregnant. Whatever happened tonight doesn't matter. I love you, you know how much, and we're going to have a baby. Come home with me now, don't get yourself into trouble."

"WHAT?" Delivering the word from deep within him, Jeremy was visibly shaking. He turned away and threw up in the gutter. Spinning back, he jabbed a finger at her. "Well, well. How did that happen if you're on the pill? What a waste of time that was for you, I have nothing now, you got yourself up the duff for nothing."

The slap that sent his head reeling came from Scotty. She squared up to him as he rubbed his cheek. "Go on, big boy, hit me back, your father should have given you a good hiding years ago. You shit. She loves you.

You know that. You bloody well know that. Julia's better at everything than you, including being human. She won't need your money. She will have a glittering career. You're an arrogant, self-centred prick, who thinks the world revolves around him, and when it doesn't, you hurt those around you. You rush around trampling people who cared about you underfoot. Those who would help you. Oh, you're a good laugh to those who don't care, but look out anyone who falls for your fake charm. Don't take my word for it, ask them." Jerking her thumb, Scotty turned her head to look at Jeremy's group of friends. "Go on ask them."

With a grin, causing his eyes to twinkle, Jeremy nodded. "Is that what you all think? Do you all think I'm inhuman? Are you only here because I'm a good laugh? Except for poor little Julia, of course, because she apparently loves me. Here. Still love me?" Pulling a photograph from his pocket, he shoved it in Julia's hands. She took one look at it and fell to her knees. Jeremy clapped his hands. "I asked you a question? Is good old tell it straight Scotty correct? Is that what you all think?"

Looking at Julia, Andrew stepped forward. "Well, you are funny, but before we discuss your attributes, or lack thereof, don't you think you should help her?"

"That's the best you could come up with? You are dismissed."

Snorting, Andrew rolled his eyes. "Believe it or not, I'm not yours to command." Taking Julia's arm, he helped her to her feet. "Come on, let's get you home." Julia was shaking, and he put an arm around her shoulder.

"Off you go with the second best, Julia. But I'll have that back first."

Andrew stopped dead and turned to look at Jeremy. "Leave it, Jeremy, before everyone here falls out with you. If things are as bad as you say with your father, you're going to need your friends. Go home, sober up."

"Not drunk, and I said, I'll take that." Ignoring Andrew and stepping to stand in front of the still weeping Julia, Jeremy held his hand out.

Irritated, Andrew snatched it from her hand before Jeremy could. His nose wrinkled. "Why did you show her that? What's wrong with you?"

"Nothing. Sharing is caring and all that."

With no warning, Andrew made a fist, pulled back his arm and punched Jeremy. Hard. Amy and Scotty rushed forward.

"I think that's enough now. Behave yourselves. This has gone too far. We're all a little excitable, we should go and chill somewhere." Amy smiled. The smile was brief as Andrew passed her the photograph. "Why?" She searched Jeremy's face. He was many of the things they had accused him of, but he wasn't a cruel man. Well, not to her knowledge.

114

"Why?" Jeremy's shoulders twitched. "Because it was there for the taking, and I thought why not?"

"That's not what I was asking, and you know it. Why did you feel the need to show Julia? You really are a spiteful little shit."

"And the compliments keep flowing. Uh oh. Scotty's having a look now, wonder what new insult she'll come up with."

Her eyes flicking from the photograph to Jeremy and back again, Scotty flung it at him and drew Julia into a hug. and She looked at him over Julia's shoulder, her eyes full of hatred. "There was no need of that. But you were right about one thing, she's better off without you." A crowd from the party in the hotel had gathered on the steps behind Susan and Chris. "You have no family, and after tonight's performance fewer friends. But still, you have an audience. Go on, take a bow."

Jeremy's face crumpled, and for a moment they thought he was going to cry, but with as much dignity as he could muster, he held out his hand towards Julia. "I'm sorry. I shouldn't have done that, any of it. Will you forgive me?"

"I can't." It was barely a whisper.

"Leave it, Jeremy. Talk tomorrow when everyone's calmer," suggested Amy, before grabbing the photograph from Scotty's hand and tearing it into tiny pieces which she threw into the air. "Go home, Jeremy."

"I made a mistake. It won't happen again. Surely, you can see that." Eyes searching the faces of his closest friends, he shook his head. "So, not my friends now, not when the chips are down and the money has run out. Well fuck you. See you all in hell."

Fishing his keys from his trouser pocket, he looked at Julia. "Last time of asking, come with me and we'll sort our way through this, stay and this is the last time you'll see me."

Looking at the tiny pieces of the photograph, Julia shrugged. "I don't know... that is ... I ..."

"Do as Amy says, Jeremy. Leave out the dramatics and go home." Scotty pulled Julia back into her embrace.

"I think Scotty is right. Tomorrow will be soon enough to see what you can salvage." Andrew held out his hand. "But give me the keys. You can't drive in that state."

"Okay, so the delectable Julia doesn't want me, any other takers. Right now, right this minute or I'm out of here." Looking along the steps of the hotel, Jeremy saw friends, acquaintances, and strangers either laughing or smirking. Only a few had the good grace to look away.

"Adios. See you never. Losers." Turning on his heel, Jeremy strode to his car. Revving the engine, he shot away from them, his horn blaring, a grin upon his face.

Ignoring the beeping from the other traffic, he flew out of Broad Street, heading for the bridge. It was the last time any of them saw him, his promise made good.

~ ~ ~

"It devastated us of course." Susan explained, "If we'd known what he intended to do we would have stopped him. If it was an accident, had we been kinder, more understanding, he wouldn't have gone and might still be alive today. It was all so horrific, we all got grades lower than predicted, except Julia, she dropped out and kept the baby."

"I know I've met him. Yesterday, in fact. He was a beneficiary of Amy's will too."

"Nice boy. Man now, of course. Despite her meagre means, Julia did such a wonderful job in bringing him up. He was so cute as a baby."

"Did you all keep in touch?"

"Most of us, yes. Especially in the beginning. We all wanted to be there for her. But work, husbands, wives, families, they all cause one to move on. Some of us stayed in touch, me and Amy, for instance. Then there were the deaths. Julia first."

"Tell me about the deaths. Why did Amy think they were suspicious?"

Susan sat a little straighter, but despite her best efforts, it took over twenty minutes between her tears to explain what had happened.

Julia Ellsworth had died first, found by her sixteen-year-old son slumped over the kitchen table. The inquest found she had taken her own life while depressed. It was a car accident due to brake failure that claimed Andrew Hemmings' life. His wife and daughter gave evidence that he had been working on the car the day before. Verdict death by misadventure. Then came Miriam Campion. Found dead by a neighbour in the garden. Asphyxiation following a reaction to eating cake with nuts in. Miriam knew about her allergy, took great care checking everything that came into the house. No one could explain why she would eat a cake she knew nothing about, or even where it had come from. Her husband and daughters were out looking for cars at the time, and no visitors were expected or seen by neighbours. Another accidental death.

Dabbing her eyes, Susan asked for a glass of water. Patsy ordered it, and she finished her summary.

"Now poor Amy. A hit and run. Not natural causes. Not by any stretch of the imagination. Amy had received a call from Miriam three weeks before she was killed, because I now believe she was, during which she suggested to Amy that if she wasn't a sensible person she'd think the people who challenged Jeremy before he drove into that wall were being bumped off."

"But why? Did any of you come up with a reason? What made Miriam think that? After all, up to that point only two people had died. And given the length of time since Jeremy's death, why would it be connected?"

"Amy agreed with you at first. She laughed and asked Miriam the same question, and they agreed it was probably because it was the anniversary of Jeremy's death that week, and Miriam was being silly. Then one day I was feeling old and lonely so I called Amy for a chat. That spooked her. She said she was halfway through an email to me telling me she'd changed her mind. That she had made her will and was going to clear her house just in case Miriam was right. Made me promise to call the police if she didn't die a natural death. I can't believe she's gone. Only a few of us left now. I could be next. I can't tell you how glad I am the solicitor is taking it seriously. I ..." Pausing as Linda entered the room. She smiled for the first time. "Thank you. I promise you, ladies, I don't think I'm being unnecessarily dramatic."

Pouring the water, Linda returned the smile. "We don't. And I promise you, if anyone can sort this out, Patsy can, even if she has to get help from almost the best police officer in Bristol. England probably."

"Are the police involved?" Looking from one to the other, Susan ignored the water proffered by Linda.

"Not yet." Patsy jumped in to explain. "My husband is a police officer. Henry Duggan, the solicitor, went to him first, old friends. I took the case because, as of yet, foul play hasn't been proven. If I think a police investigation is warranted, he'll put a team on it."

Sipping the water, Susan nodded. "That is reassuring. We have to worry about Scotty, because she got quite verbal. If the theory is right, whoever is doing this knew those who challenged Jeremy."

"I don't have her details, perhaps you'd let me have them before you leave, and I'll go and explain things."

"No need. I'm seeing her this afternoon. I'll give her your details so she can contact you if she thinks it appropriate. She's had a lot of drama in her life, one way and another, all family issues, so she might not want to invite more. But I'm going to try to get through to her. I have another appointment while I'm here, shouldn't take more than an hour. Then

117

hopefully I can get some sleep tonight, now I know you're on it and that you have police connections."

Looking at Susan, Patsy could see she was wrung out by the situation, and she smiled.

"I'll tell you what, I'll speak to Meredith tonight and run this all past him. That should put your mind at rest. He can sniff out an issue before anyone else knows there is one."

"That's gratifying. Is there anything else I can help you with while I'm here?"

"No, I'll call you if I think of anything. Let me have your hotel details and I'll let you go."

Noting down the information, Patsy got to her feet. She was interrupted by her phone ringing.

"One moment, it's Henry." She took the call. After a brief word with Henry, Patsy held the phone by her hip. "I'd like to take this, if you don't mind. I don't know whether you're right about this, but just to be sure, can you leave me the details of everyone who was there that night? Well, those that you remember, that is. You said quite a crowd had gathered. Go with Linda, she'll run through it with you."

Once alone, Patsy returned to the call with Henry Duggan. Another beneficiary had called, and Patsy took down the details. Taking the opportunity, she also updated Henry on what she had uncovered to include an abridged version of the night Jeremy died.

Duggan was animated. "Well done, Patsy. Sounds like you're making good progress. My solicitor self says this is all coincidence and there's not a shred of evidence that there has been foul play. But as a friend of Amy it sounds like she was on to something. Would you discuss it with John when you get a moment? See what he thinks."

"I was going to. Speak soon, Henry."

Patsy typed up her notes and tried to call Meredith; his message service kicked in, so she went to see what Linda had gleaned from Susan.

When she went into the reception area, Susan had gone as expected, Linda confirmed she had all the names Susan could remember, and then gave Patsy a résumé of her morning's work. Agreeing a plan of action, Patsy started back towards her office.

"Are you not having lunch? We've had ours, but we picked you up a smoked salmon and cream cheese bagel. Angel has popped out to the dentist, by the way. Shouldn't be long."

"Not hungry, that cake filled me up. Maybe later. Let's clear that backlog first, I'll speak to this beneficiary and get a meeting as soon as possible, then we'll start on those present on the evening of Rossiter's death. Although I do wish we had more than a hint of foul play."

"Will do, one of 'em is our man. I know it. Or woman, maybe. I have a dress fitting at four if that's okay, I booked it with Sharon, so I'll get as much done as I can before then. By the way, it's gone two, that cake should be but a distant memory."

Ignoring the further reference to food, Patsy nodded. "Okay, well the beneficiary James Clark is a postgrad who was training with Amy. I doubt it's him. Let's hope Harry Swinton is an older friend who might provide a few more clues. As to leaving early, no problem. Although, I thought you'd be making your own dress. You usually do."

"But not for a wedding! Really, Patsy, do you know how much there is to be done? By the way, do you think it would be cheeky if I asked the guests to dress to a theme?"

Patsy had turned to head for her office and her step faltered. She shuddered at the thought of what Linda might have in mind, particularly if Meredith was to be best man. Turning back slowly, she hoped she didn't look horrified. "A theme? What sort of theme?"

"Blimey, you've been looking a bit ropey recently, but all the colour has drained from your face. Are you feeling okay? Do you need a seat?"

"No, no of course not. You were telling me about your theme."

"And that almost made you faint? Patsy, you need to get a grip. I'm not going to ask you to wear a costume, I thought about that, then remembered Uncle David, he'd never agree to it. No, what—"

"Thank goodness, because nor would Meredith. What colour?"

"Not decided, I'm wearing lilac and … damn. I wasn't going to tell anyone! Not a word, promise me." Linda knocked the heels of her hands against her head in frustration and Patsy shook her head.

"My lips are sealed. I'm sure whatever you have in mind will be fine, but you'd better let everyone know soon, it's not far off and people may already have sorted out their outfits,.Sharon seems to have raided every shop in Bristol."

"Good point, I'll speak to the dressmaker and formulate a plan."

"Fabulous. And now we'll work. I'm off to call Harry Swinton. You do whatever is currently at the top of the list."

Once back in her office, Patsy called Swinton. He hadn't heard about Amy's death, and was a little shocked. As a result he launched into an explanation on how they'd met at the hospital. Patsy had to reject a call from Meredith while he spoke, finally, having made an appointment for the next day, she listened to his message.

"Too busy to speak to your husband? That didn't take long. A quick call because I'm up to my ears, but I've just heard they have your man, and thought you'd want to know. Speak later."

"What does that mean?" Patsy grumbled and returned his call. It went straight to his answer service.

"Husband, I was on the other line. A bit more detail would be nice. Who have you got? What has he said? Are you going to be taking over the case? Call me. Please."

Dropping her phone on her desk, she walked through to the main office as Angel came in carrying a tray of coffee.

"How did it go with Susan? Blimey, Patsy, you look like you've got the weight of the world on your shoulders. What did she say?" Angel placed the tray on her desk. "Do you need a shot in this?"

"I told her she was looking off colour." Linda chipped in.

"I'm fine. Although with everyone telling me I look like death warmed up perhaps I'll make something up. I actually came out here to tell you Meredith left a message saying they've got our man, but no more than that. I've tried to call him, but his phone is going straight to message. Give Louie a ring and see if he knows what's what."

Linda sighed as she dialled Louie's number. "Oh no. Just as we were getting into it. I wanted us to solve it." The others listened to her side of the conversation. "I see. Well call them and find out who she is, and what if any connection there was, we'll do the rest. Don't be late, we have to complete the tables tonight. Love you." Hanging up, she shrugged. "They are useless, the pair of them."

"Explain." Hit by a wave of exhaustion, Patsy took a seat in front of her desk.

"Someone called the station and said she was the one who'd hit Amy with her car. She was pretty distraught, meaning they couldn't get much out of her. Meredith and Louie were in the canteen when the duty sergeant—"

"Linda, get to the point. Who was she?"

Patsy smiled at Angel's impatience. "Do we know her? Is she anyone that's come up in our system so far?"

"I was just getting there! Am I the only one in this office that's firing on all cylinders? You two are very snappy, and it's me that's got the stress of a wedding to organise." When Patsy exchanged a look of exaggerated bewilderment with Angel, Linda rolled her eyes. "Connie Thompson, twenty-three, on her way to work. They sent someone to see her, and probably arrest her. Louie thinks it's unlikely she's connected to our case, but I've told him to find out."

"She's twenty-three. I can't see how she'd be connected. Thompson isn't a name that's come up. Looks like it was an accident. Which on the face of it is a good thing? I'll update Henry and give Susan a call, just in case the name rings a bell, if it doesn't it might put her mind at rest."

In the event, Patsy could get hold of neither Henry Duggan nor Susan. Opening her laptop, she updated her notes and added her comments. Until she spoke to Henry, there seemed little point in chasing up leads, he might pull the plug. It was almost three thirty, and making a decision, she packed up her things, collected her jacket and went through to the main office.

"No news on Connie Thompson, I take it?"

Pausing, her fingers hovering above the keyboard, Linda watched Patsy collect the cups from the desks.

"None. Are you going out?"

"Nope, we're having an early day. I can't get hold of Henry or Susan, and if he wants to call a halt given the culprit has put her hand up, there seems little point in wasting time until we know. I thought I'd come to the dress fitting with you, then I can give you my opinion on the theme. That's if I'm allowed to now I know half the secret."

"There's a theme?" Angel's eyes widened. "I've never been to a wedding with a theme before. What do we have to do?"

"That's undecided, but don't panic. Linda won't go mad, will you?"

Turning back to Linda, Patsy grinned. Linda had already shut down her computer and was struggling into her cardigan.

"No, I won't. Can't believe you'd think I would. I'm almost glad this looks like it's come to an abrupt end, it's made you take your duties as Maid of Honour seriously."

"Maid of Honour? Am I? When did that happen? And I think it's Matron if I'm married."

"It occurred to me just now, I was going to tell you soon but now you're coming to the fitting, it's two birds, one stone. I'm sure she'll be able to sort you out, you're not fussy about what you wear."

"Ask me? Not tell. And no offence taken. Angel, come on let's get locked up."

"I'm being picked up from here. Sod's law as always. I'll give him a ring and see if he can come earlier, but in the meantime, I'll finish up anything that needs doing."

"Good idea." Picking up her notepad, Linda took it across to Angel. "I've got the first one done, if you could finish the rest that would be fabulous. Go to the tab for Susan, and then Connections. Susan listed all those present on the fateful night there. If anything doesn't make sense, or you can't read her writing, make a note, I'll sort it tomorrow."

It took another five minutes for Linda to issue her instructions, making them late for the fitting. Patsy parked in the same rank as Linda and followed her to a unit at the end of the rank. The fascia declared Wonderful Weddings and other services. It wasn't inspiring, the shutter was rolled down, the only indication the place was open was the light visible behind the smoked glass window of the small entry door.

Linda grinned at her. "Doesn't look much but wait until you get inside. Stacy does gypsy weddings, and costumes for dramas, there's so much to look at."

She was right. Other than a few gasps at wedding dresses which lit up, and a few that had skirts so big Patsy wasn't convinced there was a door big enough for them to fit through, the warehouse unit was a delight to explore. They had fashioned several rooms at the front into a small reception area, a waiting room, and a very large fitting room. It was a well organised and efficient set-up. Unfortunately for Patsy, Stacy was also verbose, and within twenty minutes of entering the fitting room, she developed a headache trying to keep up with the ever-changing conversation.

Closing her eyes, she leaned back into the sofa, and let her mind run over the details of the case. Henry Duggan would probably ask if she thought it worth continuing, and she wanted to be sure to give him the correct advice. All they had was a string of coincidences, which so far they had been unable to link to any wrongdoing. Much as she'd like to see the case through to the end, she wasn't convinced it would be rewarding. She'd tell Henry it was up to him, but if it were her money she'd call it a day, and …

"So what do you think?" Linda interrupted her musings.

Opening her eyes, Patsy's smile was automatic but her mouth fell open, and for a moment she was lost for words.

"Oh my goodness, Linda. That is stunning, understated, elegant, and absolutely bloody gorgeous. If you were planning on doing anything else to it, don't! It's perfect." Placing a finger under each eye, Patsy blinked. "You've made me cry. I'm glad I saw it before the big day, or I'd be a wreck."

Linda rustled as she walked forward. "Really? You like it that much? You don't think I should—"

"No! I don't think you should do anything, except perhaps not wear black boots. What shoes are you thinking of?"

122

"I told you." Stacy was grinning from ear to ear as she fussed with the small, embroidered train that fell from Linda's waist. "I know I didn't think the flowers would work, but they do. As you don't want heels, white or lilac ballet pumps are my suggestion. Don't you think?"

Patsy was blowing her nose, her eyes still glistened, so she simply nodded her agreement.

"And for you this." Selecting a simple lilac dress from the rail, Stacy held it aloft. "Simple yet classy, and with your colouring it will look fabulous. Here, go and try it on, and I'll get the flower girls dresses out for you to see."

"But it was only decided a couple of ... forget it. I'll do it."

When she returned it was Linda's turn to make a fuss, asking if it were too simple, if Patsy wanted lace or frills or bows.

Patsy held her hand up. "It's perfect, Linda. Just like yours. Now stop fussing."

"Arms out." Stacey was giving short tugs to the garment. "Do you know, I don't think we need to do anything more. You're not planning on putting on weight I hope."

"Patsy doesn't do weight, she's always that gorgeous. I've been yoyoing up and down for months. Practically starving myself at the moment."

Spluttering, Patsy burst out laughing. "Starving yourself! I don't think so."

Linda rolled her eyes. "I am, Stacy. She's exaggerating. Show her the bridesmaids dresses. She'll love them."

Once more amazed at the simplicity of the little dresses, Patsy got teary again.

"Louie is going to cry. You might even make Meredith leak. It's all perfect, Linda."

"I know, but blimey, Patsy, you're emotional today. What's wrong with you? You only do mad or perfect as a rule."

"Probably because I wasn't emotional at my own wedding. Okay, I was mad for a while, but there was too much going on to get emotional."

The dresses were carefully packed for transportation, and they agreed that the only theme should be lilac buttonholes for the guests, and lilac ties for the groom and best man. Stacy waved them goodbye, having first supervised the loading of the dresses.

"I feel we should celebrate in some way, but I've told Louie not to be late. Would you like to come in for a drink?"

"Thank you, but no. Amanda is home tonight, so I've promised her a roast dinner. She eats rubbish when she's working nights. Thanks, Linda, that really cheered me up."

"It also put a bit of colour back into your cheeks. Was that you or me?" Linda patted her pockets as the sound of a steam train signalled she had received a message.

"Me, it's Meredith." Patsy opened the message and read it quickly. "They've been tied up tracking down a will, but he's on his way to speak to the DS dealing with the hit and run and will tell me all he knows at home. They've called it a day." She checked the time. "Wow. It's six thirty. Doesn't time fly when you're having fun! I'd better scoot or I'll be in the doghouse with Amanda."

When Patsy arrived home, the house was quiet, and she went straight to the kitchen to prepare the evening meal. It surprised her to find the lamb was in the oven, the potatoes peeled, and an assortment of vegetables prepared and ready to go. Amanda appeared silently behind her.

"I thought I'd make a start. Wasn't sure if you were doing a dad on me."

"Argh! Don't creep up on me. Sorry, got tied up with Linda's wedding. Her dress is stunning, and I'd tell you all about it but she'd kill me. Have you slept?"

"I have, maybe not enough but I want to get back to normal tonight. You look a bit flushed, have you been drinking?"

"Blimey, not you as well. I look pale, I look worn out, now I'm flushed. I feel fine, I'm tired, but other than that, fine."

"Hmm. Probably a virus, and to make sure it's not *the* virus, do an LFT."

"But I haven't got the symptoms. Oh, of course not everyone does. Where do you get them?"

"I did one myself when I was off colour, there are tests on the shelf in my cupboard. I'm sure it's fine, but better safe than sorry. You do it now, I'll get on with this. What time is Dad due home?"

"Not sure, but within the hour if he's to be believed. Can I be cheeky and grab a shower too?"

"As it's you, of course."

Patsy went to her room and stripped off, a bath would have been her preference, but that would be too cheeky. Going into Amanda's room, she sighed. Boxes packed with her things were stacked along one wall, and when she opened the cupboard the bare minimum of clothes remained on the shelves. Rummaging around the boxes of lotions and potions on the

124

top shelf, she found several test kits. If it was positive the entire household would have to self-isolate, and she'd been working closely with the girls this week. With Meredith in the middle of a murder case she prayed it would be negative. Anything else would be a nightmare for all involved. It was with fingers crossed, she grabbed the kit she needed and hurried to the bathroom.

When she came down, Meredith was heading towards the kitchen.

"Evening, I don't know what's for dinner, but it smells divine."

"Roast lamb. Hi, Dad. How's things? I'm your chef for the evening."

"Patsy, get in here quick. We've got a stranger mucking about in the kitchen. I need a beer."

"Very droll." Amanda kissed her father's cheek. "Don't get used to it, I'm moving out at the weekend."

Grabbing a beer from the fridge, Meredith took a seat at the table, and pretended he didn't know about the change of plan. He smiled at her.

"Oh, the completion of the sale came round fast. Must have a good solicitor on it. Oh yes, it was Henry, my recommendation." He held back the grin as Amanda's eyes darted to Patsy. She had hoped Patsy would have softened the blow. "Why are you looking at Patsy?"

"I'm not. How was the test? You don't look very pleased, was it positive?"

"Oh no. Negative. I was thinking about the case that's all."

"Good, well they aren't always accurate the first time, do one again in three or four days."

"Yes, I read the leaflet. Will do."

"Test? What test?"

"A flow test for Covid. Patsy's been off colour this week, and it's better to be safe than sorry."

"Oh don't tell me that. I thought we'd seen the back of it until we get another surge in the winter." He turned to look at Patsy. "Are you okay?"

"Yep, just a little tired. I'll take another test again later in the week."

"Can I get you a glass of wine?"

"Please."

Catching the glance between Amanda and Meredith, Patsy put her hands on her hips. "What was that look for?"

"What look?" Meredith swigged his beer.

"You two. You exchanged a 'we know better' look. Why?"

"We didn't, Patsy. Sit down, I'll pour the wine. Dad, go and have a shower, this will be ready in twenty minutes or so."

"Ahh, the old 'or so'. That could be an hour then. I was going to update Patsy, can I do that first or we'll be talking shop over dinner, and I'd rather talk about your new flat."

"Update me on what?" Patsy accepted the glass from Amanda and took a sip.

"The hit-and-run driver. Seriously, Patsy, where are you? Your brain is somewhere else. If I tell you, will you listen or am I going to have to repeat myself?"

"I have a lot on my mind, not least what to tell Henry to do about the case. So yes, fire away."

"The driver of the car was Connie Thompson, she works at Sainsburys on Whiteladies Road. She was late for work, but says she wasn't speeding. The rain was heavy and she was driving slowly, but Amy Cleaver suddenly appeared from behind the van and stepped out in front of her. She didn't even have time to apply the brake. Amy fell back towards the van. She didn't go over the bonnet, she didn't fall under the car, so Connie thought it was a glancing blow. It was only when she saw an article in the paper that she realised it had been more serious. Understatement if ever there was one. I don't know where you are with it all, but unless that name is connected in some way, I think you've been on a wild goose chase which is why I didn't want it." He grinned. "Does that help?"

"Indeed. I'll tell him to drop it. Thanks. I'll call him tomorrow, but while you shower, I will just call Susan and put her mind at rest." Leaving her wine, Patsy went to collect her phone.

"She doesn't sound convinced, does she?" Meredith winked at Amanda. "I'll grab that shower."

Leaving Amanda to it, Meredith went upstairs. Before getting ready to shower, he removed a box from his pocket and hid it in his sock drawer. At the end of the month, it would be Patsy's birthday and for once he was ready for it. Smiling he went to the bathroom. Once showered, he opened the cabinet to get his razor, knocking half the contents of the bottom shelf into the sink in the process. He replaced them, but scanned one that caught his interest before getting on with the job in hand.

When he arrived downstairs, the meal was almost ready, and he offered the girls wine. Amanda pointed toward her glass, but as Patsy already had a drink and was frowning, he took a seat next to her, nudging her with his shoulder.

"Cheesed off your case is going nowhere? You'll get wrinkles frowning like that."

"Not really, I still think there's something awry, but maybe not murder. I was wondering where Susan was. She was going to let me know

126

how she got on with her friend Scotty, but she hasn't. Nor is she answering her phone, it's going straight to voicemail."

"And that's your problem? Oh, that mine should be such. Is it beyond the realm of possibility that she might still be with her friend? Especially if they're close, and as to the phone, out of battery, or perhaps switched off so they can enjoy a peaceful evening. Which by the way is what I intend having, doubt I'll switch the phone off, but I certainly want some peace."

Amanda interrupted Patsy's response as she pushed open the door with her foot. "Dinner is served. We're going posh tonight, dining room not kitchen."

"Are we celebrating?" Although speaking to Amanda, Meredith looked at Patsy.

"Why are you looking at me like that?"

"Thought you might know?"

"Know what?"

"Why the daughter I never see, and who only communicates on a limited basis with her father, has not only cooked dinner, but has upgraded us to the dining room. Being an optimistic devil, I assumed there was a reason."

"I started cooking because neither you nor Patsy were here, I knew what we were having as Patsy and I actually see each other for more than a passing greeting in the hall, and I thought I'd do my bit, especially as I won't be around for much longer."

"No, Peggy told me you were moving in with Sherlock. When were you going to tell me?"

"When I saw you. But as Peggy knew, I guessed it wouldn't be necessary." Amanda grinned at her father. "Are we going to eat, or do you have more questions, and even if you do, we can sit down and do them?"

"Should I have more, that's the question." Pulling out a chair, Meredith sat down and inhaled. "That smells good. Just what the doctor ordered."

"I have no idea what you're talking about. But to bring you up to speed, Frankie and I will be co-habiting from this weekend. I am going to let out my new flat as the rental will more than cover the mortgage and it will be an investment. I've just finished nights and have three days off. Oh yes, and I've requested a place on a new cancer project, and if I get it, for most of the time I will only work nine till five for the next year, well that's the official line anyway, we know it's a pipedream, but it would mean I could escape nights for a while. My washing is done, dried and folded, I didn't get round to ironing, my car's washed and sparkles. I think you're up to date. Now eat."

Meredith didn't need the last instruction as he already had his mouth full. Although he kept the questions flowing, they had a pleasant meal with no upsets, and no distractions. When they'd finished Patsy insisted Amanda left them to the clearing up, and she disappeared to her room.

Patsy looked at Meredith. "I don't know what you were after from her, but I hope you got it. You can tell me when I get back, I need the loo, in the meantime the dishwasher is the big white machine by the sink." Ruffling his hair as she walked past, she ignored his protestations.

On her return, Patsy ignored Meredith, and instead she riffled through the cupboard. She groaned. "No rice! I'm going to have to pop out, unless of course you know of any magic way of drying a phone out, I dropped it down the toilet."

"No, afraid not. Jo did that in work, how do you women do that?"

"Because we put our phones in our back pockets, it's not rocket science, Meredith. Bugger. I'll leave it on the radiator while I'm out. Ah well, at least I won't get disturbed tonight."

"Am I allowed to disturb you?"

"Depends on why you were trying to give Amanda the third degree. You weren't very subtle, but I couldn't work out what it was you wanted her to tell you." Patsy rummaged in her bag, and locating her purse held it up triumphantly. "I won't be long, you can tell me when I get back." She headed for the door, pulling her jacket from the newel post as she went.

"I found a leaflet from a pregnancy test in the bathroom, I think she might be pregnant, hence the rush to move in with Sherlock. Not sure I'm ready to be a granddad."

Patsy paused. "It was a false alarm. You should have asked directly and saved yourself from indigestion."

"You're sure?"

"I am. Why didn't you just ask her? Right, I'm off."

The door slammed behind her, and Meredith returned to the stack of dirty crockery. He'd pretty much convinced himself that he was ready, and to his surprise he felt a twinge of disappointment.

~ ~ ~

The next morning, Patsy was up before Meredith, and hurried down to the kitchen, flipping the switch on the kettle, she removed her phone from the jar of rice.

"Fingers crossed," she murmured as she pushed the start button.

"Are you speaking to yourself now?"

Dropping the phone onto the table, Patsy grabbed her chest. "Don't creep up on me. If I've … Oh fabulous, it's opening." Retrieving the phone, she held it up for inspection. "It worked. I didn't think it would."

"Great. Toast?" Meredith pulled a loaf from the bread bin. "Unless of course you fancy making a full English? I'll take it by that snort, it's a no."

"It is. Think of your figure, and, more importantly, your cholesterol. I'll join you in a slice. Tea or coffee? Blimey, Susan Clarkson has been desperate to get hold of me, and three missed calls from Angel, I wonder why. She'll be disappointed when she hears we're closing the case. Three messages too." Patsy called her voicemail, and as she was told she had six new messages the phone rang in the hall, Meredith went to answer it.

The information from Susan made her wonder if she would close the case. As she listened to the third message she called to Meredith.

"Meredith, I think it's happened again."

Ending his call, with a curt. "Thanks, I'll get her to call you." Meredith dropped the receiver back in the cradle.

"I think you're right, Hodge. I need to know where you are with your investigation. That was Angel, she's just watched the news and worked that out. You can fill me in over breakfast."

Chapter Eleven

When Trump arrived he held the same opinion as Meredith.

"The thing is, sir, there is footage of them. It's impossible for them to have moved any distance in those areas without being picked up at the very least by a car's dashcam. We just haven't seen it yet. We'll have to pray that someone checks and brings it in."

"Praying has never got me very far, Trump, I prefer to go looking. Let's try to get another appeal out. I'm toying with the idea of *Crimebusters*. It might be useful, in particular for the row in the street, but it's not on for another two months. I want him banged up by then. I'm going to grab some coffee. Do you want one?"

"I do, thank you. Is everything else okay, sir?"

"What do you mean? What everything else?"

"Generally. You never offer to make the coffee, but when you do it's because something is troubling you."

"Well, Dr Freud, it's like this, I was merely trying to be nice. As that doesn't work, black with two please. I'll be in my office."

When Trump returned with the coffee, Meredith smiled. "Just had confirmation that the safebreaker will be at the property by nine. Let's hope it turns up something worthwhile. We need to chase the IT bods too. We need to know who was emailing him."

"Hoping has never got ... oh, forget it. I can't say it in the right tone. Would you like me to go? I'll chase the IT chaps too."

"Might do it myself. I'm hoping there's going to be a will in there, leaving all his money to some ex who happens to be tall, well built, angry, and the owner of a nice collection of overalls. Short of that, I don't know what could be in there that might be of any use."

"Fingers crossed. At least you were right about him going home."

"Who, when?"

"Did you not read ..." Leaning over Meredith's desk, Trump pulled a report from under a file. "Home telephone records."

"Thank you. I'd better have a read."

Trump left the room as Meredith lifted the report.

The itemised account was for the last six months and had only a dozen or so items. The last call made was half an hour before Jody had witnessed Kentish being murdered. It was to a local taxi firm. A note told Meredith the driver was being traced. Meredith looked at the outgoing calls. There were six, one was to Beatrix's Cheltenham address, the other five were to his business in London. The incoming calls provided little help. Two from a London call centre, one from a solicitor, and three from the oncology unit.

Placing the report in the basket on the corner of his desk, Meredith sipped his coffee and wondered why Kentish needed a solicitor at six o'clock in the evening, he doubted many firms took calls that late.

Most of the team had now arrived. He made a note to call the solicitor and check Kentish's mobile records again. They had to be missing something. He gave the team five minutes to get themselves settled before joining them to take the morning briefing.

The briefing was short and not very productive. There was little they could do except plod on with the CCTV. Rawlings wasn't looking forward to that so made a suggestion.

"Gov, I reckon we should contact his friends. We've only spoken to the wife and the boyfriend, he must have socialised with other people, perhaps he confided in them."

"Yes, that was on my list of questions for Beatrix. I also want us to speak to the staff in his jewellery shops, starting with those in Bristol. I'll call her on the friends thing, although I think it's going to be a long shot, why wouldn't they have come forward if they knew something? You give Mikey a ring, and see if he can give you any names. I'm guessing there were two sets of friends. Seaton, get a list of his businesses, and call the managers, get appointments booked in. And do the lot, there's only six, although the one in London will be a pain."

"Will do."

Back in his office, Meredith called Beatrix. It was a little after eight. The solicitor's office wouldn't be open yet, and he hoped she was up. She answered on the second ring and spoke before he had the chance.

"Hello, Beatrix, here. Do you have any news?"

"No, I'm afraid not. The investigation is moving along, but slowly, and with so few witnesses it's a hard slog."

"Oh. Then how can I help?"

Twenty minutes later, Meredith had the names of three people Beatrix considered close enough for Kentish to confide in. Although, like

Meredith, she thought they would have come forward if they knew anything. She offered to call them.

"I'll contact them, thank you. They are more likely to open up to us than they are to you. Tell me, do you know any reason that Christopher would have called a solicitor early evening last month? It was a lengthy call and it was made out of hours."

"No idea. Although I do know he wanted to change his will. It would probably be that. And Claire would take a call from him at any time. She's an old friend."

"Ah. Any idea why he was changing his will?"

"I'm guessing to include Michael. When we spoke about it, we were gossiping about Claire and her delinquent son. Christopher mentioned the will in passing."

"Who's Michael?"

"Michael Janus, Mikey. We've spoken now. He seems like a nice chap, although he would be of course, if Christopher liked him. I've invited him for lunch. Oh, is that alright? He needs someone to talk to, much like I do."

"Ah yes, we call him Mikey here, threw me for a minute. Why would it not be alright?"

"I don't know how these things work, but I'm guessing we're both suspects until you've caught who … whoever killed Christopher. I didn't want you to think we were in cahoots."

"You'll be safe to have lunch. Thank you for your time."

Giving the names to Rawlings, he looked at Seaton who held four fingers up. It was almost eight thirty, and he was surprised that so many were there, let alone answering calls. He decided to give the solicitor a call and wandered back to his office. A thought occurred to him, and rather than call the solicitor he called Beatrix again.

"This is unusual, but I know someone out there knows or saw something. If we don't get any new leads in the next week, I wondered if you'd consider offering a reward for information that leads to a conviction? I would never normally suggest it, particularly in cases like this. It brings every lunatic under the sun out, but unless one of your friends or his business colleagues gives us something to go on, it's going to be a long and painful process. But I should also say I always get my man, so if you don't think it appropriate, please say so. In fact, take a couple of days to think it over."

"I don't need to. Of course I will, if it will help. How much do you think will do it? Christopher was a very wealthy man, and although I only have access to limited funds, they are still quite substantial."

"Leave it with me, we rarely publish the amount anyway, the term 'substantial' usually does the trick. I'll leave you to think about it and we'll speak next week."

"As I said, I don't need to think about it, it will be there when it's needed. I want you to catch this man, DCI Meredith, whatever it takes. Christopher was a good man, he deserves justice."

"I know, thank you Mrs Kentish. I'll be in touch."

When he hung up, Meredith wondered if that had been sensible. There were only two or three people who might have witnessed something useful. If he went down the reward route, he'd probably end up with two or three hundred time-wasters. His musings were disturbed by Seaton.

"Louie said you wanted to see the safe being opened. He'll be there in ten minutes, just called in."

"I forgot about him. I'll toss you for it. Heads I … actually, no, you go Tom, I'm going to have a word with his solicitor."

"Will do. I'll get Louie to go and see the manager of the Bristol shop, and I'll do the Bath one this afternoon."

Nodding agreement, Meredith picked up his phone, and after introducing himself, he asked to speak to Claire. She was busy and Meredith asked for an urgent call back. To his surprise it came in less than ten minutes later.

"Claire Barnard, how may I help?"

"Did the girl who answered the phone not explain? I'm DCI Meredith, the officer in charge of the investigation into the murder of Christopher Kentish. I'm told by his wife Beatrix that you drew up his will."

"Chris is dead? That's not what I expected. When? Oh gosh, that is a shock! Apologies DCI Meredith, we were old friends. I only spoke to him a couple of months ago. Murdered, when? Why?"

"A couple of days ago. No idea why, hence I'm asking to see the will. I'm sorry, I assumed you would know."

"Accepted, but why did you think I would know?"

"It's been on the news, and Beatrix tells me she's had a lot of calls of condolence."

"Oh I see. I'm very busy at the moment, got family stuff going on, I'd love to have time to listen to the news. Poor old Bea. I'll have to call her."

"The will. I understand he made a new one fairly recently."

"Yes. I did the necessary. Do you think it's connected? Hang on, I'll put you on speaker and get it in front of me. There. Can you hear me?"

"Loud and clear." Meredith could hear a clicking and assumed she was accessing a computer file.

134

"I have the signed document in the safe, but the draft is still on here, he made no amendments, so it'll be quicker. You think this is connected?"

"I don't know. I think it might be. Have to rule out all possibilities."

"Quite. Ah, here we go. Shall I read it to you? It's quite simple, really."

"Just the headlines, who gets what, and then I'd be grateful if you would email a copy across to me." Meredith gave his email address.

"Okay, two seconds, and you can have a look. I'm assuming you're in front of a computer."

"I am."

The email arrived and Meredith opened the attachment. "I have it in front of me. Let's see now." He skimmed through the opening statement, murmuring the odd word. "Is that usual? The bit that says including that signed on the eighth of October 2011?"

"Not really, usually one would only revoke all previous wills. He wouldn't tell me why exactly, simply said he wanted it noted, that the previous one in particular was revoked."

"How many had there been?"

"Not sure, but at least two."

"What did the one in 2011 say? How did it differ from this?"

"No idea, I'm afraid. I didn't do that one. Never thought to ask."

"Are you not his solicitor? Is that usual?"

"I am now because he instructed me, but that doesn't mean he didn't use others for different things. For instance, I don't do conveyancing, so when he bought the flat I pointed him in the direction of a colleague. I'm a family solicitor mainly, divorces, wills, probate. Boring but necessary."

"And yet you didn't make his previous will." Making a note, Meredith carried on reading. "The properties, with the exception of Great George Street, go to Beatrix, his business interests are to go to Beatrix to liquidate if that takes her fancy. In which case, all staff are to be paid a year's salary in severance. That's very generous. His cousin, Jennifer Bramble, is to have first option on the London operation, see blah blah blah ..." Meredith skimmed over the next few paragraphs. "Okay, so now who else gets what?" Falling silent, Meredith read through the beneficiaries and amounts they had been left.

"Are you still there, DCI Meredith?"

"I am. Sorry, thought you'd get tired of my voice. So to summarise, Beatrix gets the bulk. His friend Michael Janus is well looked after, including getting the flat, and—"

"I know who Michael is. He told me or rather I asked, and he didn't lie."

"Okay, so five people here get relatively negligible sums, the maximum being fifteen thousand, if you can call that small. But the niece gets two hundred thousand, and generous terms of payment should she wish to purchase the London business. That's a lot of money."

"Guilt, I think. I didn't query it, you understand. He had a lot to leave. But his cousin, Jennifer's father, once owned thirty percent of the business. He was a gambler – or as Chris said, a chancer. He thought he could do better than working for a living and Chris bought him out. Jennifer was a baby at the time. The money was frittered away even before she left school. Jennifer opted against slumming it through university and asked Chris for a job once she'd graduated. Good at it too, apparently. She does most of the buying for the chain. They are … sorry, were very close."

"Do you have contact details to go with the names?"

"I do. Current as at the time of drafting the will, so I doubt they've changed."

"Do you know anything about any of the others that might be useful?"

"Not really, we only touched on them. One, Sandra Busman, was a carer for his mother, had to retire due to ill health, but still goes to visit her. Oh my goodness, his mother. That poor woman, she's very frail, I'm not sure how she'll cope with this."

"It will be tough. Beatrix was going to see her. And the others?"

"No, not really. I'm sure they'll fill you in when you speak to them. All friends or children of friends he felt worthy, I believe. But as you said, none of them are getting enough to murder him for."

"You'd be surprised, but on first glance I'd agree with you. Thank you for your time. I'll be in touch should I need anything else."

"No problem, and if you can, please keep me informed. I'll speak to Bea about the funeral and the reading of the will. Goodbye."

Hitting the print button, Meredith strode out to the printer, collected the document, and walked to the whiteboard, waving it above his head.

"We have his will. The bulk goes to his wife, Mikey, the boyfriend, gets the flat and a generous little one hundred thousand, and other than a few smaller bequests the other person getting a whopping handout is the daughter of his cousin. Jennifer Bramble. I want us to speak to all of them, starting with Jennifer. His solicitor told me he was that generous because he felt guilty. Her father had gambled away his part of the business. Perhaps Jennifer felt that guilt was well placed and held a grudge? Perhaps Jennifer is in dire straits and couldn't wait for him to pop

136

off? We need to find out. His solicitor is sending me their contact details. Hutchins, get over here and list them out in order of what they get. Hopefully, it really will be this simple, and it's someone after money."

An hour later, Meredith heard Seaton complaining he was hungry.

"You're back. What was in the safe?"

"Stuff. A few nice watches and some other bits of jewellery. A few deeds for what looks like commercial premises, a gift-wrapped present for Beatrix, a box which is yet to be opened, and paperwork. I'm going down to itemise it as soon as I get something to eat. You can come with me, that way you won't ask questions I can't answer. Not even a dry cracker this morning."

"I'll treat you to something in the canteen once we're done. I'm quite peckish myself. You should always have the answers, you know that."

"Before you go, Louie just called in. Kentish had a row with someone a while back, got him really worked up, enough to swear." Dave Rawlings rolled his eyes. "He didn't as a rule. The shop girl Trump has been speaking to said it was serious and out of character. He's on his way back, but thought it would cheer you up. It's a lead of sorts."

"I don't need cheering up. Tell him we'll be in the canteen, he can update me there. Come on, Seaton, I thought you were hungry?"

It turned out Seaton was right. Although there were some valuable items in the safe, there was nothing to indicate why he was murdered. The last item Meredith picked up was the gift-wrapped box.

He continued his dictation. "One square gift-wrapped box. Label reads Beatrix, with love and admiration, Christopher. Unopened."

"You're not going to look?"

"Nope. I doubt there's a note in there giving us a clue. Might be a birthday or anniversary coming up. I think she'd like the privilege, don't you?"

"I do. But it's true, married life is softening you up. You old softy."

"It takes a special kind of person to put up with what she has. Whatever her reasons. And I'm not soft, just considerate. You could do with taking a leaf out of my book."

"I want to stay married thank you very much." Signing the docket, Seaton pushed it across the counter. "There you go, Jamie. Seal it up."

They were halfway through a bacon roll when Trump arrived.

"Just what I could do with. I only had cereal this morning."

"Give to it us in a nutshell before you go wandering off." Meredith pointed at the chair opposite.

"I can do better than that. I recorded our conversation. When I arrived, I spoke to the manager, and he pointed me in the direction of one of the sales assistants, Cathy. I took her into the office and explained why I was there, and she was teary. 'Is it about the phone call? Did he do it?' she said. So as a precau—"

"We don't need the full tour, Trump. Put it on play and go and grab something to eat."

"Sir."

Meredith and Seaton leaned forward to listen to the interview.

"Now, Cathy, my phone is recording this conversation because I don't write very quickly, and I don't want to interrupt you. Answer my questions to the best of your memory, and as honestly as you can. I only need the facts. I don't need to know what you thought, not at this stage anyway."

"Okay. I understand."

"When I told you why I was here, you indicated that Christopher Kentish had an angry telephone conversation, during which you believe he was threatened. Would you tell me what you heard please?"

"I wasn't eavesdropping, the door to the office – this one, was open, and I was outside in the repair shop sending messages to people whose jewellery had been repaired. Mr Kentish picked up the phone and said good afternoon etcetera, just as you would every call and then there was a bit of a silence, I remember thinking I'm glad I didn't get that one, it sounds complicated or someone that likes the sound of their own voice. Then he said, and I think these are the same words, I can't be one hundred percent accurate…"

"That's okay. Just as you remember it." Trump's voice was soothing.

"Um, something like, 'You can follow me all you like, I've given you my answer.' Then another pause. 'Because you could get off your backside and show some gumption. I do understand exactly what you are saying, and I'm not unsympathetic, but no. Enough is enough.' He wasn't mad then, just sort of explaining it as he saw it. He listened again. And I didn't really understand this bit, but it's what made it all kick off, so to speak. Do you know what I mean?"

"Of course. Was he still calm at this point?"

"Very, but clipped like he was forcing himself to speak."

"Go on."

"This is from memory, but I've thought about it a lot, so I think it should be accurate. 'My situation has nothing to do with anything. There are millions of people like you, and they do all right. I'm going now, please don't call again.' I thought he'd hung up then, but he was listening to whoever he was speaking to. He swore, and he shouted. In all the years

138

I've worked here, I've never heard him even get cross, let alone shout and swear."

"What did he say?"

"Excuse my language. 'Is that the best you could come up with? Really? Well do it. See how far that gets you. Good — Are you threatening me? That would be very unwise. Get off this phone, get out of my fucking life, and get off your lazy arse!' The entire sentence was shouted, and I wondered if they could hear it on the shop floor. I don't know who hung up first, him or the chap he was shouting at."

"How do you know it was a man?"

"Oh, I suppose because he swore. I don't think he'd swear at a woman. He hated swearing, said it showed lack of imagination. Oh, and the fact he was shouting. He wouldn't have done that either if it was a woman. It was definitely a man."

"Did he say anything to you about it?"

"No. When I realised he'd finished, I went out to the shop for five minutes, then made a lot of noise coming back in. I knew he'd be embarrassed, which would make me embarrassed. I don't even think he knew I was there."

"When was this?"

"Two or three months back. It would have been a Monday or a Friday because those are the days he used to be here. It was also after lunch because the deliveries come in about two o'clock."

"Did anything else happen around that time to help narrow it down? This could be a crucial piece of the jigsaw, Cathy, if we can find out who that call was from, it may help us catch his killer."

"No, not that I can think of. It was just a normal day, much like any … wait. I think that's the day the Rolex guy, Mr Jenkins, hit the room. Two minutes."

"No problem. I'll stop the recording."

~ ~ ~

"Tell me it was Rolex guy day."

Trump had his mouth full so simply nodded yes.

"And we have the phone records on the way?"

Trump swallowed his food before answering. "Already have them, they're with Dave. He's checking them out now. They get online billing, and she downloaded me the last three months. This call was made on the second of last month, so he's starting there. Then we'll see if there were any more."

"Good man. Although we'll need to have a lot more than three months." Meredith got to his feet. "By the way, Beatrix—"

"Cathy is going to speak to her manager, he's popped out to grab something to eat, but if he agrees she'll email me her log in details and password, and we can sort the telephone data here."

"Why didn't you just say that? As I was saying, Beatrix is going to offer a reward. Hopefully, we'll have moved this along to save her the bother."

"Save us the bother, you mean." Seaton stacked the dirty crockery on a tray. "I can't believe you agreed to it this early in proceedings."

"Neither can I. Come on, work to do. It's going to be a busy afternoon. This happened two months before the murder, and that was around the same time as he changed his will. Now that is not a coincidence. If he didn't use Claire Barnard, we need to find out who it was. I think someone was taken out of the will, and that someone might just be our man."

Chapter Twelve

M eredith brought fresh coffee to the table and topped up their mugs. "To recap, Susan Clarkson has confirmed that she too thinks Amy was onto something. Especially now having met with one of the other women who was there on the night she found out Christopher Kentish has been murdered too. She couldn't get hold of you last night because your phone was out of action."

"Correct. Miriam Campion had a nut allergy, ate a piece of cake with nuts in, and was found dead in her garden. The reason that's suspicious is that the autopsy showed the cake was homemade. Amazing what they can find out, don't you think? Anyway, the reaction was so severe that she would have had trouble almost immediately. Which means either someone watched her die or left a piece of cake which she ate later. Neighbours didn't see any visitors etcetera, etcetera. Susan tells me Amy is convinced that Miriam would never have touched the cake unless it was provided by someone she trusted. Andrew Hemmings was involved in a car accident when the brakes failed. He'd been working on the car for a couple of days, although his wife didn't think it had anything to do with the brakes, and as they lived at the top of a very steep hill, thinks her husband would have been extra vigilant in that regard. It's what raised their suspicions in the first place."

"Because the wife said he was vigilant?"

"No, because the wife said he was vigilant *and* someone had popped round in the morning and ended up giving him a hand, getting something or other done. She wasn't very technical, but is convinced that it was this mystery person who caused the damage and not her husband. Although Susan wasn't sure the wife thought it was foul play, or whether she wouldn't accept that her husband had done wrong. Julia Ellsworth was a suicide, years ago. Overdose. But now they had two more of the group dying of something that everyone who knew them would have said could never happen. It set alarm bells ringing. I also found out that Amy started considering the idea more seriously when she thought she was being followed. Susan had no real detail about that, and as you know Amy didn't mention anything to Henry. Now with Kentish definitely being murdered, Susan's frightened. And on that note, I really should return her call. But before I do, what do you think? Huge coincidence, or were they on to something?"

"It's still a long shot, and the ferocity of the Kentish murder is a whole new ball game, but there may be a connection, and as you have a habit of taking cases that end up stepping on my toes, I'm going to have to look into it. But I need to work out the best way to do that. No point in my team wasting time going over ground you've covered."

His eyes twinkled, and Patsy tutted.

"Meaning, will I work for you for free? I'm sure you're not suggesting I charge Henry, who is another person I need to call."

"Meaning, we simply need to interview you. You will, as a compliant witness, give us everything you know. On a serious note, I need to get going. Make your calls, go about your business, and I'll call you in a couple of hours. Are you not eating that toast?"

"You have it. I'm going to phone Susan."

Leaving Meredith at the table, Patsy went into the sitting room. Susan had a lot to say, and Patsy had only just finished the call when Meredith waved goodbye from the doorway.

Patsy jumped to her feet. "Before you go, because it'll niggle me otherwise, I've just been told Kentish changed his will fairly recently. It might be worth you finding out what the changes were, and who if anyone might be miffed over that."

"Already on it. Although not having much luck with finding the previous will. How do you know that? Did Susan tell you, and more importantly, who told her, and how did she know?"

"Her friend Scotty, the one they were most concerned about, told her, and, no, I don't know how she knows. I will find out before we speak again."

"Good, because from what I understood from his solicitor it wasn't public knowledge."

Kissing Meredith goodbye, Patsy returned to the couch and called Henry Duggan.

~ ~ ~

Briefing over, Meredith was in his office with Rawlings, running through the names that Patsy's investigation had thrown up. He closed his notebook.

"I'm sure there's more, I'll ... Let me take this, it's the Chief Super."

Rawlings picked up the empty mugs. "I'll make a coffee."

"Good man. Sir, what can I do for you? I have an update for you, but I want to check it out before—"

Interrupted, Meredith flipped open his notebook and started making notes. He tried to speak several times but in the end let Brownlow get to the end of what he had to say.

"Are you still there, Meredith?"

"I am, I was waiting for you to finish."

"I have. Expect the case file via email shortly."

"Will do. I'm going to have to ask, sir. Am I getting assigned more officers, this will be five live cases if I take it on?"

"When, Meredith, *when* you take it on. Not sure you'll need anyone immediately, and if I had detectives sitting around looking for work, it wouldn't have come your way. What's the update?"

"I'll get back to you once I've checked out the latest lead."

"Now, please, Meredith, I'm up to my ears. While the iron's hot and all that."

"Hodge has been working on a case for a solicitor, part of his duties as executor was to find out who murdered his client, if that was the case, because she thought someone was on a killing spree. Long story short, Kentish's name came up as a possible future victim. Might be something and nothing, another coincidence, but one of my chaps will be going through what Hodge has."

"Hmm, I don't like coincidences. Your wife has a habit of getting involved in your cases."

"She does. Not intentionally, I'm sure."

"Well, I'll leave you to it. You're busy. Haven't got time to chat. Keep me in the picture, and tread carefully with the family of the Covid victims."

"Will do. I'll probably assign Trump; he's got a good bedside manner."

"As you please."

The line went dead, and allowing his head to fall onto his desk, Meredith groaned.

"Problem, Gov?" Rawlings placed the coffee on the desk and took a seat.

"There's always a problem. TRUMP!"

"God, I wish you'd give a warning." Rawlings held his dripping mug to one side and brushed the splashes from his trouser leg.

Trump appeared in the doorway. "You bellowed, sir?"

"Come in and take a pew. I've been speaking to Uncle David, he's got a job for you."

Looking perturbed, Trump took the chair next to Rawlings.

"What sort of job?"

"A murder investigation."

"Another one? Who, when and where?"

Flipping open his notebook, Meredith read his notes.

"Rebecca Burnett, fifty-five, contracted Covid-19 just after main restrictions were lifted. Took a test it was positive and had to self-isolate. She was pretty rough and phoned the Covid hotline on three occasions, the last time being three days before her son, Daniel Burnett, found her dead. She also had a daughter. That's as much background as we have. She died three weeks ago. Death was initially listed as Covid-19 but they carried out a PM as she had died alone. They found signs of petechiae – that's burst blood vessels around the eye area, in case you didn't know, and a feather stuck to the back of her throat. There were also fibres under the nails of her left hand. The pathologist thinks it's suspicious because, in his opinion, the viral damage to her lungs was not enough to kill her. Given the location of the feather, he thinks it's a possible suffocation. Funeral hasn't happened yet, but the property wasn't treated as a crime scene. Who knows what's happened in there in the intervening three weeks?"

"Were there any underlying health issues?" Trump asked, pen poised on his notebook.

"Don't know. You now know as much as I do. Give Sherlock's lot a ring and take it from there. Damn nuisance. Are the papers back from the CPS on the Hengrove case? If we can get that put to bed pending trial, it might help."

"Will do. Not sure on the CPS thing, Tom was dealing with it. I'll check. Who's working with me on the Burnett case?"

"No one. Do the preliminaries, see what it throws up, and then we'll talk again. Depending on what happens we might share the load on both."

"I need a pee, but before I go, can I make a suggestion, Gov?"

"If you think it will be useful, Rawlings, fire away."

"Why not let Patsy run with what she's doing. I can … was going to say monitor her, but I think help her out, might be a more accurate term."

"Yes, thought about that, even mentioned it to her. But can you imagine the stink if it ever comes out Bristol MIT used a PI to solve a case? The Chief wouldn't allow it, anyway."

"We're going to be short staffed. Hope he's going to pay the overtime." Now on his feet, Rawlings shrugged. "I'm sure we can find a way around it."

By the time he'd got back, Meredith had concocted a plan with Trump.

"I'll give Hodge a ring and tell her you're coming over and why. If anyone asks, you're collecting all the useful information that her lot has turned up. In reality, you'll be working from her offices on the Kentish case until we know how they are connected, if indeed they are. If Hodge or her staff need to tie up any loose ends so be it, your access to the system should speed things up a bit."

Saluting Meredith, Rawlings grinned. "Should I get my coat?"

"Can't believe you're still here, takes thirty minutes to get there."

Also on his feet, Trump followed Rawlings out but paused at the door.

"By the way, Linda asked me to remind you that the rehearsal is next Friday at three."

"Rehearsal for what? The wedding? I think the vicar knows what to do. The rest isn't complicated. Or is it?"

"I don't think so. Reverend Tucker thinks it's better those with jobs to do make themselves familiar and comfortable with the proceedings."

"Trump, I have to get you there on time, hopefully with both your eyebrows. I then have to pull a box out of my pocket and take a seat while you repeat the words you're told to." Seeing the look on Trump's face, he slapped his hands on his desk. "But if it helps Loopy calm down a bit, I'll be there if I can, as will you. Now let me make this call, or Rawlings will get there before I tell her."

"Thank you. Much appreciated. Do you want me to set the Burnett case up in the office at the end?"

"Nope. Set up over by the printer, board's small but you'll be next to Hutchins and you might need to use him. Shut the door on your way out." Meredith was already dialling Patsy.

"Will do. Good luck with Patsy."

"I don't need luck. I have charm and... Hello, wife. My call as promised. I think I have a plan of sorts. Rawlings is on his way over to you. Have you spoken to Henry Duggan yet?"

"I have. He wants us to carry on for a couple more days, as, and these are his words, '*if John is also looking into it, our information might be of some use, and vice versa, and he will have done his best for Amy.*' I will try not to get in your way."

"He is a sensible bloke. I knew there was a reason I liked him."

"What? I was expecting you to attempt to dictate what I could and couldn't do. I was ready for you."

"You'd never win. Rawlings is on his way over and is going to be working out of your office for a while, until he's collected everything that's relevant to our investigation. He might have to follow up a few leads while he's there, but on the positive side if you need anything checked out on the database you have a man that can on the spot."

"Hmm."

"What does that mean? I thought you'd be delighted, particularly as Henry Duggan wants you to carry on."

"It means my husband has just attempted to pull rank, which he doesn't have, and get me to work for him free of charge. Or did I miss something?"

"Hodge, stop being so touchy. Work *with*, not for. No one would dare attempt to tell you what to do. You know Dave, you like Dave. You have to surrender the info we need anyway, this way both investigations benefit. Don't you think?"

"Possibly. We'll see."

"Thanks, Hodge. I have to go, I have work to do, and you need to find a space for Dave to set up. He comes with his own laptop. Bye."

Feeling he'd made the correct decision, Meredith went out to let the team know of the changes, and to check the map which showed where they had collected CCTV footage. They were missing something. They knew how Kentish had arrived at the scene, but the murderer had been wandering about, both before and after, how had he gone undetected? A thought occurred to him as he rapped the board to get their attention.

"Quick update, they have handed us another case, middle-aged woman, lived alone, got Covid, got sick and died. Initially it was believed that Covid was the cause but it turns out, following a belated PM, that it could be suffocation. Trump will do the preliminaries and see what we've got. Hutchins, you'll be his back-up as and when needed, and then depending on what happens we'll look again. We currently have Jo heading up a team of fifteen uniforms out collecting CCTV. And as Hodge's case has clashed with ours yet again, Rawlings has gone over to collect what we need, see if there's a definite link. He'll probably be gone a few days. You're going to hate this but I've had a thought, and you know when I get them they're worth their weight in gold. We know how Kentish got to be at the scene, but we can't find our man before or after the event once he left Trenchard Street carpark. What if we're looking for the wrong man? After killing Kentish, what if he took off his clothes, folded them neatly?"

"Not to appear thick, Gov, but why do you think—"

"He would have been covered in blood!" Meredith said impatiently. "That was a big bag to carry for just a knife. I reckon before he left Christmas Steps, he stripped off his overalls, put something totally different on, and we've been looking for the wrong man. So we start again. We have the time of death, we go back to the recordings and see if anyone fitting his description and size is in the area – you know the drill. And as a bonus job, if I'm right he would have done what with the clothes? Dumped them? Burnt them? Taken them home as a souvenir? There's a lot of work to be done and Trump is out of the picture. I want you lot to get back to the CCTV footage and find him. Seaton you team up with Jo on that. Rawlings will carry on working on any leads as to why, and hopefully Hodge's investigation will help that. Any questions?"

There was a shaking of heads and a lot of miserable faces. Most thought they'd got the thin edge of the wedge.

"Good. Anything else need covering before I get back to finishing up on the Hengrove shooting?"

"Had the details back on the calls made to Kentish. There are repeat calls from a pay-as-you-go for both his flat and his Bristol business, and the one made on the day he lost his temper in London was from a phone box outside Paddington station. Nothing to help us there unless we get our hands on the phone. I've put a call into the lads at Paddington re CCTV for around the time of the call, but I'm not holding my breath."

"Keep me posted. Back to work, it's going to be a few long, long days coming up. Warn your better halves. Leave is cancelled for the next two weeks minimum."

With a curt nod, Meredith left them to it. He was hoping Rawlings would come up with something concrete via Patsy's investigation. Truth be known, he'd have liked to have done it himself. He and Patsy made a good team, but that wasn't possible for many reasons, so Rawlings had better be on form.

Chapter Thirteen

The chart of who was present with Jeremy Rossiter before he took his final journey looked a little like a family tree. Checking the detail one last time, Patsy nodded.

"That looks about right. Get a couple of copies printed off. Susan will be here in the next ten minutes, and Dave should be ... talk of the devil! Hi, Dave, come on in. Have you met Angel?"

Introductions over, Patsy explained that before Meredith had announced Dave's involvement, she had invited Susan to the office to run through those names present, and what if any connection they had to Jeremy Rossiter in the months leading up to the event.

"I thought you'd like to sit in, so Linda has prepared some notes and a chart we can work through to put them in some sort of order. We'll do that in my office, so if you want to make yourself comfortable and have a read through, I'll organise some tea. Linda's made a cake."

"Sounds wonderful, I think I'm going to enjoy working here."

"Oh you will, Dave, you will. You won't want to go back to the skipper, I'll guarantee it. My cake has that effect on people and when we're in the middle of a juicy case, I bake. It helps me think. There will be a lot of baking I reckon, and as Louie's on a diet, it will all be coming this way."

"Well I'm not, I'm pleased to say. What time is Susan arriving?"

"Any minute now, so you go on." Patsy held her hand towards her office door. "We're just about set up and ready to go."

"Not quite, I've not put this on." A white linen tablecloth sat at Linda's feet, and scooping it up, she followed Rawlings into Patsy's office. "We have two folding tables that form our board room. We don't use one often enough to have a permanent one, but it looks a bit naff without the cover."

The seating area in Patsy's office had been moved into one corner, and two large trestle tables were pushed together. With a practiced flick of her wrists, Linda shook out the folds and allowed the cover to float down, covering up the join.

"Very posh. Where do you want me?"

"Anywhere you like. But if you want a power cable, sit in front of the window, there's one over there."

While Dave set up his laptop, Linda placed a small vase holding a spray of flowers in the centre of the table. She placed a pile of notepads next to a box of pencils, a glass for each of those attending, and waving a carafe told Dave she'd be back.

Patsy poked her head around the door. "Everything okay? Susan is parking, so you have a little time."

"No problem, I'm not used to this treatment, it could grow on me."

"We'll see how you get on and if it works out I might try poaching you." Patsy laughed. "Can you imagine Meredith's face?"

"I'd let you tell him."

Fifteen minutes later, everyone had taken a seat around the table, with a drink of their choice and a slice of cake, even if they didn't want one. Angel sat nearest the door so she could answer the phones should there be any calls.

Patsy gave Susan a brief explanation. "This is DC Dave Rawlings. He's part of the team investigating the murder of Christopher Kentish. He's here to find out whether the connection exists between those present the night Jeremy Rossiter died and who have since died. And who you believe have been murdered. As we've already started down that road, we'll carry on our investigation, which will of course go over to the police should you be right about that connection. What we'd like to do today is to run through all of those present before Jeremy drove off, getting as much detail as you can remember, and what their relationship was to Christopher. Any questions before we kick off?"

"Not really. It all sounds perfectly sensible. But I think Scotty should be here because she'll know as much as me, perhaps more, and you'll have to do this all over again with her, won't you?"

"Who's Scotty?" Dave Rawlings ran his finger along the list. "Ah, Claire Scott. Sorry, I've found her."

"Barnard now, but I do find I slip back to their maiden names. It's my age, and all this trauma." Susan smiled briefly, then sipped her tea.

Flipping through his notes, Rawlings frowned. "Claire Barnard, the solicitor?"

"Yes. Do you know her?"

"My boss, DCI Meredith, interviewed her the other day. She prepared Christopher Kentish's will. I don't think we knew the connection to Amy

Cleaver. I wonder if she'll be able to come. Like you say, it would save time." He looked at Patsy for confirmation.

"I agree. Would you like me to call her?"

"I'll do it. She's at home this afternoon, I was going to see her. I'm not sure if she was working this morning but it's almost lunchtime. I'll call her mobile."

Claire Barnard had a light diary and rearranged the appointment so she could attend the meeting. She would take about twenty minutes to get there, so rather than make a start they adjourned to enable Rawlings to read through the notes Patsy had made. Susan followed the women back out to the main office. She sat with Linda while Patsy collected another chair.

"She'll be pleased to have this out of the way. Her son's moving back in next week, so she has a lot on at the moment. I was going over to help her get it ready for him."

"Where has he been - university, travelling?"

"Far too old. He must be approaching forty. No, he's been ill. Coming home for some TLC."

"Ah, that's nice. Claire must have been very young when she had him."

"Yes she was, but I'm glad to say she got her degree finished. She and Greg met at university, and are still together, must be true love. Me, I tried marriage twice, it wasn't for me. I much preferred the chase." Giving Linda a little wink, she flushed. "That made me sound like a trollop. I'm not, and wasn't, just picked the wrong men, I expect."

"Oh dear. I'm getting married soon, he's definitely the right man. He's perfect."

Holding back the comment she was going to make, Susan nodded. "I'm sure he is. Is it a big wedding? I ... oh, here she is." Getting to her feet, she greeted her friend. "That didn't take long. Did you have a helicopter ride?"

"Next best thing, I took a taxi, it was the driver's last job and he wanted to get home. I think my knuckles are still white."

When everyone was sitting back at the table, Patsy explained again who Rawlings was and the purpose of the meeting. She thanked Claire for attending at short notice.

"I hope I can be of help. I knew all the people there, and I can't for the life of me believe one of them is responsible for one murder, let alone a string of them."

"Stranger things have happened, I'm sorry to say. Humour me, I'm not as up to date as the ladies, so if I run through and pick a name from this chart, can you tell me what their connection was to Jeremy Rossiter, Christopher Kentish or any of the others present, and we'll take it from there." Looking down the list, Rawlings chose a name. "Penelope Vickery, now Rossiter."

The two women gasped and looked at each other, their surprise clear.

"Rossiter? Are you sure, or is it a coincidence?"

"She married Jeremy's cousin Freddie, I don't think happily, but they are still married as far as I know." Patsy passed them a copy of the chart. "Here are some brief notes we've made on what we know so far."

"Freddie Rossiter was an irritating little shit." Claire's hands flew up in apology. "Sorry, but he was. Didn't see him that often, thank goodness, but every time he was around, he was trouble. Jeremy hated him. Penny had her sights set on Jeremy, you know."

"So I believe. Tell us about her."

"Not much to tell, is there, Claire?" Susan replied. "She was doing the same economics course as Jeremy. Shared a house with Bea for a while but Bea moved in with Chris and his lot, so I'm not sure where she went, she was always around though. Troubled. That's how I would describe her, always looked as though she had the weight of the world on her shoulders."

"A miserable so and so you mean. She could turn on the charm at the drop of a hat. But her standard setting was miserable. Jeremy didn't like her much, put up with her I think, their families knew each other."

"So other than having set her sights on Jeremy, any connection to any of the others on this chart?"

When the women shook their heads, Rawlings picked another name. "Let's get Beatrix Kentish out of the way. We know she married Christopher a little while after graduation. We know it was a marriage of not quite romantic love but mutual affection as Christopher was gay. That must have been odd."

"Gay? Was he?" Susan looked at Claire for confirmation.

"I thought bi-sexual. I knew he had a dalliance with a chap in the year above, but he was with Bea so much, I didn't know if it was a drunken fling, not until years later. He was a nice chap. Quite close to Jeremy, it devastated him when Jeremy died. Greg, my husband, couldn't understand it. He too was close to Chris, one of life's gentlemen, and couldn't understand what attributes Jeremy had that Chris could admire. Greg didn't much like Jeremy."

"How did I not know any of this? I can't believe you didn't tell me. Bea was in love with Jeremy, I'm sure. I often wondered if she married

Christopher on the rebound. Was it Christopher in the picture you tore up that night?"

"No. But thinking about it, neither Christopher nor Bea were shocked when they found out about the content of the photographs. Do you remember after we put Julia to bed? They came to see how she was. But then, Christopher was close to Jeremy. I'm surprised he didn't tell me then though." Claire sighed as the memories returned.

"Are you? Perhaps he thought it was irrelevant, or more likely private. Hated gossiping, poor man, of course we loved it." Susan cast a guilty glance at Rawlings. "I was shocked that night when they told me about the photograph, much as I am now to find out about Christopher. Perhaps that's why he didn't gossip. But you saw a lot of those two, didn't you?" Susan returned her attention to Claire.

"Yes, I was quite close to Bea having lived with her, and as a consequence Chris. In fact, it was Chris who introduced me to Greg. That was a little before Jeremy died. Chris and Greg played on the squash team together. He'll be devastated when he hears the news of Chris's death. He's away picking up our son, and I didn't want to do it over the phone. I could kick myself, I saw him off and on over the years, I did his will fairly recently, and we always talked about getting together but what with Greg's job, my work, and of course Sean, we only made it once, and that was years ago."

"Greg is your husband, and Sean is who?" Rawlings interrupted Claire's musings.

"Oh, sorry, our son. He lost a friend to suicide while at university and it hit him hard. His solution was to mess about with drugs, the messing about became a habit, he relapses from time to time. We've just experienced a particularly nasty episode, but he gets out of rehab at the weekend, and for once has scared himself enough to agree to come home."

There was a slight warble in her voice, and Rawlings moved the conversation on.

"Thank you. For completeness, let's talk a little more about Beatrix. We've established that she had a thing for Jeremy, that she was best friends with and later the wife of the ... sorry, Christopher. Anything else we should know? Anything that may have stuck in your mind?"

Both women shook their head. It was Claire who voiced her opinion.

"Bea was one of life's nice people. My brother had a huge crush on her, I saw him more when I was at University than I have since." Claire smiled and looked at Susan. "He's coming to see Sean, he'd like to see you again too, I'm sure. Sorry, I'm wandering, Bea had opinions, and she could become furious if it was a human rights issue at stake, but she tried to live by three simple rules. She told me her grandmother drummed them into her. First, give everyone the benefit of the doubt, second, don't believe gossip, and do unto others, etcetera, and that old favourite, if you have got nothing nice to say, shut up!" A memory made Claire laugh. "Bea said that to some women who were gossiping on the bus in front of us. We laughed so much, I thought one of them was going to have a coronary. In fact, I would challenge you to find anyone who has a harsh word to say about her."

Susan grabbed Claire's arm. "Except Penny. Do you remember that night in the club, can't think of the name, the gangster chappie?"

"Do you mean Capones?" Lifting the envelope in front of her, Patsy pulled the out the photographs and chose one. "This club?"

"Oh my God. Were we ever that young? I don't have one photograph from that time, other than my graduation one. No idea what happened to them." Claire was smiling from ear to ear. "Have you more?"

"Oh yes, I've seen them. Amy kept everything." Taking the photographs from Patsy, Susan passed them to Claire.

They allowed Claire a few moments to look at the photographs. Her smile fell away, and she looked at Rawlings.

"Jeremy aside, those were happy times. They were good people, a few misguided of course, but no one is perfect, but they were good. Not murderers. Oh, I'm sure one or other of them could have been driven to a crime of passion, but not systematic murder. That's why we're here. We could talk for the rest of the day, but neither Susan nor I will deliver you anyone capable of murder. I'm sure. Look at Andrew, he was captain of the rugby team, could drink more beer in one night than the rest of us could drink in a week, and yet never a cross word with anyone. Now he's dead. If someone is bumping us off, I'll guarantee it's not any of these people – meaning us, I suppose."

"I understand what you are saying, Claire, but this may progress to a police investigation, and the more we know about everyone, the clearer the picture becomes. Susan, you referred to something happening at the club. What was it?" Rawlings had no idea whether any of the information he was collecting would be useful but he had to keep the women on track. Nice as it was working out of Patsy's office, his time here was best spent getting information.

"Call me Sue, please. I'm not sure what started it, but Bea had been to the loo. I remember the club was over three floors, and the dance floor was at the bottom where we all were.. She appeared at the top of the stairs and had only taken one step when Penny grabbed her arm and swung her round. Bea's face told me she was angry, so I watched them. Bea stepped back up to talk to Penny, who was poking her, and the next thing I knew, the finger jabbing stopped and Penny slapped Bea before storming off. Bea didn't come out for a few days, and after that the two avoided each other. I don't know what it was about. I asked, but Bea said Penny was just drunk."

"Oh yes, I remember being told about it, but I wasn't there so can't help."

Finishing his notes, Rawlings smiled. "So other than being a gentle giant of a rugby player, tell me about Andrew. How did he fit in?"

"He was marvellous, everyone's sensible older brother in a way. Oh, don't get me wrong, he partied just like the rest of us, but he could handle it better, and if there was any trouble, he would calm it down before it escalated. Jeremy seemed to have this knack of winding people up, even if it wasn't intentional. But I suppose that was borne out of his boisterousness, and as I've said, his arrogant persona. He created several skirmishes that would have spelt trouble had Andrew not been there."

"Were Andrew and Jeremy good friends?"

"I suppose they were. Andrew, being the sensible one, didn't get into everything Jeremy wanted to do. But they had a laugh, and for the best part, Jeremy accepted he was the voice of reason. Other than that, he was simply 'around', just like the rest of us." Knowing Rawlings wanted more, Claire shook her head. "To the best of my knowledge, he never fell out with anyone. He punched Jeremy that night, after he gave Julia the photograph, but Jeremy deserved that. Other than that, he was only ever violent on the rugby field."

"What about you?"

"In what way?"

"How did you get on with everyone? Anyone you disliked or had a falling out with?"

"No one I disliked, not really. Some of them could irritate, but can't we all, but none so much that I disliked them. I probably had words with most of them over the years. I have the unfortunate habit of speaking my mind. Although now in my mature years I think I have that under control."

"Is that why Amy and Sue were concerned about you?" Patsy joined the prompting.

"Were they?" Claire turned to Susan. "Is that true?"

"Absolutely, can't you remember what you said to Jeremy that night? How you spoke to him, and encouraged Julia to walk away?"

"Oh. Yes. Well, I only said what everyone else was thinking, but I suppose compared to everyone else I was quite forthright. But if that's your theory wouldn't they have come for me first? As I remember it, Christopher stayed up on the steps with Bea. Amy was trying to keep the peace. Andrew was being sensible, as he always was. I think you are way off the mark with that, don't you?"

"Possibly. But don't you think it has to be more than a coincidence that four of the people outside the hotel that night died in unusual circumstances? Because I do, and so did Amy." Susan looked at Patsy. "You agree with me, don't you?"

"I think it's odd, yes. And I do think you two should be conscious that it is a possibility. Don't talk to strangers, accept cakes, or unexpected help, etcetera. It sounds like I'm making light of it, but if you are being picked off one by one, whoever is responsible is very persuasive when not being very violent."

They spent the next twenty minutes going over more questions about Jeremy and Christopher, but none of the information gathered gave them any clues as to why Christopher was murdered. Rawlings called it a day.

"Thank you, ladies. We'll keep you informed of any developments. Don't forget, if you are concerned about your safety, you should call us."

Patsy looked at Susan. "What are you going to do? I know you came to Bristol so quickly because you didn't feel safe at home. Will you go back?"

"No, I'm delighted to say Claire has invited me to stay at hers. I can help keep an eye on Sean while Claire and Greg are at work. And Greg is a hulk of man. I'm sure he'll protect us, now we're officially at risk."

"We are not!" Claire threw her hands into the air. "When was that established? Don't you go filling his head with this nonsense, he's got enough on his plate, what with Sean and … anyway, calm down or you can go home."

"My lips are sealed. Let's hope I don't have to say I told you so."

"Well, if you're right, one of us won't be around so that might prove difficult. Come on, these people have work to do."

Patsy bit back her smile as Susan looked horrified. She walked the women towards the door, ignoring the jerking of Linda's head as they passed through the reception. Once the door had closed, she turned back to Linda.

"What on earth is wrong with you? Have you developed a tic? You're jerking about like a mad woman."

To Patsy's surprise, Linda jumped to her feet, and grabbing Patsy's arm, yanked her towards the kitchen.

"What the—"

"Hush. I don't want Dave to catch on."

"Catch on with what? Because the way you're behaving a blind man could … what are you doing?"

The door closed behind them, and Linda pushed Patsy into the toilet. Sitting on the cistern was a laptop.

"You have to go and give that to Dave. You don't know how it got here, etcetera, but he needs to see that now."

"Whose laptop is it? And it would be hard to tell him where it came from given that I don't know."

"I think it belonged to Christopher Kentish, actually that's a lie. It does. He didn't want to dump it again as he's trying to … anyway, it belongs to the murder victim, it's going to be crucial evidence, and a well-wisher who wishes to remain anonymous dropped it off."

"Okay, so Trevor dropped off a what – stolen laptop? Why did I have to be manhandled in here to be told?"

"How do you know it was Trev?" Linda thought for a moment and shrugged. "Okay, I gave that bit away. You know what he's like, he wouldn't even hang around for you. I had to meet him in the supermarket's carpark and even then he wouldn't get out of the car, he passed it through the window. I was worried someone would think we were doing a drugs deal or something. He said—"

"Don't worry about what he said. If this is Kentish's machine, he's going to have to say how he got hold of it. Come on."

This time it was Patsy who grabbed Linda by the arm, and picking up the laptop, she marched her through the office. Angel grinned as Patsy pulled Linda towards her office.

"Shall I make coffee?" She called as Patsy used Linda to push open the door.

"Yes." Patsy kicked the door shut behind her.

Rawlings looked from one to the other. "What's going on?" he asked.

"This." Patsy placed the laptop on the table and pushed Linda onto the chair in front of it. "This, I am informed, is Christopher Kentish's laptop. Linda, will now open it up so we can have a quick look before you take it off to the powers that be, and find out where it came from."

"You what? Are you… Oh, it's the Gov, hang on."

Rawlings answered Meredith's call, his eyes not leaving the laptop.

"Yes, Gov. Okay, I don't think the women had anything too crucial to say, although I'd like to speak to Bea Kentish, just to get her thoughts on the theory that they are all being bumped off."

He listened for a while. "Yes, that's about the sum of it, although Patsy has just marched Linda in here with what they claim to be the victim's missing laptop." Rawlings held the phone away from his ear and shouted over Meredith. "I'm putting you on speaker." He pushed the relevant button and placed the phone on the desk.

Meredith's voice boomed out. "Are you there? I asked how the hell you lot got hold of that and why I'm only just hearing about it?"

Patsy leaned towards the phone. "Meredith, it's me. It's no use shouting at Dave, this has only been in the office for minutes, and—"

"Save it for when I get there. I'm on my way. Tell Loopy she'd better have something nice waiting for me, I'm not happy you're in possession of crucial evidence."

The call was terminated. Linda buried her face in her hands. "Oh no. He's going to think I was in cahoots with Trev or something. All I did was take the call and pick it up. What would he rather I did, let it get dumped? Think what might have been lost, think what—"

"Linda, shut up and get us into that thing. Then go and cut him a large slice of cake or something."

Linda got to her feet. "The password is now password. I hope the cake will be enough. I can't fall out with the skipper, not with the wedding coming up and him being the best man."

"Is he? I never knew that. He's not mentioned a stag do to me."

Patsy took the seat Linda had vacated. "I'm sure it can't only be me who wants to know what's on here. Linda, you're being dramatic, Dave, concentrate."

"I am not. I want peace and harmony."

"In which case I suggest you work out how you're going to explain to Trev you had to give him up. Because you know Meredith will make you tell him, and better they knock on his door than he sees his face on *Crimebusters*."

"Oh my God, I'm doomed. My wedding is doomed. If I smoked, I'd have a whole packet now. But I'll settle for a slice of cake. Do you think I should get him a sandwich or a pasty or something?"

Ignoring her, Patsy logged onto the laptop, and Dave pulled up a seat and tapped the screen. "Go to documents first. Actually no, go to emails, the old will is top of the agenda, he might have emailed a copy, or ... no, go to—"

Patsy swung the keyboard to face him. "Would you like to do it, because to be honest, Dave, you're as bad as Linda. What's wrong with everyone today? It seems like common sense and rational thought has gone out the bloody window."

"Sorry, you carry on. I'll get you a drink. Tea or coffee?"

"Water."

158

Patsy was already clicking through the files in the document folder and allowed herself a smile as Dave spoke to Angel.

"I wouldn't take that in there at the moment, anyway she would like water, I think the Gov has been giving her lessons."

"Oh dear. Linda said much the same."

"Where is she?"

"Gone in search of a banquet to keep Meredith happy."

"Well, that's a lost cause. Meredith rarely does happy, and I don't think today will be the day. I'll grab the water. I need to pay a visit."

"Tie a knot in it," Patsy shouted. "I've found the will and guess who features in it."

Chapter Fourteen

Meredith paced around what little room there was in Patsy's office, stopping every few moments to rap the table with his knuckles when he felt a point needed to be driven home.

"And you didn't think to get his address?"

"Meredith, I have no new ways to say this, but slowly, and for the record before I also become irrationally irritated, I thought Henry Duggan would have it. Now, change the subject, remember you have a team of professionals on this, or we'll have to have a domestic in front of the staff." Patsy was fuming, and only just kept her temper under control. She pulled out a chair and pointed to it. "Take a seat, and I'll ask the questions."

"I'm happy pacing, thank you." Meredith pushed the chair back in with his foot. "It helps me keep calm."

Linda banged her hands on the table. "Look, Skipper, can I establish that none of this is my fault. I'm merely the messenger, wrong place, etcetera. Don't shoot me. I don't want that getting lost in the mix while you two are having a domestic."

"Loopy, at this moment I'd like to wring your neck, but as you've kindly supplied me with nourishment, I'm holding back. But you are correct in thinking I am a little miffed because, like my dear lady wife, you also don't take addresses of suspects. And for the record, we don't do domestics." Meredith relented, and pulling the chair back out, dropped into it. "How long do you reckon we'll have to wait for him to call?"

"Trev is not a suspect. He deals in ... that is, he works in IT. He reconditions old hardware and sells it on. Not a crime, Skipper, and he is very useful to know. I'm telling you, if you scare him off it will be at the cost of the business."

Meredith chewed his lip as he looked at Linda. There was much he wanted to say, but knowing he'd get nowhere if he riled her, he held his tongue.

The will had revealed that Marcus Ellsworth had been a beneficiary in Christopher Kentish's original will but had had his bequest greatly reduced in the second. There were a few other minor changes, but Ellsworth would have been twenty thousand pounds better off had Kentish not changed the will. When Meredith issued instructions for his arrest, he found that the only known address they had for Ellsworth was a PO Box, and that despite believing he had a job, Patsy didn't know what or where. They had the mobile number, but Meredith wanted it tracked before they alerted him by calling.

Thwarted for the moment on this avenue of inquiry, Meredith turned his attention to the origin of the laptop. He listened to the explanations of who Trev was and how they used him, and it upset Linda that despite telling Meredith that Trev was a valued contact of the late Chris Grainger he hadn't calmed down. When she explained they didn't know where Trev lived or if he had business premises and they only had a mobile telephone number, she thought he might explode.

She telephoned Trev, who as usual didn't answer but called back a few minutes later. His temper matched Meredith's when he realised Linda had told the police he'd brought her the laptop. Ignoring Trev's tirade, Linda explained the reason for the call, and he only calmed down when Meredith snatched the phone from Linda, and explained in no uncertain terms, that he wanted to know the origin of the laptop within thirty minutes, or he would have a warrant out for his arrest for obstructing a murder enquiry.

Trev had asked Meredith to bear with him and promised to call back within twenty minutes. Meredith checked the time, Trev had four minutes left. To fill the time, he turned to Rawlings.

"Nothing of any use from the two women you met? Is there any point in you being here?"

"Honest answer is I don't know. Like you, I don't like coincidence, and something niggles to say these are all connected. What I'd like to do is speak to the widow and get her thoughts about the night Rossiter died, and the theory that those who were present are being killed one by one. I'd also like to speak to that girl, Connie Whatsit, and find out if she's connected in any way. As she came forward voluntarily, and it appeared to be an awful accident, albeit she didn't stop, the station she reported to haven't questioned her at all. There seems to be little else I can do that's of any use, so we might as well tie up those loose ends."

Linda's phone rang, and she snatched it up. They listened to the one-sided conversation. "Trev, it's me. Ah, don't be like that. Okay, okay. Yes, I have a pen. Oh, that sounds reasonable. No, I didn't mean it like that.

The skipper is as good as gold. You don't … no, no, don't hang up until I've spoken to him. He'll go ape." Linda placed her phone against her chest.

"He's spoken to his customer, and it appears they pulled it out of a skip on Hampton Road."

"Now we're getting somewhere," Meredith was on his feet. "When?"

"The skipper says when? Right. Hold on." She looked at Meredith. "He thinks yesterday afternoon, that's when he got the call asking if he was interested."

"Stop calling me Skipper and tell him to answer your calls promptly if he knows what's good for him." Meredith was already dialling out, and Linda ended the call with Trev while Meredith barked instructions. "There was a skip on Hampton Road yesterday. Someone pulled Kentish's laptop out of it. Get over there and search it, find out who hired the skip, and find out if there are any cameras nearby. I'm on my way back."

He snapped shut the laptop and picked it up. Walking towards the door, he jerked his head and Rawlings followed him. "I'm going to move this along, try to see those women today. Who knows what else this laptop might throw up? Anything interesting and I might need you later. On that note, take Hodge with you in case I need you back at the station." He turned to look at Patsy. "I take it that's okay with you?"

"I expect so, I'll check my diary. I take it you'll keep me informed about Marcus Ellsworth. I wouldn't want to step on your toes, knowing how sensitive they are."

"I take it by that, you mean compromise my investigation. Yes, I'll keep you informed." He held his hand up to halt Rawlings. "Give me five, Dave, I need a word with the wife."

"Oh, you've moved me back to marital status." Patsy pointed to the door. "Shall we take this outside?"

Meredith pulled open the door and stood back to let Patsy exit. He ignored the exchange of grimaces between Linda and Dave. Allowing the door to close behind him, he took Patsy's hand and pulled her to face him.

"Have I done something? Because if I have, spit it out and let's clear the air. We've both got enough on our plates."

"I can't believe you have asked that question. What? Done anything apart from being rude, irrational and downright bloody irritating?"

Meredith's lips twitched. "Yes. Because I'm always like that. You, on the other hand, are not, and you're doing a good job impersonating me."

"Well, perhaps I'm not in the mood for it today. It can be wearing, listening to you rant about ridiculous stuff. I'm tired and … look, I can't even be bothered to have this conversation. Shall I apologise, we'll both go about our business and by the time I see you this evening, you'll have talked yourself into being a normal human being?"

"And that's it? There's nothing else?"

"Like what? No, Meredith, there is nothing else. I'll see you later."

Meredith studied her face for a moment. "I'd like to believe you, and for now I'll be the one to apologise and I'll leave you to it. Whatever it is, remember I love you, that I've always been a miserable bastard, but I'll get better with age." He pulled her into a hug, kissed her and, leaning behind her, pulled open the door. "I'll keep you informed. I promise."

"Thank you."

Back in the office, Patsy looked at Rawlings. "Who shall we do first? Beatrix or Connie thingy?"

"Beatrix, I reckon. More related to our case. Everything sorted?"

"In what way?"

"With the Gov. Not that it's my business, so apologies, but we rely on you to calm him down."

Patsy rolled her eyes. "He's calm. Give her a ring, let's hope we can get there today."

Beatrix Kentish was at home all afternoon and told them she was available for a visit. They left twenty minutes later. They had almost reached Cheltenham when Meredith called.

"A quick update. They collected the skip a couple of hours before we got there. Currently trying to contact the driver, but the office says as he's not answering his phone he might be at the tip. I've got men there to try and stop it being dumped. Keep your fingers crossed. In other news, someone we believe to be Marcus Ellsworth had been sending begging emails of a sort. Kentish only answered two of them. He ignored the third, which he received two days before he changed his will. I've issued a warrant for his arrest. Seaton is trying to call him now, but his phone now seems to be turned off and goes straight to voicemail. I've got men on the way. I hope your description was accurate, Hodge. Might have to get you to do an E-Fit. What news your end?"

"Nothing as yet, Gov, on the way to see Beatrix Kentish. I'll call you if we pick up anything useful. How's Louie getting on with the Covid death?"

"Not good. Following their mother's death, and knowing no better, the three siblings took it upon themselves to start clearing the house out. They've destroyed the bedroom, which was the possible crime scene. He's going to interview them, find out if there was a will, and make a recommendation, hopefully by the end of the week so we can have him back. Because even if someone did kill her, we're going to have a hell of a job proving it. But I know Trump won't give up if he thinks there's a chance."

"Much like yourself then. I'll call you if we find anything useful. We're nearly there."

As they pulled into a parking space outside the substantial Georgian villa, a black Mercedes was reversing out, and squinting at the driver, Rawlings leaned forward for a better look.

"Someone you know?" Patsy released her seatbelt.

"I hope I'm wrong, but he looks like the E-Fit of the bloke arguing with Kentish outside his Clifton address."

Patsy shifted in her seat to get a better look, but only managed a fleeting glance. "That's not good, not good at all. Have you got a copy of the E-Fit?"

Rawlings skimmed through the photographs on his phone and finding the E-Fit handed it to Patsy. Her eyebrows rose.

"I didn't get a good look, but the set of the jaw and the hair colour are right. How do you want to handle this?" Patsy knew what she would do but felt it pertinent to let Rawlings take the lead. He considered his options for a moment.

"I'm going to start with what we came to do. Ask her about Rossiter and whether she thinks there is any merit in the theory that members of the group are being killed for some reason. Then, I'll ask her if she recognises the photofit and take it from there. Life is never simple, Patsy, but how simple would this be if it was him?"

"Depends why he was here, and what he is to Beatrix. If it is him, is she party to it?"

"No I wouldn't think so. Well, never say never, but that woman was genuinely upset when the Gov interviewed her. Oh well, only one way to find out."

Beatrix showed them into an elegant but comfortable living room. They both declined a drink as they settled down on the overstuffed sofa. Patsy smiled at Beatrix.

"You have a wonderful home. I'm sorry for your loss, we will try not to take up too much of your time."

"Thank you on all counts, although it seems I have a lot of time on my hands at the moment. I don't feel much like socialising, but I am starting to climb the walls here. So, please, take your time and don't worry about me. Detective Rawlings tells me you're a private investigator

165

and your cases have crossed somehow. It all sounds very intriguing, and I have to say I'm surprised the police are working with you. Is that usual? Not that it makes a difference to me."

"Patsy was a police officer and used to be one of our team. When she realised her present investigation could compromise ours, she brought it to our attention. It's a long shot, but stranger things have happened, hence our visit. If we're here together, it will save you having to be disturbed twice."

Beatrix Kentish was satisfied with the explanation and nodded her acceptance. "As I say, intriguing, fire away."

Patsy took the lead. "A solicitor, whose friend and client believed she might have been murdered, hired me. Sounds odd, but her will left clear instructions as to the action he should take if she died of anything other than natural causes. She was hit by a car that didn't stop, so here I am."

"Are you speaking about Amy? I spoke to Susan a couple of days ago, and she mentioned it, but given Christopher's death we didn't get into details. She phoned to give condolences and to ask to be kept informed about the funeral. We haven't seen each other for many years, but I did think she wasn't her usual self, not the one I remember anyway. Is she involved in some way?"

"Yes. Susan, like Amy before, believes that several of the people who were present the night Jeremy Rossiter drove off to his death have been murdered. Possibly. They have no idea why, other than they didn't do enough to stop him leaving."

Beatrix's hands, which had begun to shake, came together, and she held them against her lips as though praying. Her eyes were wide, her brow furrowed.

"Are you okay, shall I continue, or would you like a glass of water?"

Her hands fell back to her lap. "No, please continue. It's been a horrible week, and this is the second time I have been carried back to those days, and spoken about Jeremy. It's all so mind boggling. But I'm fine, who else has died? I don't know about water, I think I might need a stiff drink. Please tell all."

"Okay, I know this is difficult to take in, and I haven't yet accepted this theory completely, but I'll run through the deaths and what the others have said, then you can give your opinion." On receiving a nod, Patsy drew in a breath, and ran through who had died and how the others had all died in a way that appeared to have been an accident, which could not be the case with Christopher.

"No." Beatrix blinked back the threatened tears. "Christopher aside, it strikes me that although you say the others could have been accidents,

166

poor old Julia couldn't have been. Have you considered the possibility that the other two might have taken their own lives? Eating something that could have killed them, crashing a car, stepping out into the road. All could have been intentional. I doubt that is the case, but it is possible."

"Yes, it is. But as Amy had already made instructions if her life was taken by unnatural causes, my instinct also tells me that's unlikely. Our main question for you is, can you think of any reason someone would want all those present on night of Jeremy's death dead? However twisted their reasoning might be?"

"No. Not at all. There were a group of us outside, but we were all friends. Close friends. I'm sure none of us has that sort of evil in us. I haven't seen some of them for a while, but even so, why kill? What would there be to gain? And after all this time. I think it's far more likely to be a horrible coincidence."

"Yes, that is a possibility. If you would, I'd still like you to think back to that night, and who was there, and who, except Julia, would be most upset by Jeremy's death? Who might feel that perhaps the others, maybe all of you, needed to pay for the loss of Jeremy?"

Beatrix covered her face with her hands and let out a groan.

"This is so hard. Thinking of Jeremy. He was such a force of energy. When you were with him, anything seemed possible. Any problem solved, any goal achieved." A smile made her eyes light up. "Well almost, unless your goal wasn't the same as his of course."

Rawlings returned the smile. "Was he the man that both you and your husband loved?"

"DCI Meredith has been talking, I see. Yes, yes he was."

"Were any of the others in love with him?"

"Probably all of them, in one way or another. He had a way of drawing you in. Not Andrew, though. Andrew was as straight as a die, although they were still very close in that macho, matey way handsome young men have. But I think Jeremy genuinely cared about Julia. She was the only one that he acknowledged having a relationship with, rather than just a series of romps I mean. Julia was the only one that might have been able to hold on to him, money or not. Poor Julia. Although what made him show her that bloody photograph is anyone's guess. That was cruel, and he wasn't cruel."

"Did you see the photograph?"

"No, but we were told about it. For a moment, Christopher was worried it might have been him, but the reaction of the others made it clear it couldn't have been. I'm guessing whoever took the photograph did so with blackmail in mind."

"I think you're right."

"Do you know who?" Beatrix leaned forward. "It would be nice to have that mystery cleared up after all this time."

"We believe it was Penelope Rossiter."

"Never heard of her. Was she a cousin?"

"No, her maiden name was Vickery."

"What? Our Penny Vickery? Who did she marry?" As the realisation hit, Beatrix's eyes widened. "Freddie. Oh dear."

"You don't like him. Patsy didn't much either."

"He was as miserable, sneaky and boring as Jeremy was fun, open and entertaining. Chalk and cheese. I don't know what Christopher would make of this. Penny Vickery sending compromising photographs of Jeremy to his father ... to what end? Because she didn't like him outshining Freddie? Because that would never change."

"Because she wanted to marry Jeremy, her plan backfired, and she ended up with Freddie instead."

"Serves them both right. They probably deserve each other. I didn't like her much, but she tried to blackmail me too. In a much more minor way of course, she was being spiteful, but I managed to put her in her place." Beatrix paused to look from one to the other. "Do you think this is Penny's doing? She was never fully integrated into the group, never had a best friend, just flitted around."

"As far as I'm aware she's lived in France for many years, which doesn't rule her out but . . . Let's look at it a different way. Had Jeremy lived, how would that have changed things? In the immediate years following university, would anyone have been affected in a positive way?" Patsy held her hands up. "I'm sorry, I know that's an impossible question, and I'm not phrasing it very well."

"Not at all. Christopher and I would never have married. Not if I thought there was a chance I might regain Jeremy's attention. That would have been sad. As odd as our marriage was to others, it worked for us. It was a good marriage, I ... I feel lost."

Rawlings allowed Beatrix a moment, he could see this was going nowhere useful, and decided to bring that line of questioning to an end.

"I'm glad you had each other. I don't think this is going to get us any new information, and we're not here to upset you, so just a couple more questions and we'll leave you in peace. Do you know Marcus Ellsworth?"

"Julia's son? No. Visited them both not long after he was born and remembered his birthday the first few years. You know how it is. I know

168

Christopher bumped into him a few years back and felt sorry for him, so I think gave him some money. I saw that look. Why do you ask? What aren't you saying?"

Rawlings held his hands up. "We're not holding anything back, but we've discovered that Marcus Ellsworth was a beneficiary in your husband's will. The original bequest had been for twenty-five thousand pounds, it was reduced to five thousand pounds in the latest will. We wondered if you knew why?"

"I don't. How odd, twenty-five thousand pounds is a lot of money, perhaps Christopher thought better of it, after all, we didn't really know the boy, or perhaps I should say man." Her hand on her chest, Beatrix looked from one to the other. "Do you think he's connected to any of this in some way? Oh dear."

Patsy assured her that they didn't know any more than they had told her, and that the purpose of their visit was to see if there was any connection, but that nothing she had told them had led to any firm conclusions. She brought their visit to an end.

"I promise we will keep you informed of what we find, but the more I discover, the less likely I think Amy and Susan's theory is likely to be true. That said, you were there that night, so until we are absolutely sure I'd suggest you are careful about who you let into the house. Is there someone who can come to stay?"

"Oh dear, this seems to be going from bad to worse, but yes, I have a friend who will stay. You just missed him. He felt it would be unseemly for the grieving widow to be seen to have a man friend, bless him. I tried to explain that you knew about our arrangement, and had met Michael, but he still felt obliged to make himself scarce."

Rawlings pulled his notebook back out of his pocket. "Does he live here? Can we take a name?"

"Harry Scott. No, he doesn't live here. Christopher and I live here. Lived. He has a flat on the other side of town, but he's been staying here since … well since Christopher died. Should I call him? He's gone to see his sister Claire. I think he was going to tell her about us, now it doesn't need to be a secret anymore. He's due back this evening."

"I'm sure that won't be necessary, but keep the doors locked until he gets back. I don't suppose you have a picture of him, do you?"

"A picture? Of course, but why?"

"We'll have a car keep an eye on the place, don't want them jumping on the wrong man." Rawlings attempted a smile.

Beatrix only had one photograph Rawlings was interested in. It had been taken several months earlier at a friend's wedding, and he stood hand in hand with Beatrix. She forwarded him the photograph. With little more they could say, they took their leave, and Rawlings was on the phone before he reached the car.

He tossed Patsy the keys. "You drive, head back to Bristol. I have to … Gov, how's the search for Ellsworth going? Because it seems he bumped into Kentish a while back and was given money. Sounds fishy to me, especially given the phone conversation, and the argument in the street etcetera. And I'm sending you a photo. Beatrix Kentish's man friend is a lookalike for our E-Fit. He's slender though, not well built. Have a look. We're going to his sister's house, he's there now, let me know if you want me to pull him in."

"You have been busy. No luck on Ellsworth yet, I'll keep you posted. Invite the boyfriend in for a chat, if he refuses, nick him. Do you want me to send help?"

"No need. We have the 'help us protect your girlfriend' angle, and I've got Patsy."

"Let me know when you're on your way back."

"Will do." Rawlings held out his hand. "Change of plan, that was quicker than I expected, the Gov didn't have much to say. You find out where Claire lives, and we'll take it from there. What did you think of the likeness?"

"Not perfect, but too close to ignore. I'll call Susan for the address."

Chapter Fifteen

S usan answered on the third time of trying.

"Hi, Susan, sorry to bother you again so soon but there are a couple more questions. Rather than drag you both back to the office, we'll come to you. I don't have Claire's address though."

"Oh, so you want to come here? I'm sure she won't mind."

Patsy took the address and added an extra twenty minutes to their expected time of arrival.

"It won't take that long to get there, not unless you know about some traffic we're going to hit on the way."

"Susan is bound to mention it, and I didn't want Harry to do a runner if it is him and he thinks we've put two and two together. His likeness and his eagerness to get away from Beatrix's, despite her reassurance that his presence wasn't an issue, is starting to build a case against him, don't you think?"

"I was just thinking the same. Much as I want it to be him, so we can put him away, I don't know what it will do to Beatrix. Poor woman."

"Doesn't bear thinking about. Oh, I missed a call from Marcus Ellsworth while I was speaking to Susan. Should I ring him, do you think? With you lot looking for him, I might be able to coax him to make contact."

"Did he leave a message, if not let's deal with this first."

They arrived at Claire's home and seeing the black Mercedes parked on the drive, Rawlings blocked it with his own car. Patsy nodded approval and climbed out.

"I'll leave the talking to you unless it becomes necessary to get involved."

"With Susan there, you'll be hard pushed to stay quiet."

They were ushered into the house by a bright and bubbly Claire, who showed them through to the family room at the rear of the house. The doors to the garden were open, and Susan was talking to a man with pale skin, and a look of bemusement as the words kept flowing. Harry Scott was nowhere to be seen.

Susan paused to greet them. "Come on in, we've been on tenterhooks waiting to see what news you have. But first can I get you a drink? I've already topped up the others."

Rawlings refused for both of them, and in the absence of Harry Scott looked at Sean. "Hi, how are you doing? Dave Rawlings." He leaned forward and shook Sean's hand. "Nice to meet you. Sorry to interrupt proceedings."

"You're welcome. Anything that shuts these two up, I don't think they've paused for breath yet." Sean's strong and steady voice belied his painfully thin frame and deathlike pallor. "Have a seat, they can focus on you instead." He patted the sofa next to him.

"I will. But first, if I may, can I use the toilet?"

"Of course, but I think Harry is in the downstairs one. Oh no, here he is." Claire smiled at her brother as Patsy and Rawlings took in his features. "This is DC Rawlings and Patsy Hodge, we were getting to the point of our meeting with them, but I'm sure they'll be far more succinct, so over to you."

"I hope so." Sean murmured, much to the amusement of the others.

Harry Scott held out his hand. "Nice to meet you, Patsy, you too, DC Rawlings."

When Rawlings took Scott's hand, he kept hold of it. "Have we met? You look familiar." Scott's eyes darted towards the door, and the hand Rawlings was holding went limp. It was clear he knew there was something wrong. Dave pointed his free hand at him. "Yes, yes, I know where. Rather than bother the others, can I have a quick word? Won't take long."

Harry Scott nodded. "Yes, sure. Let's go into the dining room."

He held the door open for Rawlings and pointed at the door further down the hall. "In there."

As Rawlings shut the door behind him, Harry started talking.

"I've been waiting for you to catch up with me. Ever since I heard about Chris's death, I knew you'd come."

"Heard about it? Are you saying it wasn't you who killed him?"

Harry bellowed out a laugh. "Me. Hell no, I've considered it a few times, but wouldn't do it to Beatrix. She'd never forgive me, and I'm probably not clever enough to get away with it, so what would be the point? I know it sounds bad, but when he was diagnosed with cancer, I thought halleluiah, but it wasn't bad enough to kill him, and the treatments were working. Yes, it suits me that he's gone, but I wouldn't have wished that on him. A quick heart attack or being hit by a truck, but not attacked in the street by a knife wielding yob."

"Then why do you think I'm here?"

"Because of the row I had with him. I know he was with his boyfriend at the time, so I thought Mikey would have told you about it."

"Fill me in."

"Christopher and a few very trusted friends are the only people who know about my relationship with Beatrix. I'm too old and too tired to keep up the pretence, and I had, on a regular basis, asked him to release her. The last time was a week before he died. I knew about his boyfriend and I knew it was serious because he bought him a flat, and I thought now's the time. There's no one left who will care if you're gay, straight, black, blue or sky dive naked. Let her have a normal life, let me have a normal life. He refused, it got messy, and I threatened him. Or nearly. I told him to watch his back."

"And this was the week before?" When Harry nodded, Rawlings pulled his notebook out. "What's your telephone number?" He jotted it down as Harry called it out. "And did you also go to see him the week before? Have a row on Sion Hill, and get told off by the neighbours?"

"No, I don't know what you're talking about. Who said I was there?"

Rawlings pulled his phone from his pocket and opened the E-Fit. He turned it to face Harry.

"This is an E-Fit of a man seen arguing with Christopher Kentish the week before he died. It also fits the description of—"

"That's not me, it's nothing like me, other than the dark hair. That's … Hang on, finish what you were going to say."

"I think I'd like you to finish, that's what? Or should I say who?"

Rawlings could see Harry's brain working overtime. His eyes were darting around the room, they seemed to settle on something and then he looked at his feet.

"I'm not saying any more until you finish your sentence. It also fits the description of who? If you don't want to tell me, then I'd like to leave. If I'm under arrest, I'd like to speak to my sister."

"I thought she only did family stuff. You're not under arrest, yet, but I would urge you to cooperate."

"She's still a solicitor. I'd like a word, please, in private."

Rawlings pointed at a chair, "Take a seat." When Harry hesitated, he shook his head. "If you would like me to arrest you, I will. I'll take you straight to the station where you will be held for a minimum of twenty-four hours, probably longer as murder is a serious charge."

"I haven't murdered anyone, don't be so—"

"Sit."

As Harry pulled out a chair, Rawlings turned away to call Meredith, he paced to the fireplace, stopped and turned back to Harry. "Have you got your phone on you?"

Harry patted his pockets and shook his head. "No, it's in the kitchen on charge. Why?"

"No matter."

Rawlings sent a text to Meredith and then forwarded it to Patsy. Walking to the door he pulled the key from the lock. "Stay here. And don't be doing anything stupid and frightening your sister. Think of Beatrix."

He left the room, leaving a protesting Harry in the dining room. Rawlings was locking the door as Patsy entered the hall closing the door behind her.

"Are you sure?" she asked.

"Yep. Positive."

Patsy looked at the door to the dining room. "Have you locked him in?"

"I have, I don't want him speaking to anyone."

"He could climb out of the window you know."

"Don't think he will. He'll quieten down in a minute, he's got a lot to talk about."

"What—" Patsy was interrupted by the arrival of Claire.

"Is everything okay out here? I thought I heard shouting."

"Your brother is a bit angry, he's on the phone."

"Harry never gets angry. Who is he talking to?"

Rawlings shrugged. As predicted Harry had fallen silent so Claire looked at Rawlings. "Not sure what you were speaking to Harry about, but no doubt all will be revealed. My husband will be home shortly, shall we get on?"

Patsy thought on her feet. "Of course. Dave, I'll leave you to it, and shout if there's anything I need to ask."

Rawlings nodded agreement, and Patsy led the way back through to the family room. When everyone was seated, she crossed her fingers she could string her story out long enough. She told the two women that she and Rawlings had met with Beatrix and the only person Beatrix thought might be capable of murder was Penelope.

They asked what Penelope would gain, and Patsy thought it would be revenge. Beatrix had admitted that all the girls had been a little in love with Jeremy, but only Penelope had paid for his death. She'd been drawn into a loveless marriage with a man she didn't much like, and perhaps

174

thought if the others had stopped him leaving that night, and not been so forthright he might have stayed, made everything alright with his father, and married her.

Patsy drew in a deep breath. She could feel the phone vibrating in her pocket and knew messages were coming in, but in a bid to keep the women occupied she ignored it.

"So," she concluded, "the main reason for coming here was to get your thoughts on that theory."

"Rubbish. Jeremy had no interest in Penny at all. Even if we'd managed to stop him, he'd have sorted things out with Julia, or perhaps moved on to a new crowd, but certainly not Penny." Claire nudged Susan. "I can't see it can you?"

Susan shook her head. "Not really. Jeremy needed someone vibrant, Penny was hardly that."

"Who is this Jeremy?" Sean joined the conversation. "You two make him sound like a saint. And, because I have no idea what this is about, what is the Penny woman not capable of?"

Relieved she didn't have to spin another tale, Patsy let the two women interrupt each other as they listed the possible way their friends had been murdered.

Sean was bewildered. "I know my brain is addled most of the time, but really? Mum you're an intelligent woman, you don't believe any of this do you? If that's the case you two are also on his, or her I suppose, hit list. Run through that again, how did they all die?" His smile grew as Susan again listed the demise of her friends.

"It's not amusing, Sean. These people were our friends and they're dead."

"No that's not amusing, what's amusing is that you've come up with this theory. What about suicide, accident, accident, suicide?"

"Well, yes possibly, but what are the chances?"

"Well, perhaps you were just an unlucky group, how did Uncle Harry get involved?"

"He's not. Why do you ask that?" Sean's mother frowned. "He came down a lot, but that's because he had a thing for Beatrix."

"So, why did the police officer want to speak to him?"

"Nothing to … Oh." She looked at Susan. He wouldn't be a suspect, would he? Well, I'll tell you what, let's find out." Getting to her feet before Patsy could respond, Claire left the room, and as Rawlings was standing with his back to her reading something on his phone, she did a quick sidestep and turned the knob on the dining room door. "Why is this locked?" she demanded, rapping on it. "Harry, what's going on?"

The doorbell rang, and Rawlings went to open it. "Saved by the bell, come in, Gov."

"DCI Meredith, would you like to tell me what the hell is going on?"

"Of course, is there somewhere we can talk?" Meredith placed a hand on her arm, and although he smiled his eyes held the pity he felt.

"Cut to the chase, Meredith. Why are you looking at me like that?" Shrugging away his arm, she banged on the door again. "Harry, is there something you'd like to tell me?"

Meredith tried the door and looked at Rawlings. "Have you got the key? Unlock it."

He allowed Claire to go in first, her brother was staring out of the window, he looked over his shoulder at her. "I'm sorry, Claire. I think this might be my fault."

"What is? Why is everyone speaking in riddles, and where's bloody Greg when you need him? Never around when I want him."

"Mum, what's happening now?"

"I have no idea. How long did your father say he'd be?"

"About two hours. He was going to the gym, then the supermarket to pick up some steaks for the barbeque. What's the time now? Is he late again?"

"He's always bloody late. What?"

Susan had appeared at the door and held her finger up. "I thought you'd like to know there are men in your back garden. What's going on?"

"I have no idea. DCI Meredith is about to enlighten us, if he doesn't, and he hasn't got a warrant, he can bloody get out." Claire looked at her brother. "What have you done?"

Harry couldn't look at her, instead he turned to look out of the window, his head bowed.

"Am I allowed to say I'm getting worried. Just out of rehab and I've landed in an episode of Morse or something." The chair scraped along the floor as Sean pulled it out and dropped into it. "Are you Meredith? If so, would you please, before my mother blows a fuse, tell us what's going on, and where my father is?"

Meredith held up a finger as his phone rang. "Take a seat all of you." He walked into the hall, rolling his eyes at Patsy as he left. He returned minutes later looking less worried.

"I'm sorry to tell you this but a few minutes ago Greg Barnard was arrested on suspicion of murder. He's being taken to the station, and I'm guessing he's going to need a solicitor."

Claire jumped to her feet. "Murdering who? Amy? Andrew etcetera? Don't be so ridiculous. Why?"

"I don't know about them yet, but this arrest is for the murder of Christopher Kentish."

"Noo." Susan held on to the vowel, her hands on her chest. "Surely not, why?"

"Yes why? Greg was good friends with Christopher, he introduced us for God's sake. Why would he kill him, and so violently?"

"I don't know, sorry but I don't have the answer to that at the moment, and I can't stand around here and speculate. The sooner we speak to him the sooner I might have some answers. I know you don't do criminal cases, so if he has a solicitor, or if you would like to arrange one for him, please get in touch with them. I will speak to you later, but now I have to leave." He pulled Rawlings to one side and lowered his voice.

"Find out where she says he was that night, if there's been any ill feeling etcetera. Let me know if you find out anything interesting, wrap it up with Hodge, and I'll see you back at the station later."

With a curt nod Meredith turned and left. He paused to lean into Patsy who was hovering in the hall. "There's nothing you can do here, wrap it up and get out, or you'll probably get dragged into something dangerous." His eyes twinkled. "Our cases have crossed yet again."

Patsy was now walking to the car with him, and asked, "Do you think he killed the others?"

"I really have no idea, nor will I until I find out why he killed Kentish, but young Jody was near hysterical, so I think we have our man. Took me five minutes to calm her down. She saw him coming towards her in the supermarket and freaked out. Managed to get a photo though. That one came in two seconds before Dave's. Got to go. Don't know what time I'll be home."

"You never do. I'll grab some pizzas on the way home."

Chapter Sixteen

Meredith nodded, and Seaton hit the record button, made the necessary announcements of who was present, and read Greg Barnard his rights.

"Can you stop doing that? Christopher was my friend. I haven't seen him for a few years, what reason would I have to kill him? The first I knew of his death was when you told Claire and she told me." He jabbed his finger towards Meredith. Turning to his solicitor, he asked, "James, do they not need evidence of some description? Are they able to arrest people willy-nilly on the say so of some hysterical teenager?"

"We can, Greg, yes. May I call you Greg?" Meredith rested back in his chair, stretching his legs to the side of the table. He glanced at James Tovey. "Tell him."

"I'm afraid they can. They can question you for up to twenty-four hours. After that they need to either charge you, get a judge to agree to an extension, or let you go. My advice has not changed."

"But if I say 'no comment' repeatedly won't that make me look guilty? I want to get out of here. Claire will be fuming, what with Sean just home. God knows how he'll react to this. Surely if I speak to them it will be over sooner."

"Exactly." Meredith answered with a smirk for the solicitor. "Let's start with the basics. Where were you on the evening of the fifteenth and early hours of the sixteenth?"

Barnard's hand moved towards his pocket. "I'd tell you, but I don't have my phone. If you'd get my phone back, you can look at my diary."

"Come on. It was only a week ago. I'll get your phone, but humour me and give it some thought. How often are you out at three in the morning?"

"Rarely."

"There you go, so rarely you'll know if you were at the top of Christmas Steps on the sixteenth."

"I wasn't."

"Where were you?"

"At home in bed, I don't remember there being any good late-night films on."

"See how—"

"Unless, of course, that was Thursday." Barnard moved his head back and forth, counting back the days. "Yes, it was. I was at a friend's house. I'd gone to dinner, had too much to drink so slept in the spare room."

"Most people would call a taxi. I take it this friend can vouch for you, what's his name and contact …" Meredith raised his eyebrows. "I take it, it was a man?"

"Yes of course. I'll need my phone."

"You can't remember his name?"

"Johnny Isaac. His number will be—"

"Yep, I got that. Address?"

"Bell Barn Road, I don't know the number it's on the corner with … nope, forgotten that too."

"That's convenient, around the corner from me. Woodland or Coomb Bridge? Unless it's on the corner with the main roads?"

"None of those rings a bell. It's a private road, in an awful state."

"Ah, that will be Cheyne Road. Tom, would you get someone round there please? Detective Sergeant Seaton is leaving the room." Meredith waited until the door had shut. "So why didn't you get a taxi, and what were you celebrating?"

"I was drunk, I just needed to sleep. Why do you think I was celebrating?"

"Do you have an open marriage?"

Barnard's face hardened. Gone was the perplexed expression, his eyes had narrowed and the hand resting on the table curled into a fist.

"What the hell? Where did that come from, and no, but what relevance is that to you and your trumped-up charges?"

"We haven't charged you. Yet. I ask because if it were my wife she'd say get into a taxi and get your arse home, and like most wives, she'd have a hundred questions about why I needed to stay out. How did Claire take it?"

"She's a grown woman and trusts me. When I got home, I apologised for not calling. She was miffed because when she woke up and found I wasn't home she was worried. After telling me I shouldn't drink so much, she went to work. I showered and did the same. No rows, no dramas. Does that disappoint you?"

"It does a little, yes. Because if she had been miffed, she might have checked out your story. Perhaps she did, I'll find out." Meredith pulled

180

his phone from his pocket and texted Rawlings. Placing the phone face down on the table, he smiled. "That shouldn't take long."

"Who did you just text? My wife?" The fist had curled again.

"No, my colleague, he's with her now."

"Why? How dare you frighten my wife with such nonsense!"

"We were already there."

"What? Why?"

"On another matter, I might come back to that." Meredith looked up as Seaton returned. He announced it for the tape and asked. "All done?"

"Car on the way, Gov."

"Good. Let's move on. Why did you—"

"No, let's discuss what other matter you were discussing with my wife. Was it Sean? He can't have done anything?"

"Who's Sean?"

"Okay, not Sean. Why are you at my home?"

Meredith rubbed his brow as though weary. "Mr Barnard, Greg, we will get to why you needed to be away from home that night, but as you asked …" With a sigh, he flipped open his notebook. "Do you know of a Jeremy Rossiter?"

Barnard's body stiffened, and a look of disgust flitted across his features before he frowned and held out his hands. "Yes. He died years ago, what's that got to do with me?"

"Nothing, I hope, you've got enough on your plate. It was your wife we wanted to speak to, as luck would have it, we picked you up at the same time."

Barnard's knuckles rapped the table. "You know what I mean. What did you want to speak to her about? What has a man who has been dead for thirty-odd years got to do with my wife?"

"I don't know, and it's a long story which I won't bother you with. But it was also connected to Christopher Kentish, and he met a violent death. Your reaction to that question was violent. Another coincidence? Why does the mention of Jeremy Rossiter cause such a reaction?"

"There was no reaction." Barnard looked to his solicitor for support. "Is he allowed to make things up?"

"It's called fishing." Tovey tutted and looked at Meredith. "May I have a word with my client?"

Meredith grinned, dragged in his legs, and getting to his feet, he suspended the interview, stopped the recording, and opened the door.

"Good timing. I now have a few more things to check out. Ten minutes."

Whistling, he strode along the corridor to the incident room.

"Do you reckon we've got our man, Gov?"

"I know it. I also think he might be the man Patsy is looking for. I told Dave to wrap that up, but I think they need to keep digging. Our Mr Barnard might be responsible for a string of deaths."

Back in his office, Meredith called Rawlings.

"Where are you?"

"Just about to leave, you'll love what I found out. I'll drop Patsy back to her office, then come back in."

"You're going to tell me he wasn't home that night. I've got Hutchins on the way to check out his alibi. What did the wife have to say?"

Rawlings read from his notebook. Greg Barnard had left the family home after dinner to go to the gym to play squash with his friend Johnny Isaac. He didn't return home that night as she found out when she woke the next morning. He claimed to have gone to Johnny's to watch a Lions' rugby match, had too much to drink and stayed the night. Claire had asked why he hadn't called her, and Barnard had claimed he was that drunk he passed out. Probably because he'd not eaten much that day. Claire had phoned Sue Isaac to apologise, but she hadn't even realised Greg had stayed the night until mid-morning when her husband asked her if Greg was okay when he left. They checked he wasn't there, the bed had been made, and the shower room window open.

"So, alibi established, except of course he could have slipped out. Dave, hang on, I need to speak to Hutchins, I'll call you back in five."

Instructions issued, Meredith called back.

"I mentioned Jeremy Rossiter to Barnard. It was like I'd shoved something somewhere nasty. It could be he's the man Patsy's after. Don't come back in, carry on with your original plans. But now you can chuck the name Barnard into the mix. What was next on your agenda?"

"We're going to see Connie Thompson, see if she's connected."

"Sounds good. Text me if anything interesting comes in." Meredith hung up and turned to Seaton. "Come on. Let's see what else we can get. But first I'm going for a ciggy."

"It'll kill you, you know."

"Yep, but we've all got to die of something, I … Change of plan, you go back in on your own for a while. Tell them I'm following up something the wife said."

"Will do."

Meredith had his cigarette and went to watch the interview in progress. Jo Adler shook her head as he entered.

"He's gone no comment. Tom is doing his best, but I don't think he'll change his mind. Who's Rossiter? Because that's what made him shut up. Is that what Dave is working on?"

"Yep. Give them another twenty minutes, if I'm not back you go in and start questioning him about the deaths of this lot. Tell him they were all connected to Rossiter and I'm getting the dates to find out where he was when they were murdered. Might be enough to get him talking." Tearing the list of names from his notebook, he turned to leave.

"Where are you going? You like to be involved."

"To find out if they know what was in that skip yet. To speak to Hutchins, might even track down this alibi with him, and I also want to know if and where Barnard's phone was used that night. If we can get one more thing to tie him in with today, we've all got a chance of going home tonight."

Chapter Seventeen

Rawlings returned to the dining room to find Claire Barnard on her feet, pacing from the window to the fire.

"Was that Meredith? What did he say, is Greg coming home?"

"Take a seat, just a couple more questions."

"I've told you where he was. Surely, a quick conversation with Johnny can sort this ridiculous mess out?" She pulled out a chair, sat down and folded her arms across her chest. "Fire away because I've had enough of this, and I need to get back to Sean. God knows what he'll say when he hears why his father isn't coming back. Is Harry still here?"

"I think so, yes."

"Good. Because I want to know what he said that led you on this wild goose chase."

"It's not what he said, in his defence he was shocked. I showed him this, as we mistakenly thought it might be him, and he looked at that." Rawlings showed her the E-Fit then pointed to the picture on the mantle. "I called it in but it was unnecessary, the witness to Christopher's murder saw your husband in the supermarket and phoned the police. It was a positive ID."

The colour drained from Claire's face and there was a tremor in the hand she raised to cover her face.

"The witness could be mistaken. Because why? Why would Greg kill Christopher? He's not seen him for years."

"That's what we hope to find out. There are several lines of enquiry that might reveal that."

"Greg is not gay! Is that what you think? My husband didn't know Chris was gay until I told him he'd been murdered. He was genuinely shocked. Initially he denied it was possible, said he'd have known. But Christopher was very good at keeping secrets. It was like Greg had lost him twice."

"I'm sure you're right. Did your husband know about Amy and Susan's theory? That an investigation was underway to see if the deaths were linked?"

"No. Why would he? I only found out about it myself yesterday. We are both busy people and with Sean coming home there was a lot to think about. It never occurred to me to discuss it with him. Why do you ask?"

Rawlings ignored the question. "How well did Greg know Jeremy Rossiter?"

"A little. He knew him, of course, but Greg was very sporty and tended not to drink and party like the rest of us. How is that relevant?"

"Was he there the night Rossiter died?"

"No. As I remember he was up north somewhere for a rugby match. Detective Rawlings, if you're trying to link Greg to this thing Susan and Amy dreamed up, true or not, Greg was not even Jeremy's friend. To be honest, he didn't like him." For the first time since she'd demanded her brother's release, she smiled. "If Meredith thinks he's tied up with any of those deaths, he's very much mistaken, and that news tells me Greg will be home soon."

"I hope so for your sake. But why would he react to the mention of Rossiter's name do you think?"

Claire frowned. "React in what way?"

"In DCI Meredith's words, 'It wlike I'd shoved something somewhere nasty.' I think we can assume a severe reaction."

"I have no idea. None … is that all?" The smile was gone, and Claire got to her feet.

"For now."

"Then I'll let you see yourself out. Goodbye."

Rawlings watched her leave the room before closing his notebook. Something had just registered with her, and she needed space to process it, and he said as much when Patsy appeared in the doorway.

"I understand we're going. Claire looks mad as hell, which is going to make the others even more jumpy that they were before. What's the latest?"

On the way to the car, Rawlings explained Barnard's reaction at the mention of Rossiter and that he thought something had occurred to Claire which she hadn't shared, although she'd found the thought of her husband being involved in the other deaths amusing. Before heading back into town, he set his sat nav for the address Connie Thompson had given.

"This is getting interesting. I don't think she'd protect him if he was involved, she possibly needs to speak to him first. I'm going to return

186

Ellsworth's call because with Barnard in custody, I doubt Meredith will want to see him today, but it will be another loose end tied up."

Ellsworth picked up the call on the third ring.

"Hi, Patsy, thanks for calling back. I was calling to find out if you'd made any headway with your investigation and had handed it over to the police because they'd called me. But I've been in to see them now, on my way home. Seems I was a suspect in a murder, they didn't tell me who. I had an alibi for the time in question, so they took details of where, when, who, etcetera, and then someone came in had a whispered conversation and they kicked me out. Don't know what happened, but the end result is that I don't need you."

"That's good to hear. I'll let you get home. My day is far from over."

"Oh dear. How's your investigation going? Any news?"

"At the moment yes, although it's unlikely that it will be for much longer, we'll know more later. The murdered man was Christopher Kentish."

"Who?"

Patsy and Rawlings exchanged glances. Beatrix believed Ellsworth had already received money from her husband, so how could Ellsworth not remember him?

"Christopher Kentish, he was at university with your parents. His wife seemed to think you knew him."

"Kentish? Ah, yes. You mean Chris, sorry, use of the full name threw me. Blimey, I haven't seen him for years, he helped me out when I was trying to get my business up and running. Poor man. Murdered! I don't know how you cope with all this death."

"I guess you were released as it looks like his killer is in custody. There was a witness to the crime, and she saw him in a supermarket so he's currently being questioned."

"Well, that is a relief. I wonder why they thought it was me? Perhaps I look like him."

"Because you were a beneficiary of his will and had to be eliminated."

"How decent of Chris. I'm sorry he's dead though. It was a long time ago but from what I remember of him he was a decent man. Life is shit sometimes. I'll let you get on, thanks, bye P... Oh, I don't suppose the man they have could be connected to the other deaths, could he? As you said, Chris went to university with my parents so . . .. Sorry, too many questions, I'll leave you to it. Although, if it was him, you can end your investigation."

"It's possible, you're right. Still some ends that need tying up for good measure. I'm on my way to see the woman who knocked over Amy

Cleaver. A formality really, my investigation will go on hold until we know more from the police."

"Good luck, and thanks again."

The call over, Patsy leaned back into her seat, closed her eyes and let out a long sigh.

"Are you okay? That sigh was heartfelt."

"A bit tired. I was hoping Meredith would get home at a reasonable time tonight. Peggy's coming to dinner. She'll be put out if he doesn't make it, and I've got to get some shopping in."

"I'll take you shopping before I drop you home. Nearly there, like you said it's just a formality, so shouldn't take long."

Connie Thompson was not at home and not answering her phone. Her neighbour told them she was probably still at work, so they headed for the supermarket.

"We're going to hit the commuter traffic, but at least you can pick up some shopping while we're there." Rawlings turned to look at her. "We can always leave this until tomorrow if you'd rather?"

"No, let's get it sorted today, we're almost there now."

"No problem. Get your shopping first. I'm starving, I could do with a sandwich or something to keep me going. You've hardly had anything either, there's a café on the corner of the shopping centre, we could grab something first."

"No, I'm fine. You grab something while I shop."

Thirty minutes later, the shopping was done, Rawlings had eaten, and Patsy was cursing silently as they spoke to the store manager. She told them they'd missed Connie by twenty minutes, she'd left immediately her shift had ended. Rawlings thanked her and asked if Connie was working the next day.

"Yes. She's due in at eight. Shall I say you were here?"

"Yes, of course." Rawlings smiled as he turned away. "Thanks again."

"Is everything alright?" The manager wanted to know more but tried to hide her interest. "You won't cart her away or anything? I'm already short-staffed."

"Nothing for you to worry about. Only following up on a car accident." Rawlings stepped away. "We'll catch her at home."

"Accident? She never said. Was she a witness?"

"No, she was driving, as I say, just a formality. Thanks once again for your help."

Patsy also stepped away, knowing if they left now, she could get dinner on within the hour.

"Driving? Is she learning again?"

188

Rawlings frowned and stopped walking. "Learning?"

"Connie failed her test three times. The last time must have been four years ago. Vowed never to try again, said it wasn't for her." It was the manager's turn to frown. "Oh dear. I haven't got her in trouble, have I?"

"Not at all. Now, if you'll excuse us, we must get on."

This time when he turned away Rawlings kept walking.

"I take it you didn't know she didn't have a licence." Patsy asked.

"Nope, and I'm not sure anyone else did. I'll check what the score is once we're in the car."

Rawlings was surprised when Meredith took the phone from Hutchins.

"How are you two getting on? Anything to tie Barnard to the girl who was driving?"

"Not yet, can't locate her. She's the reason for the call. Her manager tells us she hasn't got a licence. Did we know that?"

"Not that I know of. Hang on." Meredith gave instructions to Hutchins. "If she hasn't, you're going to have to bring her in. Are you still with Hodge?"

"I'm here. How are things? You sound very chipper. Do you think he's responsible for the other deaths?"

"No idea. Since I asked about Rossiter, he's clammed up. Tom will give it another half an hour and bang him up for the night. We need something else on him, but as luck would have it we've found the skip, it's been tipped but we know where. Messy job, but a team are there now, and one of the houses near where the skip was located has a camera. It's a long shot, but it might have caught something. Trouble is, the neighbour tells us the owner commutes to London twice a week, and it looks like today is one of those days. We've left a note."

"Sounds positive, Gov. I take it Barnard's alibi checked out?"

"Not watertight. His mate didn't get up until mid-morning. Has no idea what time Barnard left, or indeed whether he stayed there all night. The wife didn't know anything, only that someone had used the guest shower room. I'm waiting for his phone records to see if we can put him in the vicinity."

"Can I take it that as your man has gone to no comment, you might actually get home this evening? You might remember that Peggy is coming to dinner."

"I hadn't forgotten. Can't promise seven thirty though."

"Do your best. Oh, hang on, Connie Thompson is ringing me. Stop speaking a moment."

"Hi, Connie, thanks for … Bugger, I missed her, that was a voice message." Patsy's phone pinged, and she listened to the incoming message. "We won't be seeing her tonight, she's on her way to Bath to visit a friend and said tomorrow at three would be the best time to catch her once she's finished work." Patsy turned to Rawlings. "Home, James, and don't spare the horses. That's me done for the day, Meredith. I'll expect you home soon."

"I'll do my best. Rawlings, get off home, there's not much you can do here tonight, I'll see you in the morning. We'll have a briefing and depending on what's happened, we'll decide if Hodge can go it alone."

Chapter Eighteen

The next few hours saw the recovery of the overalls, socks, and a T-shirt, all soaked in blood, which had been disposed of in a black plastic sack. Also recovered from the tip was a set of three keys on a blue leather fob, and a brown leather wallet complete with cards and cash. Everything else recovered from the tip location was set aside as for the moment they had no connection to the crime. The clothes were sent to forensics.

Meredith waited while the key recovered from Kentish's neighbour was collected from evidence. Taking it, Meredith chose the correct type of key, and holding the evidence bag so the other items fell away, he matched the key.

He grinned at Hutchins. "Get this off to forensics pronto. I want to know whose fingerprints are on them. We're almost done for the night, but I'm going to have a final word with Barnard, but I'd like to know if there's a trace of him on those first. Give his solicitor a shout." Meredith checked the time. "If I'm lucky, I might get home for dinner." He clapped his hands. "You lot can get off home. Not much you can do tonight. Hutchins has volunteered to be night duty officer. Thank you and see you in the morning."

Any prints that had been on the key fob were wiped clean, and Meredith's hopes now rested on some DNA evidence being on the clothing or the sack. But undaunted, he strutted into the interview room with Hutchins wearing a smug smile on his face.

"Evening. Let's get on with it shall we, I have somewhere I'd like to be."

Recorder on, he announced those present and reminded Barnard of his rights.

"Earlier this afternoon we located the contents of the skip in which the clothes worn by Christopher Kentish's assailant, the keys to his house and his wallet were dumped. We already had the laptop. All these items are with forensics, and it's looking promising. Hair was seen attached to the inside of the black bag, and there's a partial fingerprint on the key fob at least. Who knows, there might be more than seen at first glance."

"And you're telling my client this why? Do either the fingerprint or the hair belong to Mr Barnard?"

"I don't know yet, but as I say I have somewhere to be so I thought I'd give him a last chance to come clean. I have my own theory on why he killed Kentish, a spurned lover might get more sympathy from the jury."

Barnard thumped his fists on the table. "I did not kill Kentish. I am not his lover, and I am not talking to you. So if that helps you get away earlier, please be my guest."

To Meredith's surprise, he folded his arms and closed his eyes.

"As you like. I should have the preliminary results by ten o'clock, I'll see you then. You know there's nothing wrong with being gay. I know it's difficult with a family, but people are more understanding these days. Look at Phillip whatsit on the telly, he's got more fans now than he did before. Mind you, he didn't kill anyone, not that I know about."

For a big man, Barnard flew from his chair with remarkable speed, and caught Meredith off guard. He grabbed hold of Meredith's shirt, tearing off two buttons in the process, before Hutchins had him back in the chair, and stood behind him to avoid a recurrence.

"I am not gay." Now calm, his tantrum over, he closed his eyes again.

Meredith brushed his hands down his shirt front and smirked, "Methinks you do protest too much, sir. That's assault added to the charge. Hutchins take him back down."

"May I remind you that you haven't charged my client with anything."

"Yes, but that's only a matter of time. See you in the morning."

When Hutchins returned, he joined Meredith in watching the tape of the interview.

"Did you notice?" Meredith asked as Hutchins pulled up a chair.

"The flinch when you noted the skip contents? Yes, I did."

"Well done, you're getting good at this. What do you reckon, do you think they had a relationship?"

"No idea, but your 'Methinks' comment made his solicitor smirk, so there might be something in it. Whatever the forensics turn up, I think we have our man."

"We do. I'm going to call it a night. My wife is expecting me for dinner. I want to know about any developments. Text me, I'll call if I want more information."

"Will do. Night, Gov."

Meredith felt satisfied with what they had achieved that day and didn't mind that he was going home to dinner with Peggy. He was quite looking forward to some banter with the old girl. A song he liked came on, and he increased the volume. When it finished, the local news came on.

"Police have confirmed that the man arrested in Morrisons supermarket this afternoon is helping them with their inquiries into the murder of jeweller Christopher Kentish a week ago. Mr Kentish's body was discovered on Christmas Steps. It was a violent attack. No charges have yet been brought, but a witness to the arrest, who doesn't wish to be named, claimed the man was sixty-one-year-old Greg Barnard. Mr Barnard is well known in Bristol and the south-west for his charity fund-raising. Police have refused to confirm this, and his wife declined to comment."

Meredith switched off the radio. If he didn't believe Barnard was guilty, he would have found the witness who didn't want to be named and put the fear of God into him.

Opening the door, he emptied his pockets onto the hall table and hung his jacket on the newel post.

"Patsy, get the flags out, he's home!"

Peggy had been flipping through a magazine in the living room and getting to her feet she allowed Meredith to pull her into a hug.

"I was expecting a fanfare too." Meredith winked at her and turned to greet Patsy, who had appeared in the doorway behind him. She had a phone clamped to her ear, and he rolled his eyes at Peggy. "Never stops working. Something smells good. What did you have?"

"Her phone has not stopped. We had a lot to discuss, so we waited for you. I did most of the work because it's difficult to prepare food when you're holding a phone."

Patsy slid her phone into her back pocket and kissed Meredith.

"Do you know the press have got hold of his name? I've had Claire on twice, and that was Susan. She's convinced Claire and Sean to go to Wales with her, at least for the night, or until such time as he's charged or released. The press are camped outside. Have you charged him yet? What happened to your shirt?"

"Barnard did, didn't like me suggesting he might have been romantically involved with the victim, and no, not yet. Can we eat? I'm starving, barely eaten a thing all day."

"Me too, although I don't believe you. It's ready now, do you want to shower first?"

"Nope. I want to delight in eating and Peggy's company. I'll shower when she's gone. You might join me then."

"You're not embarrassing me, Meredith, so pack it in and get out of the way. I really am starving."

They had a pleasant meal with Peggy amusing Meredith with tales from the eighties. Although she only mentioned her husband by referencing them as a couple, it was good to hear her speak about her past with such warmth.

"Did you know Barnard?" he asked as he accepted a slice of cheesecake from Peggy.

"Not that I recall. I remember Claire, though. Good laugh, like most of the girls in Jeremy's crowd. Didn't know his cousin, Freddie. They were fun times, and it's a shame so many of them have gone, however it was they went." Peggy fell silent, as her husband was one of those who had lost their life too young. The silence was broken by Patsy's phone ringing.

Patsy got to her feet. "I'll only answer it if it's my father, I promise." She returned seconds later. "Marcus Ellsworth again. He can leave a message or wait until tomorrow. He's very needy. Nice chap, but I'll be glad when these cases are over. I think he thinks I'm his font of all knowledge. What was that look for, Peggy? I have finished work for the day."

"I think Peggy's rolling eyes and snorting mean Mr Ellsworth might be attracted to you."

"Don't talk rubbish. He wants to know what's going on, he's the nosy type. I'll answer the next call to prove it."

"It is a compliment, you know, not an insult. Am I getting coffee? I brought after-dinner mints."

"I'll do the honours. You're a bit touchy, wife. Have I not been giving you enough attention?"

"I'm not, but no, you never do. It's lucky I'm used to it, or perhaps I'd be glad of attention from Ellsworth."

"Is he charming?" Peggy had a mischievous twinkle in her eye.

"Not really, just a nice chap. Good looking I suppose, smart, and I can't put my finger on it, I think he would be irritating. I've got enough irritation in my life. Let's not talk about work, I'm turning into Meredith. Tell me about Pablo, how's he getting on at nursery?"

"Oh, famously. One of his teachers is Spanish and between them they are teaching the others Spanish nursery rhymes. His grandmother is delighted. By the way, his birthday's coming up and they are going to have a party. You two are invited and, Meredith, as his godfather your presence is required."

"And I shall be there. All you have to do is make sure no one gets murdered in the weeks before, and—" A knock at the door interrupted him. "Who's that at this time of night? If it's Ellsworth I might have a word."

"Oh, that'll be my taxi. Time has run away with us. Never even got my mints." Peggy lifted her bag from the floor. "You answer it, I'll get my coat. What day next week? I can't do Wednesday."

"Well that's nice, a weekly dinner date. You arrange it with Patsy, because I can't guarantee attendance one way or the other, but I'll do my utmost."

As Meredith walked Peggy to the taxi, Patsy loaded the remaining dishes into the machine and ignored the vibrating phone. It pinged as Meredith returned, and she picked it up.

"Ah finally, he's got the message and left one."

Patsy played the message so Meredith could hear it.

"Sorry, Patsy, it's late I know, but I'm out of Bristol tomorrow and just wanted you to know that I know the man who they say was arrested for murdering Christopher Kentish. You won't believe this, but he was also one of the crowd you've been speaking to. Don't think he was friends with my father because he tracked me down to ask about him. I got the impression he didn't much like him. A weird man, very touchy-feely. I didn't like him at all. Anyway, I thought that might be relevant, and that your other half might want to ask him about it. That said, my imagination might be running away with me. Not used to all this murder and intrigue. Take care. Oh, it's Marcus by the way."

She looked at Meredith. "You see, he doesn't fancy me."

"Of course he does. Any man would be mad not to, and he doesn't sound needy just trying to help. It is a good shout after all we're considering it. Also, interesting that he says he was touchy-feely, odd. But enough! Leave your phone down here, get upstairs and get in that shower."

"I've already showered."

"And that makes a difference to me why?"

Grinning, Patsy hit the light switch. "Come on then, before I fall asleep."

Chapter Nineteen

T he next morning Patsy found herself unable to go back to sleep once Meredith had woken her when he was searching for his socks. After ten minutes of tossing and turning, she went to join him in the kitchen.

"Sorry I woke you. But it was your fault, your method of distraction last night stopped me being my usual organised self." His eyes twinkled as a dishevelled Patsy pulled out a chair. "Have you come to distract me again?"

"No. I came down to join you for breakfast." Patsy stole a slice of toast and lifted his orange juice. "You need another glass."

"In which case, we'd better talk shop. I've been thinking, I want you to visit this hit-and-run driver as soon as. If she is anything but kosher, I need to know. Am I dealing with one or a bunch of murders? Is that okay with you? I know you weren't scheduled to see her until three."

"Fine. She starts work at eight. I'll try to catch her before she leaves for work. I'm guessing no news on your forensics."

"Not anything definitive, no. But when I spoke to Barnard I lied about some hair being stuck to the bag he used to dump the clothes. Turns out it wasn't a lie. Now we have to wait for the DNA results. It's going to take a couple of days, so if that's what nails him, I'm going to have to apply for an extension. Unless of course the owners of the camera come home and we find him dumping the clothes. His shoes, one has to assume he dumped them too, Kentish's watch, and wedding ring are still missing. There's a chance whoever took the laptop out of the skip took those too and just missed the wallet. Might try to get an appeal on the news. I don't know why that's always so difficult, can't they see that helping solve a murder is more interesting than some parrots in the park, or the latest moan from the farmers?"

"Meredith, you're going off course to moan again."

"I do not moan. I simply point out the shortcomings I have to deal with on what feels like an hourly basis. If you're going to be like that, I'm off." He finished the orange juice and kissed her. "Speak later. I'll try not to be late."

"Bye, husband. Love you."

~ ~ ~

Patsy rang the doorbell for Connie Thompson's flat at seven thirty. She'd already tried to call and had left a message. She cursed when there was no reply and headed for the supermarket. The same manager came out to greet her.

"If you're after Connie, you're out of luck. She's called in sick."

Patsy raised her eyebrows, Connie wasn't at home and she doubted she was sick. She forced a smile. "Ah well, it was worth a try. Nothing serious I hope."

"Dodgy tum. I'm sure she'll be in tomorrow."

"Let's hope so."

Patsy called Meredith and updated him. "So unless she was avoiding me, I reckon she had one too many last night and stayed over in Bath. Going to see her at three as was originally arranged. I'll be at the office if you need me."

"I always need you, Hodge, it's just some settings are inappropriate."

"Ha, ha. You must be in a good mood. You're trying to crack jokes. Wish me luck, I'm off to see the seating arrangement."

"Good luck. I hope she's not taking Louie's mind off the job in hand. I'm off to interview Barnard and see what his reaction is to Ellsworth's touchy-feely comments. And as if on cue, Tom is signalling his solicitor has arrived."

"Okay, well… you've hung up again." Patsy dropped her phone on the passenger seat and headed for the office.

Meredith hit the button of the recorder and made the necessary announcement.

"I'd remind you, you're still under caution. I hope the breakfast wasn't too bad this morning. I eat anything but the breakfast here would test even me."

Barnard looked at him and gave a slight shake of his head. "Strangely enough, I've—"

James Tovey held up his hand. "My client will not be answering questions, DCI Meredith, so might I suggest you charge him or release him."

198

"You might. Not sure I'll take you up on that suggestion. I will, however, ask your client why he went to the bother of tracking down Marcus Ellsworth, and upon doing so, in Mr Ellsworth's words, got very touchy-feely?"

Barnard's lips barely moved. "No comment."

"Did you have a relationship with Mr Ellsworth?" Meredith waited a beat. "I'm sorry, you're going to have to say something."

Once again, Barnard took them by surprise and was on his feet. Meredith followed seconds later, and Tovey sat with his mouth gaping.

Barnard waved his finger at Meredith. "And that's where you're wrong. I'm not even going to say no comment until I get out of here, with this exception. I do not do touchy-feely. I am not gay. If that's what Ellsworth said, well he's more… actually, forget it. Take me back."

Meredith left Barnard facing the door and hands on the table, spoke to the recorder.

"For the purposes of the tape, Mr Barnard is disproportionately sensitive about any implication that he is gay, which begs the question is he homophobic? Perhaps Christopher Kentish died because he made one approach too many. Food for thought. Mr Barnard will be taken back to his cell while we track down friends and family who might shed some light on Mr Barnard's prejudices. Interview ended at ten fifteen."

Aware that Barnard wanted to respond by the twitch of his head, Meredith asked, "Unless you want to speak to me, do you?"

When Barnard ignored him, Meredith instructed Hutchins to take him back to the cell. "Join me in my office when you're done. We need to divide this list of associates, there are many so it's going to be a long day." Holding the door open, he swung his hand into the corridor. "See you later, Mr Barnard."

Meredith banged down his phone as Hutchins returned.

"Where's Jo? She spoke to Ellsworth, he's not answering his phone again. Think we're going to pay him a visit."

"To find out what he meant by touchy-feely?"

"Exactly. You'll be after my job next. JO!"

Hutchins winced and shuddered. "I don't think I'll ever get used to that."

"Gov?" Jo Adler appeared behind Hutchins and patted his shoulder. "You won't."

"How did you get Ellsworth in here, and where's his address, he's not answering the phone?

"Did you leave a message? He's one that doesn't answer unknown numbers."

Meredith rolled his eyes and redialled. He smiled when the call was answered first time and explained he'd like to meet. Arrangements were made, and Meredith got to his feet.

"He's out on appointments but has a break at eleven thirty. We're meeting him at a coffee shop."

"Which we?" Jo asked.

"Why, have you got something better to do?"

"I hope so. I'm working with Tom on the unlisted telephone calls to the victim. We're waiting for a call back from a taxi firm, but I think we've got him."

"Explain."

"Finally got the schedule of calls made on the pay-as-you-go numbers that also called Kentish. On the night Kentish was murdered, a call was made to a taxi firm a little before midnight. Tom reckons if the pickup is in the vicinity of Bell Barn Road, we've got him."

Meredith rubbed his hands together. "Good work. Come on, Hutchins, you're buying me a coffee."

Meredith watched Ellsworth walk into the coffee shop and look around. He stood and waved him into the booth they'd chosen at the back of the shop. After thanking him for seeing them so promptly, he got straight to the point.

"I want you to tell me about your meeting with Greg Barnard. Patsy Hodge tells me you believe he could be responsible for a string of killings. Why do you think that? What happened at the meeting to make you think ill of him?"

"I thought Patsy was married to you? Do you not call her your wife? She's very naughty. I didn't say I thought he had, I said he knew the crowd that were there the night my father died, so you might want to check him out. Or words to that effect. That said, he was odd. He didn't know my father was dead at first, and he'd gone to a lot of trouble to track me down."

"I find it surprising he didn't know your father was dead, perhaps he lied for some reason. I'm sure we'll find out why in time. I'm going to throw some random questions at you. Just give an honest answer."

Ellsworth nodded and rested back against his seat.

"How long ago was your meeting with Barnard? And how did he track you down?"

Ellsworth explained that around six months before, Barnard had told him he'd been to Caversham, Ellsworth's previous address, only to find he'd moved back to Bristol. As they didn't have his new address, Barnard had done various online searches until he got the correct street address, and then made various visits until he saw him. When asked what was so important, he said he was trying to trace a friend from his university days, and he thought my mother and father might know where they were. When told that both parents were dead, he'd thrown his arms into the air and pulled Ellsworth into a hug, stroking his hair and murmuring 'poor boy'. Once Ellsworth had managed to push him off, he asked who it was that Barnard was trying to find as his mother had addresses for a few of those she went to university with, although it was years out of date, but it might be of use. They had a brief discussion, and Barnard said he didn't want to be a nuisance and that he had to go and visit his son. He wished Ellsworth a happy life, gave him another hug, catching Ellsworth's hair on his watch in the process, and left.

Ellsworth had been so intrigued, he'd then done his own internet search and found that he'd married Claire Scott, one of his mother's friends, and they had a son who was the same age. With a shrug, Ellsworth asked, "Did that help? I can't think that it did, I'm as bemused now as I was back then."

"It certainly is odd. Why did you think I might be interested in him?"

"Only because he's been arrested for murder, and Patsy, or rather Amy thought my father's friends were being killed for some reason and he was looking for one of them." Ellsworth tilted his head. "Do you know you're a very difficult man to read? I don't know if you are genuinely interested in the answer, or you already know and are testing me."

"How would I know?"

"Because you've been speaking to Greg Barnard, and you asked to speak to me yesterday. I'm assuming for the same reason. But Barnard was more likely because I have an alibi and I'm assuming he doesn't."

"Remind me of your alibi." Meredith winked to show he wasn't totally serious.

"I was working. I do promotions. That night I was at Starlights, the little club under the shops on Queens Road, promoting the latest brand of schnapps. Youngsters love a shot. At two am I called it a night, packed up the stall and counted the takings. I got twenty percent of the take, which wasn't too shabby. Going to try to talk the owner into doing another night with a different brand, only I'll supply it and he'll get the smaller cut." Ellsworth smiled. "They close at three and he'd ordered food for the staff, I was invited to stay, and it was past four before I left. In a taxi because I did have a couple myself."

"Ah yes. Mr Valero confirmed. Did Barnard ask about Kentish?"

After only a little consideration, Ellsworth shrugged. He didn't think so but wouldn't swear to it. Then Meredith asked how Ellsworth knew Kentish.

"I know of all of their crowd. My mother lived in the past. We used to see a lot of them when I was young, but the years passed and people have their own lives to get on with, they drifted off. Then of course she died. I think they all carried a measure of guilt over my father's death, and some of them have kept in touch one way or another. Mr Kentish was one of them, Patsy tells me he's left me something in his will."

"Which is why we wanted to speak to you. But you seem to have a cast-iron alibi, so congratulations on your windfall."

Ellsworth smiled and asked, "Is that it, because my next meeting is in twenty minutes and although it's only up the road, it's a bugger to park and too far to walk."

"Only one thing." Hutchins joined the conversation. "Your address, just so we've dotted all the i's."

"Well, I've been sharing with various friends since I came back to Bristol, but currently 78a Pembroke Road. BS8 3... Oh I can never remember the end bit."

Hutchins flipped his notebook closed. "That'll do. Thank you."

They watched him leave as Meredith drained his coffee.

"What do you reckon?"

"His alibi is watertight. It was more than just the owner. He didn't kill him. But this is a long shot so hear me out. As he said, he's the same age as Sean Barnard give or take a few weeks. What if Greg Barnard was after his hair? He's not touchy-feely, and he hugged him twice, stroked his—"

"Hair tangled it in a watch. Bloody hell, you're on fire today, Pa. Come on, Barnard's brief is going to love us. You can call him on the way back."

When Hutchins pulled out his phone, he was smiling. Pa was the nickname Meredith had given him when his first child was born, the second was due any day, and when Meredith used it, it meant he was pleased with him.

Back at the station, Meredith checked through the progress on the other lines of inquiry, and although nothing concrete had come in, he didn't get frustrated. Convinced Hutchins was onto something, he was itching to get into the interview room, and time was running out. All he had to do was work out why Jeremy Rossiter's being Sean's father, would lead to the brutal killing of Christopher Kentish. That would come.

It was almost one thirty by the time he hit the record button.

"I've had a meeting with Marcus Ellsworth. I wanted to know why you got touchy-feely with him. I thought you were in denial in some way, but then the genius to my left sussed it out. DNA."

Barnard jerked as though electricity had shot through his body.

"And that reaction tells me I'm right. So I'll leave you for a moment. I need to send someone to get a sample from Sean."

"No." It was barely a whisper.

"Are you going to talk to me?"

"Yes, but only on the understanding—"

"Greg, I really should caution you, you don't need to answer these questions."

Barnard flipped the caution away and asked for Meredith's word that if he told the truth about his meeting with Ellsworth, Sean needn't be bothered. Meredith agreed, and Barnard explained that he'd overheard a conversation between Claire and one of her friends which made him question the paternity of his son. When he thought back to that time, he knew if he wasn't the father then Jeremy would be. Claire didn't sleep around, but Jeremy had once boasted, when they entered a pub, that his harem was waiting for him. Sitting at the table had been four girls, one of them was Claire. Someone had joked that he wished and Jeremy said he didn't need to wish because it was true.

At the time Barnard had thought he was exaggerating, and he wasn't actually dating Claire, that happened shortly after, but that call had brought it all back and he had to know. The only way of doing that was to ask or get proof one way or the other. He'd considered approaching Freddie Rossiter but decided if he were to keep his actions a secret, Ellsworth would be his best bet. He got hair samples from both Ellsworth and Sean, and with a few lies and forged signatures sent them off to be tested. The results came back, they were half-brothers.

It hadn't changed his feelings for his son, but their relationship and probably Sean's health would be ruined if the truth were revealed, so he hadn't said anything. When Meredith asked about Claire, Barnard said he'd never confronted her. He knew she'd never cheated on him, and he doubted she knew herself. At least that was his hope. By not asking her, he didn't need to deal with it.

Meredith leaned back and crossed his legs at the ankle.

"Very admirable. I know your son has issues to deal with. How did that bring you to Kentish?"

"It didn't. I'm simply telling you why I met with Ellsworth. Who, by the way, has something to hide. I don't know what, but he moves about from one place to the other, like he doesn't want to be found. My search probably took me to ten different addresses. Perhaps he doesn't pay his rent. He knows Kentish by the way, he mentioned him."

There was a knock at the door and a happy looking Seaton passed him a sheet of paper. Meredith knew what it would be before he looked at it. He thanked Seaton and looked at Barnard.

"Do you know what's on this sheet of paper?"

"DCI Meredith, how on earth could my client—"

"Okay, I'll help. During our investigation we found that Christopher Kentish received calls from several pay-as-you-go phones, these as you know can't be traced very easily to the person using them. However, when we ran a check on those numbers, we found that one of them had been used at around midnight on the night Kentish was murdered. We checked the number, and it was a taxi firm. We've just got confirmation of the location it collected the fare from. If I turn this over, where do you think that will be?"

Barnard's eyes betrayed his worry, but he simply shrugged his shoulders in response. When Meredith revealed it had been Bell Barn Road, the same road that Barnard had stayed on, he shrugged again. Meredith returned the gesture.

"Fine. We'll get a warrant, and we'll search your business, your home, your gym locker and anywhere else we might find associated with you. But in the meantime, Hutchins here will formally charge you. We are of course going to have to speak to your wife about the paternity of your son, because she may know of a reason—"

"I'll give you a full confession if you give me your word that neither of them ever finds out. They will need each other, and Sean is fragile enough as it is."

"For me to try to bury that you will have to tell me why you killed Christopher Kentish."

"Say he tried it on with me, say he was trying to blackmail me into having sex with him, how hard can it be to make up the why?"

"I mean the real reason. You were friends with Christopher Kentish, maybe not so much recently, but he introduced you to your wife. What happened to make you rip his heart out?"

His eyes closed, Barnard tilted his head as though looking at the ceiling.

"Because he knew. He knew before we were married. He knew when I struggled to earn enough to keep my young family. When Sean went off the rails. When I was at my wit's end on how to help Sean When I hated myself for resenting him. When I considered leaving them because we had

204

no fucking life of our own. Christopher Kentish knew. He should have told me. He betrayed our friendship, and he told me it didn't matter."

"Would you not have married her if you had known the truth?"

"The honest answer is I don't know. I certainly wouldn't have wanted to take on Rossiter's baby, but I loved her. Kentish said he helped Claire come to a decision about a termination. He told her to have the baby, and to lie to me. Do you know how I found out? What he did, I mean?"

"Tell me."

~ ~ ~

On a beautiful spring morning, Greg Barnard called goodbye to his wife from the downstairs toilet. Door locked, he sat with the DNA results in his hands. The sheet fluttered as his hands shook. He couldn't face her; he couldn't speak to her. If he did, he might say something which couldn't be taken back, after all she might not have known.

Waiting until he heard her car pull off the drive, he unlocked the door and went into the kitchen, called work and said he had a stomach bug. Claire wouldn't question that, not when he'd been in there for over half an hour. Glad that Sean wasn't around, he poured a shot of brandy into his now cold coffee and emptied the cup. Pulling his golf clubs from the hall cupboard, he stowed them in the car and headed out of town. Keynsham has a golf range, and he could take out some of his frustration while he considered his options.

The range wasn't full, and he made his way along to his allocated position. His heart sank when someone called out to him. He turned and was surprised to see Christopher Kentish. For a moment he forgot his woes and pumped his old friend's hand.

After exchanging a brief greeting, they agreed to meet in the club house for coffee once they'd finished. Thrashing the balls had done nothing to lift Barnard's spirits, and he regretted the arrangement as he made his way to the bar area. Kentish was already seated.

"I've ordered coffee as I remember you take it black, but just in case a pot of cream too. I have to say, Greg, you're wearing a little better than me, life must be being kind to you."

"Life hasn't been kind to me for about twenty years. It's been an effing nightmare for the best part, but I'll take the compliment."

"I'm sorry to hear that, my friend. Nothing to do with the lovely Claire, I hope?"

"No, our s... that is, our son, Sean. He has addiction issues. Alcohol, as a teenager, got him dry, then he found drugs in his early twenties. No

205

reason needed, no trauma, just if he likes something he doesn't know when to stop."

"I'm sorry to hear that. How is he now?"

"In rehab. Doing really well, he's such a lovely person, someone you can be proud to call your … son. Then just when you think things are settled, BOOM. Everything blows up. Sorry, Chris, you don't want to listen to all this crap."

"Not at all. It's the person you should focus on, the one who loves you. Sean. The rest, well, I can only imagine what you've been through, but you've survived, and fingers crossed this will be the last time. Bea had a cousin with a horrible addiction, turned her into the most disgusting evil creature, hated everyone and everything. There was no reasoning with her. No idea what happened to her, she just broke off all contact with her family. It sounds as though your boy loves you, and he's in rehab so he's trying."

"Yes, but despite his age it still feels like he's a teenager finding his feet, and sometimes you have to remind yourself how old he is. I don't need reminding I feel every bloody year of it. Let's change the subject. How is our lovely Bea?"

"Lovely. Don't think she has any other settings. Currently learning Italian, she's already mastered French, German and Spanish. She has different cogs to me, I am still at grammar school basics. We really must arrange a get-together. Ah, here's the lovely Lucy with the coffee, and yes, little biscuits in packets. Are you still with the same firm?"

"Yep, senior partner, gets more boring the closer to the top you get. But the money is a godsend when you are supporting a grown man. I don't need to ask about you, how's business? I do my bit you know, always go to your shop when it's a special birthday or anniversary."

"Good. Ups and downs, the pandemic was a blow, but we survived, had a little put by you know. Listen, I'm sorry, but I'm going to have to make a move. Let's make a date for lunch."

They agreed on a date, and the meeting left Greg Barnard feeling a little more positive until they said goodbye in the carpark.

"See you Wednesday, I'm glad Claire chose right, you are a good father."

"What does that mean? Chose me over whom?"

"No one. I meant she could have married someone else, and you were the right man for her."

Barnard stewed on those words for the next week, and when he entered the restaurant he was confrontational. He demanded to know what Kentish meant and asked what he knew that he hadn't been told. All

206

the while knowing the answer. Kentish denied all knowledge until the month before Barnard killed him. Kentish had been very patient with what he called Barnard's insecurity, but finally he blew.

"Greg, for God's sake, man, pull yourself together. What difference does whatever happened all that time ago make? You love Claire, she loves you and together you have a son whom you both adore."

"But is he mine?"

"Yes, I've just said that. Look—"

"LIAR!"

"You know?"

"Yes, I know. I've had a DNA test, not just to prove he's not mine, but I found Rossiter's other bastard and confirmed it. You were supposed to be my friend."

"I was and I am."

"But you knew and didn't feel it appropriate to tell me."

Kentish got to his feet. "No. Claire spoke to me in confidence. You asked her to marry you before you knew she was pregnant. She wanted to say yes, she loved you. But she'd had the pregnancy confirmed, and the scan indicated the baby had been conceived in the month before she started dating you. She told me that meant it was Jeremy's, and he was dead. She didn't know what to do, and I suggested she tell you. When I asked how it went, she said you were so excited and happy she was pregnant she didn't have the heart to tell you the rest. She'd decided to abort and tell you it was a miscarriage. It was breaking her heart. The guilt and the knowledge would have dragged her down, so I told her if you were happy and she was happy to get on with it. My lips were forever sealed. So, Greg, what would you have done?"

"I'd have told her to tell the bloody truth. You know I didn't like Rossiter. I still have no idea what you all saw in him. But I've sacrificed so much … for what. For a broken heart, a broken child, and now probably a broken marriage. Fuck you, Chris. I hope you sleep soundly in your bed tonight. I'll be lying awake wondering if someone else's son has slipped out of the complex and is looking for his next fix or working out the easiest way to top himself. Yes, we've had three suicide attempts."

"I'm leaving. You're being ridiculous. Sean is your son. I told her not to abort and not to tell you, so don't blame Claire. If you want someone to blame, blame me."

"Oh, I do."

But the truth was he also couldn't bear to be in the same room as Claire, and all because Christopher Kentish had told her to deceive him. To lie, and in effect ruin his life. The more he thought about it, the more his hatred grew. His heart was broken. When Claire received a call from the clinic reporting that Sean had gone missing again, he began to plan a murder. When he had it all worked out, he carried a bag with the equipment ready to take his chance, when he felt ready to take a life.

He became ready when by chance he saw Christopher kissing a man on the doorstep of a house off Park Street. Not only had he ruined Barnard's life, but he was ruining Bea's, too. The next day, instead of going to the gym, he waited there again, and the next, and the next, until they appeared. Laughing, joking, hand in hand. He went home and pondered what to do. When he decided it was to kill his friend, he knew he had to be careful, so he purchased a pay-as-you-go phone. There were enough true crime programmes on television for him to know his own phone could be traced.

Knowing Claire would miss him if he disappeared at night, he orchestrated the visit with a friend. Feigned drunkenness and having stumbled into the spare room, called Kentish. The attack itself was a blur fuelled by his fury, but a girl appeared and screamed. He saw the look of horror on her face and knew the image would live with her for a long time, so after she ran off, he carried the body further down Christmas steps. Saw the bin and thought it an appropriate resting place. Initially, he removed only the keys, wallet and watch from Kentish, but thought being found naked in a bin would add to his humiliation. Once stripped, he looked down at Kentish's body and panicked. What had he done? What had this evil man driven him to? In another fit of fury, he shoved the knife back in and tried to remove the heart. Heartless, naked and in a bin. A fitting end, he thought. Now he needed to cover his tracks. Stripping off the top layer of his clothes, he carried clean shoes until he was almost on the Centre before he put them on. He flagged down a taxi and got dropped off around the corner from Kentish's home.

There was no guilt as he made as much mess as he could to make it look like a break-in, and for good measure he stole the laptop and some cufflinks. When he looked at the bed in which Kentish had probably cheated on his wife with other men, he wrote his message and left the heart. On his journey to meet Kentish he'd noticed a skip on Hampton Road, and once he'd cleaned up, he walked back into the heart of Clifton and found another taxi. He dumped his bloodied clothes and the items he had stolen and walked to Whiteladies Road where he found the final taxi. Back at his friend's home, his absence hadn't been noticed, and the door was still on the latch. He crept in, showered, and headed home.

~ ~ ~

Meredith got to his feet. "Thank you for being honest with me. I might need to speak to you later, but for now you'll be taken back to the cell. It will probably be tomorrow before you go before the magistrates. As you're pleading guilty, I doubt much of this will come out. But you might want to consider telling your wife the truth, because to be honest, I'm not sure she'll understand otherwise. Hutchins take Mr Barnard back to the cell."

"Wait. That's it? I just go to prison and don't get to see my family beforehand?"

"I'm afraid that's the price you pay when you kill someone. Your solicitor will get in touch with your wife. Once you're on remand, she'll be able to visit."

Allowing his head to drop onto folded arms, Barnard wept as Meredith left the room.

Chapter Twenty

B ack in his office he considered what he'd heard. He knew how it felt to be told that a child you had loved and cared for wasn't yours. In his case it hadn't been true, but he could remember the absolute desolation he'd felt. Would he have taken it as far as murder in similar circumstances, he doubted it.

With a heartfelt sigh he sat at his desk. His first call was to Chief Superintendent Brownlow.

"Meredith, sir, thought you'd like to know I've charged Greg Barnard with the murder of Christopher Kentish, and he's pleading guilty."

"That's splendid news, Meredith. Congratulations. I'll get a press release out. Now, about the wedding, have—"

"Sorry, sir, I'll catch you later, his solicitor is beckoning me. I'll let you know if it's anything worth hearing."

Dropping his phone onto the desk, Meredith wondered how people became so invested in a wedding. He'd been married three times, and each time, with the exception of setting a budget, he'd simply agreed to everything that was suggested. All he'd wanted to do was be married and have a family. All the frills and fancies were an unnecessary distraction. He pulled out his notebook and looked at the notes from his meeting with Ellsworth and frowned, that was familiar.

He called Patsy. "Barnard just confessed. Long story why, I'll tell you later, but have you still got the tapes that Amy Cleaver left Henry Duggan?"

"They're at the office. Call Lindhe'll have filed them. What is it? Do you think Barnard might be involved?"

"It's possible but I need to check something out. I thought you were in the office, are you bunking off?"

"I wish, I feel absolutely lousy. I'm in my car, off to meet Connie Thompson. She'd better be there this time."

"I'm going to send Rawlings to meet you. Don't go in until he gets there. If she hasn't got a licence, we'd better arrest her formally, that's manslaughter."

"I did wonder why you hadn't already done that."

"Because, my lovely wife, you told me she wasn't answering her phone, she wasn't at home, and she'd bunked off work. I knew you were going to see her, and I always intended sending someone with you. I'd have told you before now but I got tied up solving a grisly murder."

"You lie so easily. If you were intending to do that you wouldn't have asked why I wasn't in the office. Get off the phone and let me get going. Tell Dave I'll see him there."

"I will. See you later."

Meredith despatched Rawlings to meet Patsy and called Linda.

"Loopy, I hope you're not busy. Patsy tells me you can put your hand on the tapes made by Amy Cleaver. I need an urgent favour."

"I'm always busy, Skipper. PHPI has been in all morning and given me another stack of work, just when I'm up to my ears in the wedding stuff. Talking of which, have—"

"Life and death, Loopy. Can you do it now?"

"In which case yes. But if you don't get a decent pudding it's because I got distracted. What do you need?"

"Can you play me the tape. Someone said something to me today and I've got a niggle in the back of my brain that it relates to something on the tape."

"Will do. Anything in particular, we've stored them on the system so I can word check the document."

"You can? I knew there was a reason you were my favourite."

"Well what is it?"

"You're ready?"

"Skipper, life and death remember?"

"Yep. Something like a measure of guilt." Meredith listened to Linda's fingers typing the words.

"Exactly that. Are you ready, I'll play bit around it too."

Meredith agreed, and seconds later he was listening to the voice of Amy Cleaver.

"I'm too ashamed. I should mention that I also feel a measure of guilt, we all do, and in my own way I've paid the price of my actions, or lack of them. The question is, I suppose, was that enough?"

"I knew it! Shit. Loopy, got to go. RAWLINGS!"

212

Meredith was dialling out when Hutchins appeared.

"You sent him out, Gov. Anything I can help with."

Meredith held up his finger. "Patsy, it's me. I think—"

"Meredith, wait. You'll never guess who I've just seen speaking to Connie Thompson."

"Ellsworth?"

"How did you know that?"

"Because I'm a brilliant detective. Is he still there?"

"No just getting into a blue Honda Civic can't see the registration without getting out of the car, hang on."

"No. Stay in the car. We don't want him focused on you."

"Hang on, he's pulling away, I'll try and get a photograph …Get off the phone and I'll send you a copy."

"Is Rawlings there yet?"

"Not as I can…Oh yes, he's walking towards me. Did you get the photograph?"

"Don't know. Tell him to arrest her, even if he has to kick the door down. Don't want any more no-shows."

"You sound worried."

"And I shall remain that way until we have him. You led us to him, Patsy. I have no idea why in his warped mind he has to kill these people because they've done nothing, you on the other hand will be dripping in guilt to him, because you led us to him. Come to the station, I want you where I can see you, and you have to give a witness statement that they were together." Meredith's tone was firm. With Patsy having had her life threatened on two previous cases, he was taking no risks.

"Ah, so sweet. It won't happen a third time, Meredith. Even I'm not that unlucky."

"Just do it. I'm going to circulate this photo."

"Okay, I … You've gone again haven't you."

Patsy waved at Dave and climbed out of the car. "He hung up on me again. Ellsworth is involved, I just saw him speaking to Connie Thompson, and Meredith had already worked that out. No, don't ask me how. Anyway, you're to arrest her, and with or without a warrant, take the door down if necessary."

"Better get on with it then."

As Meredith predicted, Connie Thompson ignored the constant ringing of the bell and rather than break the door down Rawlings gained access via a neighbour. They asked to see his ID, then hovered in the hall as Patsy and Rawlings climbed the stairs to the first floor.

Rawlings banged and kicked the door when Connie didn't answer his polite knock. Patsy put her hand on his shoulder to stop him before dropping to her knees to look through the letter box.

"Connie, it's Patsy. I'm not sure why you won't come out, but it's very important you speak to the police. You need to explain your side of the story, without doing that you're looking at a life sentence for murder."

The door was yanked open causing Patsy to fall forward.

"Murder? He said it would be nothing like that."

Rawlings stopped her there, arrested her, and cautioned her.

"You said murder again. It wasn't murder. He said if you caught me out, it would be death by dangerous driving at worst, and that I'd get a suspended sentence and possibly lose my licence."

"But you don't have a licence. You shouldn't have been driving at all."

"I wasn't driving. I was at work! He was driving, he asked me to put my hands up to it because if he lost his licence, he'd lose his job. I'm crap at driving so it made no difference to me, and it was an accident, and for five K who wouldn't?"

"He paid you?"

"Of course, do I look stupid?"

Patsy and Rawlings exchanged a glance which answered that question. Rawlings told her to grab her keys and asked if she had a solicitor.

"I'm hoping I won't need one. I'm going to tell you everything, don't worry." When she saw the handcuffs, her voice went up a pitch. "Cuffs? I told you, I wasn't driving."

"Even so, you still committed an ... Do you know what, shut up. Save it for the interview."

As they exited the block they had to fall into single file as a dustbin partially blocked the path. Seeing her opportunity, Connie made a run for it. Dave was manhandling the dustbin, so Patsy did the honours and chased after her. Connie hit the road with a thud and was still cursing when Patsy hiked her to her feet.

Rawlings walked towards them applauding. "Well done, Patsy. I knew you'd be ... SHIT. Look out."

Hand on Connie's elbow, Patsy looked in the direction that Rawlings was pointing. As Rawlings reached her the car hit all three of them as if they were bowling pins. Connie went up and over the roof, Rawlings across the bonnet and into a lamppost, and Patsy took the impact side on, ending up on the bonnet of a parked car.

She lay still assessing her pain and thinking how quiet it was. That lasted mere seconds before she heard an almighty collision. Her last thought before passing out was the hope that he hadn't killed anyone else.

Chapter Twenty-One

Patsy winced as she attempted to turn over. Her eyes opened and her hand grabbed her leg.

"It's broken." Meredith's voice was gentle, and he smiled as she turned her head to look at him, taking in her surroundings as she realised she was in hospital.

"Ellsworth?"

"Yes. I've let Seaton deal with him. I don't think I could control myself."

"Blimey, that's not like you. You must be getting sensible in your old age."

"You were my top priority."

"God, I'm thirsty, is there any water?" Seeing the cards on the cabinet, Patsy frowned. "What time is it? How long have I been out?"

"About half two."

"In the morning?"

"The next day."

"Did they have to operate or something?" Patsy's hand tapped the dressing on the splint lightly, and she looked at Meredith. "Another battle scar for you to kiss better?" Attempting to push herself up on her elbows, she groaned and dropped back onto the pillows. "Come closer and kiss me."

As Meredith lowered his head she took hold of his face, her palms warm against his cheeks. "Are you crying, Meredith? Don't blink, it's too late." Her hands left his face and covered her mouth. "Not, Dave, please don't tell me that."

Kissing the end of her nose, Meredith cleared his throat. Now she was looking for it, she heard the warble in his voice.

"He's not good. His body is battered and bruised, but his head took the brunt after colliding with a lamppost. Major bleed, they've operated to relieve the pressure, and hopefully stem the bleeding, but," he coughed again "they can't tell how much damage has been done."

"Oh no, I don't know what to say, I'm so sorry." Patsy brushed away her own tears. "What about Connie? Dave tried to push me out of the way, did he get her too?"

"Connie didn't make it. Died a little after midnight last night."

"And all for five grand." Patsy saw his frown and knew he didn't have that information. "I'll tell you all about it later. How did you catch Ellsworth?"

"I sent Hutchins over to help out, I didn't want you involved." His smile was brief as Patsy grimaced. "He saw him drive into you, and drove at his car, putting it passenger side on at the last moment. He didn't reckon on kamikaze Ellsworth, who also floored the accelerator. He had to be cut free. And do you know that bastard barely had a scratch."

"And Hutchins?"

"Bruised but walking wounded. His is the one with the flowers and soppy verse. They had a girl by the way."

"Oh, how lovely. As I'm indisposed you must buy a card and a gift. Thank God it wasn't more serious. Can you imagine, a new baby and a husband in hospital, or worse."

"Not worth thinking about."

Reaching up, Patsy wiped away a tear. "What else, Meredith, there's something else."

"Not now, when you're better."

"I am better. I have a broken leg. My brain is functioning." She watched the internal conflict in his eyes, and on the third cough, insisted. "Meredith. What else?"

"When they brought you in, you were losing blood. Saturated. I saw the clothes they cut away."

"Am I going to be able to walk? Has something crucial been damaged?"

"Yes with crutches, but only for a while because of the plaster." Meredith smiled at his poor humour.

"Then what? Meredith, just tell me, because you going all coy like this is scaring the whatsit out of me."

Taking her hand, Meredith brought it to his lips and kissed it.

"You don't know?"

"No. Of course not. Why would I ask?"

"You were pregnant. About three months they reckon. We lost the baby." Kissing her hand again, he screwed his eyes shut, but still a tear escaped.

"Oh."

"You really didn't know?"

Patsy shook her head.

"Not even an inkling? You have been very tired, pale, grumpy. All those clues."

"No."

"That injection you have isn't much cop. You might not get periods, but if it's not one hundred per cent, you don't get a warning. I'm sorry, Patsy. So sorry."

"Why?"

"Why? What sort of question is that?"

"It's the, why are you sorry, question. Because I didn't know, because I lost the baby, or because we lost the baby?"

"Oh."

"Meredith, I need a moment, go and grab me some grapes and Lucozade or something."

"But—"

"Please."

Nodding, Meredith kissed her hand, placed it back on the bed as though it might shatter. "Twenty minutes be enough?"

Nodding, Patsy tried to smile. Unable to watch, Meredith left as requested.

Patsy gazed at the clock on the wall opposite and wondered if Meredith would give her that long. At ten minutes her face crumpled, at fifteen she wept. At twenty minutes she dried her eyes and tried to control the jerky tremors taking control of her body. She knew she must look a mess, but she needed to be calm to speak to Meredith.

At thirty minutes she dozed off, exhausted and not willing to rethink the 'what ifs'.

When she woke up there was someone at the end of the bed. Her eyes went to the clock. It had been sixty eight minutes.

"I'm sorry, I dozed off."

"Hi, Patsy." Amanda brought the chart with her, and after kissing Patsy's forehead, took her pulse. "How are you feeling?"

"Numb."

"That's understandable. Can I get you anything, you should be okay to eat now, something light? Don't move too much, you won't be plastered until tomorrow, when the swelling has gone down."

"No, thank you anyway. You could help me sit up a little. Did I miss your father, did he say what time he's coming back?"

"He's not sure. He sent Eve home to see Ellen. I'm sure he won't be long."

"How is Dave, has there been any change?"

"Not good I'm afraid, he had a seizure earlier, but he's stable now."

"What are his chances?"

"Too early to say."

"Amanda, your best guess."

"Seventy thirty he'll survive. But in what condition - it's too early to say."

"How's Meredith?"

"Honestly? Lost. He's sitting in with Dave talking about Ellen, and telling him why he should survive, and that he'd lost a son, and he didn't want to lose a friend as well."

"It was a boy?" Patsy's voice was barely a whisper.

"Oh God, he told me he'd told you. I'm sorry, Patsy."

"He told me about the baby, but not that it was a son."

"You didn't know? I thought you must have. I thought you were waiting to get past the three-month stage before telling anyone. Oh, Patsy, I'm so sorry."

"Meredith would have wanted a son."

"He would have wanted any child if it was with you."

"You think?"

"Of course, Patsy, he worships the ground you walk on. He would love it."

"You think he'll want to try for another one?"

"Patsy, this is a conversation you need to have with Dad. I can't answer for him, but I'm guessing he'll say whatever you want will be perfect with him."

"That's the problem, I don't know what I want. On one hand, I feel devastated having lost something I never knew I had, and on the other, I'm asking if it was for the best. Your father was half expecting to be a grandfather and would have been happy about it. But becoming a father again. I don't know."

"Speak to him. I'm going now, I'll send him up."

Before she could leave, a shattered Meredith pushed open the door and smiled at Patsy. "I'm late, and I forgot the grapes."

"How's Dave?"

Meredith shook his head and walked to the window. "Another seizure, although not as bad as the first, they've sent for Eve. I can only stop a few minutes. I need to get back down there."

"I'll go. Dad, take a breather, you've been up all night." Amanda waved at Patsy and left them alone.

"Do you need space? I'll understand if you don't want to talk."

218

"Oh, I want to talk, why, what if, how, when, and so many other bloody things, but I need to be here for Eve. It's not looking good, bloody awful in fact."

"Come here. But be careful."

Patsy held out her arms, and Meredith carefully lay down on the bed next to her. His head on her chest.

She stroked his hair. "We are not discussing anything, not a bloody thing until Dave gets out of here."

"He might not."

"He will one way or another. And that's when we'll talk."

"It could be months."

"I know. Now hush."

"Thank you."

"Shh. Grab five minutes, Amanda will call when Eve gets back."

"You don't want me to give you Linda's request about the wedding then?"

"No."

Patsy stared at the clock. Meredith's breathing slowed, and after five minutes she felt the warmth from his dribble on her chest. It lasted for another five minutes. The door opened and Amanda apologised.

"Sorry, Dad, the consultant is in with Dave and they're going to run more tests, and do another scan to see if the seizures have caused further damage. Eve's back and looks lost, I think she needs you."

"Bring her here. She can have both of us," Patsy answered. "We can keep her busy until he comes back to the ward."

Amanda nodded and left the room

"I love you, Hodge. Still coming to terms with—"

"Hush, and I love you too."

Before Eve arrived, there was a tap on the door and Linda's face appeared.

"Can I come in? Amanda said it would be okay for five minutes."

Meredith climbed off the bed. "Come in, Loopy. I'll go and find Eve, but only five minutes."

Patsy smiled as Linda unpacked a carrier bag. It contained everything one would expect to find next to a hospital bed. "Thank you."

"You're welcome. Don't stop me talking, PHPI, I've got a lot to say, and only five minutes. First, the wedding. Did Meredith give you my request?"

"No, what request."

Linda rolled her eyes, "I knew he had too much on." She perched on the edge of the bed. "I asked if, when they did your cast, you could bear in mind the colour of your outfit," she held her hand up to silence Patsy, "but that doesn't matter now, we've postponed the wedding, so have what you want."

"You've what? Linda, I can't believe it. Why?"

"Because we want everyone we love there, and that includes Dave. He's going to be here a while and I'm guessing will need rehabilitation, so until he's ready to come … Second, and this is the only time I'll mention it, I'm so sorry about the baby."

Without warning, Linda lunged forward and scooped Patsy into her arms, she patted Patsy's back as she spoke, and it was obvious she was controlling her emotions.

"I know you are devastated. Of course you are, can you imagine the child you two will produce? But you can try again in a few months. These things happen for a reason, although for the life of me, this one has me stumped. But while you're processing your grief, keep an eye on the skipper. He was in such a state, Louis said they had to restrain him from going in to see Ellsworth. Uncle David told him to take compassionate leave, but he wouldn't listen. I'm running out of time, but just to let you know, you will have a baby. You've got to, who else would have me as a godmother?"

Patsy's head remained clamped against Linda's shoulder and she merely nodded. As unexpectedly as she'd grabbed her, Linda released her and headed for the door. She paused, wiped her cheeks with her palms and turned back to face Patsy.

"My five minutes is up. I'll be in tomorrow with a good book, or some knitting or something. Bye, my lovely Patsy."

Patsy looked at the closing door. Meredith wanted a baby.

Chapter Twenty-Two

Nine months later, Marcus Ellsworth was led back to the dock. The Jury had finished their deliberations and had reached verdicts on all the charges. There had been little but circumstantial evidence on some of counts, but they came together and formed a picture.

Marcus Ellsworth had benefitted by the death of all those he had killed. When his mother died, he'd inherited a decent sum of money that was held in trust until he was eighteen, but until then he was penniless, and his mother's old friends had given him several large handouts to tide him over. Once he got his hands on the inheritance, he was wealthy. He developed a standard of life and wanted to maintain it. The trouble was he couldn't stick to one thing or another and by his thirtieth birthday he was broke. He decided to go begging again, he got some money, but some of those who knew his parents had little or nothing to give, they had their own commitments, and most of their money was tied up in property and investments, but a few promised him a bequest, which gave him the foundation for his evil plan.

Christopher Kentish had become tired of his requests for handouts and had fallen out with him. As a consequence, he'd reduced the amount he left him, although still unable to cut Jeremy's son out altogether. Meredith's team believed he probably orchestrated his mother's death, but had no proof, although the prosecution used that as a starting point.

"Will the foreman, please stand."

Meredith gripped Patsy's hand.

"If they can't see it was aout the money ..." Meredith's free hand made a fist. "In Miriam's case only two hundred quid, but he didn't know that." He fell silent as the foreman of the jury was asked to stand.

The clerk cleared his throat. "Have you reached verdicts on which you are all agreed?"

"Yes."

221

"On the count of the murder of Andrew Hemmings, do you find the defendant guilty or not guilty?"

"Guilty."

On the count of the murder of Miriam Campion, do you find the defendant guilty or not guilty?

"Guilty."

"On the count of the murder of Amy Cleaver, do you find the defendant guilty or not guilty?

"Guilty."

"On the count of the murder of David Rawlings, do you find the defendant guilty or not guilty?"

Dave Rawlings murder was the most clear-cut, and the verdict should be a formality, but Meredith's grip tightened on Patsy's hand, and he held out his other to take hold of Eve Rawlings'. There was a buzzing in his ears, and time seemed to stand still. He held his breath and pulled Eve to him as the foreman answered.

"GUILTY."

There should have been one more charge, but the law doesn't allow for the killing of an unborn child. Meredith pulled the two women to their feet, and they shuffled along the bench seat. The judge wouldn't pass sentence today.

Eve needed to get home to Ellen, and Meredith had a best man's speech to cobble together.

Dave Rawlings had died six months ago, and he still had to have that conversation with Patsy. Perhaps today was the day.

222

AUTHOR'S NOTE

Thank you for reading A Measure of Guilt. I hope you enjoyed reading this story as much as I enjoyed writing it. If you did, I'd be grateful if you would be kind enough to leave a review, or contact me with your thoughts and any comments. Constructive reviews are invaluable to authors. If you would rather contact me personally the details are below.

If you would like to read more of my work, then please sign up for my newsletter, where you will receive regular offers and news of new releases. http://mkturnerbooks.co.uk/

ABOUT THE AUTHOR

Having worked in the property industry for most of my adult life, latterly at a senior level, I finally escaped in 2010. I now work as a consultant for several independent agencies, but I dedicate the bulk of my time to writing and, of course, reading, although there are still not enough hours in the day.

I began writing quite by chance when a friend commented, "They wouldn't believe it if you wrote it down!" So I did. I enjoyed the plotting and scheming, creating the characters, and watching them develop with the story. I kept on writing, and Meredith and Hodge arrived. In 2017 the Bearing women took hold of my imagination, and the Bearing Witness series was created. I should confess at this point that although I have the basic outline when I start a new story, it never develops the way I expect, and I rarely know 'who did it' myself until I've nearly finished.

I am married with two children, two grandchildren, two German Shepherds and a Bichon Frise, and we live in Bristol, UK.

I can be contacted here, and would love to hear from you:

Website: http://mkturnerbooks.co.uk/

https://www.facebook.com/mkturnerbooks

Printed in Great Britain
by Amazon

79809593R00133